MRS. JEFFRIES
APPEALS THE VERDICT

EMILY BRIGHTWELL

BERKLEY PRIME CRIME, NEW YORK

THE BERKLEY PUBLISHING GROUP
Published by the Penguin Group
Penguin Group (USA) Inc.
375 Hudson Street, New York, New York 10014, USA
Penguin Group (Canada), 90 Eglinton Avenue East, Suite 700, Toronto, Ontario M4P 2Y3, Canada
(a division of Pearson Penguin Canada Inc.)
Penguin Books Ltd., 80 Strand, London WC2R 0RL, England
Penguin Group Ireland, 25 St. Stephen's Green, Dublin 2, Ireland (a division of Penguin Books Ltd.)
Penguin Group (Australia), 250 Camberwell Road, Camberwell, Victoria 3124, Australia
(a division of Pearson Australia Group Pty. Ltd.)
Penguin Books India Pvt. Ltd., 11 Community Centre, Panchsheel Park, New Delhi—110 017, India
Penguin Books (NZ), Cnr. Airborne and Rosedale Roads, Albany, Auckland 1310, New Zealand
(a division of Pearson New Zealand Ltd.)
Penguin Books (South Africa) (Pty.) Ltd., 24 Sturdee Avenue, Rosebank, Johannesburg 2196, South
Africa

Penguin Books Ltd., Registered Offices: 80 Strand, London WC2R 0RL, England

This is a work of fiction. Names, characters, places, and incidents either are the product of the author's imagination or are used fictitiously, and any resemblance to actual persons, living or dead, business establishments, events, or locales is entirely coincidental. The publisher does not have any control over and does not assume any responsibility for author or third-party websites or their content.

MRS. JEFFRIES APPEALS THE VERDICT

A Berkley Prime Crime Book / published by arrangement with the author

PRINTING HISTORY
Berkley Prime Crime mass-market edition / May 2006

ISBN: 0-425-20969-5

BERKLEY® PRIME CRIME
Berkley Prime Crime Books are published by The Berkley Publishing Group,
a division of Penguin Group (USA) Inc.,
375 Hudson Street, New York, New York 10014.
The name BERKLEY PRIME CRIME and the BERKLEY PRIME CRIME design are trademarks belonging to Penguin Group (USA) Inc.

PRINTED IN THE UNITED STATES OF AMERICA

10 9 8 7 6 5 4 3 2

This book is dedicated to Jeong Hong Lee,
also known as Joseph Lee,
a truly intelligent man who understands the importance of heroes,
and, of course, to the Immortal Admiral Yi Soon Shin

CHAPTER 1

———

"I expect it's just as well that we missed that one," Mrs. Jeffries said as she put the newspaper to one side and picked up her teacup. "They seem to have caught the fellow fairly easily, so there isn't much of a mystery to the crime." Mrs. Hepzibah Jeffries was a plump, middle-aged woman with auburn hair and dark brown eyes. She was the housekeeper to Inspector Gerald Witherspoon of the Metropolitan Police Force.

"From the account I read, it seems a simple robbery gone bad," Betsy, the blonde-haired maid agreed. She put the cone of sugar she'd just brought in from the dry larder on the worktable and got the sugar hammer out of the drawer. She laid the heavy wooden utensil next to the cone so the cook would have it at the ready. "But it's odd that someone was actually killed. Most robbers simply grab a purse and make a run for it."

"Perhaps the husband put up a fight," Mrs. Jeffries speculated. Crime was an important topic around the household, and even the ones they weren't directly involved with were discussed at great length.

"Maybe he put up a fight, but it was the poor woman that was killed." Betsy came to the table. "Did Smythe say what time he'd be back?"

"He didn't say," Mrs. Goodge, the cook, said as she came out of the hallway and shuffled over to the table. She was an elderly, portly woman with gray hair and spectacles. She'd cooked for some of the finest households in all of England, but she wouldn't trade being a cook to a simple police inspector for a position as head chef at Buckingham Palace. "But I imagine he'll be back for his morning tea," she continued as she took her seat. "There's not much he can do at the stables on a day like today. It's not fit for man nor beast out there. Oh good, I see you've got the sugar out for me."

"Do you want one of us to pound it off for you?" Mrs. Jeffries asked. "With this weather it's gotten very hard." She knew the cook's rheumatism had been acting up, and smashing just the right amount of sugar off the cone was difficult if your joints ached.

"Ta, Mrs. Jeffries, I'd appreciate the help. Good gracious, what's all that racket?" she broke off as heavy footsteps pounded down the back staircase.

A moment later, Wiggins, the footman, burst into the kitchen. "I'm goin' to kill that bloomin' bully." Wiggins was generally a good-natured lad with dark brown hair, pale skin, and round apple cheeks. He didn't look very good-natured at the moment. "The mean old thing's gone and chased Fred under the table on the landing again."

"You didn't hurt my lamb, did you?" Mrs. Goodge glared at the footman. "Where is he? What have you done with him?"

"Last I saw he was sittin' on the top of the bannister hissin' at my poor Fred."

"Fred's got to learn to keep his nose to himself," Mrs. Goodge cried. "Samson would leave him alone if he did."

"It's your fault," Betsy told him. "You're the one that brought the cat here. If you'd left him in Richmond—"

"He'd 'ave starved to death," Wiggins said defensively. "I was tryin' to do a kindness. Fat lot of good it's done me."

"Of course you were," Mrs. Jeffries said soothingly. Samson was a big, orange tabby that the footman had brought home when they'd finished their last case. The staff helped Inspector Witherspoon with his cases, not that he had any idea they were helping, of course. The cat had belonged to the victim and was universally hated. In order to save the animal from certain death, Wiggins had rescued it. But there was a good reason the beast had been so disliked in its previous household: he had a nasty disposition.

Mrs. Goodge and Samson had taken one look at each other and it had been love at first sight. Unfortunately, the animal's disposition hadn't improved in regards to the rest of the household, especially Fred. He was a mongrel dog that Wiggins had brought home several years ago and he earned a solid place in the hearts of everyone, including the inspector.

Fred hated Samson. Even worse, he was just a bit scared of the cat. Samson knew it as well and delighted in laying in wait for the poor mutt and then springing out and swiping one of his big paws across Fred's nose. Fred, occasionally wanting to assert his territorial rights, would sometimes gather his courage and shove his nose under the cat's tail. This usually resulted in a great deal of screeching, running, clawing, barking, or yelping, depending on who managed to get the upper paw, so to speak.

"And I for one am very grateful," Mrs. Goodge said quickly. "It's nice having a companion like Samson. Keeps me company at night when the rest of you have gone up to bed. When you get to be my age, you don't need as much sleep as you young people."

Wiggins instantly felt like a worm. Poor Mrs. Goodge loved Samson, and here he was making a silly fuss. She'd spent most of her life on her own, moving from place to place as her positions changed, and he was acting mean and nasty. "Samson's all right," he said as he took his seat. "But I wish he and Fred could learn to get along."

"Fred's got to stand up to him," Betsy said. "I do wish Smythe would hurry and get back. It's awful out there." She and Smythe were engaged. He was the coachman and a big brawny fellow who'd been all over the world on his own, but she still clucked over him like a mother hen.

"I expect he'll be here soon," Mrs. Jeffries said. Just then, Samson walked into the kitchen. He gave a meow, glared at the rest of them, and hurried over to Mrs. Goodge, who obligingly pushed away from the table to make room for Samson on her lap. "There's a good boy," she said as he jumped up and settled himself down. "You see, he's sweet as a baby lamb." She looked at the others. "I can't think why everyone makes such a fuss about him."

"That's because he's not clawed you." Betsy grinned. "He got a good lick in on my hand last week."

"You got too close to his food dish," the cook said. Not wanting Samson's hair in their tea, she eased her chair farther away from the table. "You know what he's like about his food dish. He's a sweet one, he is. You just have to be gentle with him."

Betsy glanced at Mrs. Jeffries and Wiggins. None of them had the heart to point out that Samson wasn't in the least sweet and that the minute her back was turned he was his usual nasty self. The cook loved the old beast far too much to ever see him for what he really was!

Fred stuck his nose around the door, spotted Samson on the cook's lap, and then dashed over to Wiggins. He wedged himself as close to the footman's chair as physically possible. A moment later, he leapt up, his ears cocked toward the back door, and charged off.

Samson hissed at him as he ran past.

"He's probably heard Smythe." Wiggins stared at the disappearing brown and black dog. Fred began to bark as they heard the back door open. "That's odd: Fred doesn't bark at Smythe." Surprised, Wiggins got up and started for the hall.

"Easy, Fred, this is a friend. You're a good guard dog, that's right," Smythe said.

Samson, obviously put out by the commotion, suddenly leapt from Mrs. Goodge's lap, hissed in Fred's direction, and then ran toward the cook's quarters.

"Thanks, mate. I thought for a minute he was goin' to have my guts for garters," said another cheerful voice.

Fred, followed by two men, trotted back to the kitchen and settled next to the footman's chair. Smythe was a tall, muscular man in his mid-thirties with black hair, heavy features, and dark brown eyes. His companion was a short, chubby, ginger-haired fellow wearing a porkpie hat and a long black greatcoat with a bright red scarf wound around the neck.

Everyone looked at Smythe expectantly.

"This is my friend, Blimpey Groggins. 'E's got something 'e'd like to discuss with us," the coachman said hesitantly. Smythe wasn't sure bringing Blimpey to the house was a good idea, but he'd not really had much choice. Blimpey had been waiting for him outside the back garden gate and had insisted he needed their help.

"How do you do, Mr. Groggins," Mrs. Jeffries said as she rose to her feet. "Would you care for some tea?"

"Ta, ma'am," he replied politely. "I could do with a cuppa. It's right cold and miserable out there."

Everyone waited until the two men had taken off their coats and settled into chairs around the table. Smythe squeezed Betsy's hand as he slid into his spot next to her.

"I'm Hepzibah Jeffries," the housekeeper said formally. "And this is Mrs. Goodge, Betsy, and Wiggins." She pointed to each of them as she said their names. "You already know Smythe, of course."

Blimpey nodded at each of them. "Cor blimey, Smythe, your lady is a pretty one."

Smythe blinked in surprise, but Betsy, not in the least offended, laughed. "Why thank you, Mr. Groggins," she said. "That's very kind of you."

"Would you care for a bun?" Wiggins shoved the plate of buns toward their guest. "They're real nice. Mrs. Goodge made 'em fresh this mornin'."

"Thank you, lad," Blimpey helped himself and then looked at Smythe expectantly.

The coachman cleared his throat. "Blimpey needs our 'elp," he began. Blast a Spaniard, this was harder than he'd thought it was going to be. He had to tread carefully here. He didn't want to say too much, but on the other hand, he had to tell them enough so they'd know they could trust Blimpey.

"Is Mr. Groggins in need of domestic assistance?" Mrs. Jeffries asked softly.

"Call me Blimpey," he said quickly. "And no, I'm not needin' domestic assistance of any kind, thank you. I'm wantin' your help to prevent a huge miscarriage of justice, so to speak, and you've not got much time, either."

"Miscarriage of justice," Mrs. Jeffries repeated.

"Not got much time," Mrs. Goodge echoed.

"What's 'e on about?" Wiggins muttered.

"For goodness' sakes, Blimpey, give 'em a bit of more information than that," Smythe said irritably.

"I fully intend to do just that," Blimpey replied, "but I thought it important to let everyone know right away that we can't be dillying about here. The lad's life is at stake." He turned to Mrs. Jeffries. "There's a man by the name of Tommy Odell that's going to meet the hangman in less than three Sundays unless you and your lot help."

"Why do you think we can help this man?" she asked calmly. She had a very good idea why he thought they could help, but she wanted to learn a bit more before she said too much.

Several people in London had figured out that Gerald Witherspoon's household staff were helping with his cases, but those few were trusted friends. She needed to know how Blimpey Groggins had learned their secret.

"Because it's my job to know such things," Blimpey

said. "I'm a broker of sorts, Mrs. Jeffries, only instead of stocks or coal or tea, I deal in information."

"What kind of information?" Wiggins asked curiously.

Smythe held his breath. This was the rough part. If Blimpey said too much, then everyone at the table would soon figure out that he'd been using Blimpey as a source for all their cases. On the other hand, if Blimpey didn't tell them enough, they'd have a hard time taking his concern seriously.

"All kinds," Blimpey grinned proudly. "I can honestly say that my customers come from all levels of our fine society. Just last week I had an insurance company hire me to find out if a warehouse had been deliberately set afire."

Wiggins leaned forward eagerly. "And 'ad it?"

"Nah. Much to the insurance company's annoyance, the fire was an accident. The warehouse owner had just taken in partners and didn't need to burn down the building. Mind you, it did work out for the fellow—now he gets a brand new building—but that's neither here nor there. The point is, in the course of my work, I'm often privy to information that works both sides of the road, so to speak."

"What does that mean?" Mrs. Goodge demanded. She eyed their visitor suspiciously.

Mrs. Jeffries was fairly certain she knew exactly what it meant, but she said nothing.

Blimpey shrugged and took a quick sip of his tea. "There's no delicate way to say this except to just come out and say it. Sometimes I get information about the less respectable members of our society, and recently I've come across something that leads me to believe a great miscarriage of justice is about to take place, namely that poor Tommy Odell is goin' to swing for a murder he didn't commit."

"And how do you know Mr. Odell isn't guilty of this crime?" Mrs. Jeffries asked.

"Cause I know Tommy—he's a pickpocket, not a killer." Blimpey shook his head in disgust. "I know that sounds odd to you lot, but Tommy's a good lad. He'd no more take a life than he would cut off his own hand. But they caught him with the goods so they laid the blame on him. He didn't do it. I need you lot to prove it before they hang him."

"When is he due to be executed?" Mrs. Jeffries took a sip of her own tea.

"April ninth." Blimpey shook his head sadly. "He's a nice bloke, is Tommy. Wouldn't hurt a fly."

"That's not much time," Mrs. Goodge mused.

Mrs. Jeffries gave her a quick, surprised look. The cook was the one person she thought might balk at helping someone like Blimpey, or even believing him in the first place. "Why do you think we can be of service?" she asked softly. "Shouldn't you take your concerns to the police?"

Blimpey stared at her for a long moment and then said, "I've just told ya, Mrs. Jeffries. My business is information. Did you really think you and the others in this house could help Inspector Witherspoon solve over twenty murders without some of us catchin' on? Don't be daft. There's plenty that know what you've been up to, but as you've also got a reputation for gettin' it right and keepin' innocent people off the gallows, most of us keep what we know to ourselves."

"And you think we can help Mr. Odell?" she replied. Her voice and manner were very calm, but inside her spirits soared. She wasn't certain she liked people knowing what they'd been up to, but in all honesty it was rather exciting to know there were people who recognized and approved of what they'd done.

"If you can't, the lad's a goner," Blimpey said bluntly. "I'd 'ave been here sooner but the missus and I was out of the country." He smiled self-consciously. "We had us a bit of a holiday. We went to the South of France to get away from the miserable weather, and when I got back yesterday I found out poor Tommy Odell was in the nick and facing the grim one. So I come along here and waited for Smythe, hoping you'd be able to help."

"You and Smythe are old friends?" Betsy asked.

"We go back a bit. Blimpey grinned. "Smythe used to work for one of my old customers, Euphemia Wither-spoon, your inspector's late aunt. She was a character, she was. Nice woman, too. Sad to see the likes of her go."

"Could you give us a bit more of the circumstances of Mr. Odell's troubles?" Mrs. Goodge asked. "I've not heard of any murders done recently."

"It was in the papers." Betsy pointed to the newspaper lying at the far end of the table. "He was sentenced last week."

"That's right, but the murder itself were a couple of months back," Blimpey said easily. "Just after that baronet out in Richmond was killed. A woman named Caroline Muran was shot during a robbery. She died. Her husband was coshed on the head, but he lived. Mrs. Muran's bracelet was stolen as well as the husband's watch. That's how they nicked Tommy: he'd sold the watch to a pawnbroker and it was spotted by a copper."

"How did Tommy get the watch?" Smythe asked.

Blimpey shrugged. "He's a pickpocket. He claimed he lifted it hours before the killing. Look, I know it don't seem right, my wantin' you to help a thief, but thieving isn't murder."

"You're convinced he's telling you the truth?" Mrs. Jeffries pressed.

"Of that, I'm sure." Blimpey nodded emphatically. "Tommy takes care of his mum. His biggest worry about facin' the hangman is who is goin' to take care of her when he's dead. Can you help or not?"

"Would you mind giving us a few moments to discuss it?" Mrs. Jeffries asked. She had no idea what they ought to do. They'd had people come to them for help before, but those had all been murders that were unsolved. How one went about trying to prove someone was innocent when they'd already been convicted was quite a different kettle of fish.

Blimpey pulled his pocket watch out of his pocket. "I've an appointment nearby at eleven o'clock. If it's all the same to you, I'll be back around noon."

"That will be fine." Mrs. Jeffries nodded.

They waited until Smythe had seen their guest to the back door before they started talking. "Sorry I wasn't able to give you any warnin'," he said as he slipped back into his seat, "but he waylaid me at the back garden gate."

"That's quite all right," Mrs. Jeffries said. She surveyed the faces around the table. Everyone looked as bemused as she felt. "Am I right in assuming we're all a bit surprised by this latest turn of events?"

"Cor blimey, it's the last thing I expected to come walkin' in on a rainy day," Wiggins admitted. "But on the other 'and, it's a bit flatterin' to know that there's people out there that know what we've been up to and think we're doin' a right good job."

"Yes, well, that's true," the housekeeper replied. "But we mustn't let it go to our heads." In truth, though, she was as pleased by the knowledge as the footman. Modesty might be a virtue, but recognition was very gratifying indeed.

"But it is nice," Betsy grinned. "I mean, I know we don't want all and sundry knowing our business, but a bit of recognition is exciting."

Mrs. Goodge nodded vigorously in agreement, whether she was agreeing with Betsy or Mrs. Jeffries wasn't apparent. "But what are we goin' to do about this problem?" she asked plaintively. "It doesn't seem right not to do something, especially if the fellow is innocent."

"We don't know that for a fact," Smythe muttered. He still wasn't sure how much the rest of them might have gleaned from Blimpey's arrival today.

"How well do you know this Blimpey Groggins?" Mrs. Jeffries asked.

Smythe shrugged, trying to look casual. This was the one question he'd been dreading. He didn't fancy lying about his relationship with Blimpey, but on the other hand, his pride wouldn't stand for him admitting that he'd gotten most of his information on their last dozen cases directly from Blimpey. "I know 'im well enough. Truth of the matter is, I've used him a time or two when we were really stuck on a case. His information is always good."

"Yes, but does that mean the pickpocket is innocent of murder?" Mrs. Goodge exclaimed. "That's what we've got to know."

"Even if 'e's innocent," Wiggins said slowly, "'e's still a criminal. Seems to me that ought to be taken into consideration before we make a decision."

"Wiggins, I'm surprised at you." The cook stared at him in disbelief. "Surely you're not saying a man ought to be hung over stealing a pocket watch."

Wiggins blushed and looked down at the tabletop. "Course not, but well, it's not like 'e's a workin' bloke that was pulled in off the streets for a crime 'e didn't commit. Oh, I don't know what I'm sayin'. Course we ought to 'elp this feller if 'e's innocent. Especially now, bein' as we've got a bit of a reputation for upholdin' justice."

"I'm not sure we can," Mrs. Jeffries murmured. "The crime was weeks ago, the trail is cold, and frankly, even if we found out who the real killer might be, we'd need irrefutable proof of guilt before we could get an execution stopped."

"We've got to try," Mrs. Goodge said stoutly. "If we turn our backs on even one innocent person, then all the good we've done will be undone. Take my word for it, I'm old and I know these things."

"Don't look now, sir, but Inspector Nivens just came in." Constable Barnes struggled to keep the contempt out of his tone as he stared across the crowded canteen. Barnes was a tall, gray-haired policeman who'd been on the force more years than he cared to recall, and he was now working almost exclusively with Inspector Gerald Witherspoon. He considered it part of his job to shield his inspector from the likes of people like Nivens.

Witherspoon glanced up from his lunch of boiled cabbage, carrots, and stringy beef. He looked at Barnes out of a pair of deep-set blue eyes obscured by a pair of spectacles. His thinning hair was dark brown and graying a bit at the temples, his complexion pale, and his nose a shade on the long side. All in all, he didn't look like a man who'd become famous for solving murders. He looked like a person who ought to be in charge of the records room, which is precisely what he'd done before Mrs. Jeffries had come to be his housekeeper. "Inspector Nivens is here in the police canteen?"

Barnes grinned. "Surprising, isn't it. He usually eats lunch with one of his fancy political friends at a private club. I expect he's come to gloat. They sentenced that pickpocket for the Muran murder yesterday."

"Sad business, wasn't it." Witherspoon agreed with a shake of his head.

Barnes nodded. "Murder usually is, but at least this one's got Nivens what he's wanted. Let's just hope he doesn't let solving one murder go to his head."

Witherspoon took a quick bite of cabbage. "Be fair, Constable, he did solve the case."

"The killer fell into his lap. That case wouldn't even have been assigned to him if he'd not stumbled across the victim's watch in that pawnshop. From the pawnshop to the killer was so easy even a child could 'ave done it." Barnes snorted in derision. He loathed Nivens. The man was a boot-licking bully who'd used his political friends at Whitehall to muscle his way up the Metropolitan Police ladder. The rank and file police constables hated the fellow; Nivens blamed others for his mistakes, took credit for others work, bullied subordinates, and was suspected of skirting the edge of decency in getting confessions out of suspects. "Now that Odell's been convicted, he'll try and use that as a way of getting assigned more murders."

"He's in division K," Witherspoon murmured. "If there's a murder in that district, it'll probably come to him."

Barnes shook his head. Sometimes the inspector was so innocent. "Most of the murders they give you aren't in your division," he pointed out. "But you get them because you're good at what you do, sir. Oh blast, he's seen us and he's coming over."

Witherspoon took another quick bite of his food. By the time he'd swallowed, Nivens was at their table. He nodded curtly at the two men. "Witherspoon, Barnes."

Nivens was a middle-aged man with dark blond hair and cold gray eyes. Clean shaven, he was of medium height with a slight portliness that couldn't be disguised by the expensive black greatcoat he wore. A black bowler hat dangled from his fingers, and there was a copy of the *Policemen's Gazette* tucked under his arm.

Witherspoon smiled politely and Barnes contented himself with a grunt.

But Nivens appeared not to notice the tepid reception. "You'd best be on your toes, Witherspoon." He whipped out the newspaper and waved it at the two policemen. "You're not the only one who can catch ruthless killers. You ought to read what the judge said to Tommy Odell when he was sentenced for Caroline Muran's murder."

"I have read it," Witherspoon said softly.

"I'd like to go to the execution," Nivens continued. "Too bad they did away with public hanging; it would be a deterrent for others, show them what happens when they disregard the law."

"Murder is a horrific crime," Witherspoon commented. He didn't wish to engage in a debate with Nivens, but he didn't agree with him, either. He wasn't in the least sorry that public executions had been banned. The idea of watching someone die, even someone who might deserve the punishment, was grotesque. He couldn't imagine any human being enjoying such a spectacle.

"Do you ever want to see any of yours hang?" Nivens continued chattily.

"No."

"I wish I could be there," Nivens said eagerly. "It isn't fair that they'll let the press into the hanging shed but they won't let us in to watch. I'd love to see that nasty little woman-killer swing from the neck until he's as dead as that poor woman he shot."

Witherspoon lost what remained of his appetite. He pushed his lunch away.

"It's odd that a pickpocket would be carrying a gun," Barnes said. He watched Nivens carefully and was rewarded by seeing an angry flush creep up the man's fat cheeks.

"You sound like Odell's counsel," Nivens snapped. "But the fact is he was carrying a weapon. When the husband tried to fend him off, Odell panicked and shot the woman."

"Why didn't he shoot the husband?" Barnes asked. A lot of coppers had wondered about this case; there was something really odd about the whole business. "Why bash him over the head if he had a gun? You know as well as I do that you can't count on knocking someone out, even if you strike them with something like a brick. But a gun is generally very reliable, especially at close range."

Nivens shoved the newspaper back under his arm. "How the devil should I know why the fellow acted the way he did. Like most people of his class, he's stupid. He pawned Mr. Muran's pocket watch less than a mile from where he'd done the killing." He glared at them. "You'd best watch what you say, Constable Barnes, the chief inspector won't want questions about a closed case being bandied about. The department is still smarting over the licking we took from the press over those Ripper murders."

"Constable Barnes was simply making a comment," Witherspoon said quickly.

"*Humph,*" Nivens snorted. "Then I'll thank him to keep

his comments to himself. I'll not have the two of you wandering about asking questions about my case. Do you understand? This was my case; I solved it and I won't let you or anyone else ruin it for me."

"I assure you, Inspector," Witherspoon said earnestly, "we've no interest in this case whatsoever."

Nivens said nothing for a moment, then he turned on his heel and stalked toward the door, almost knocking over a constable who had the misfortune to wander in his path.

"I want to make sure you all understand that we've no guarantee we'll be successful if we undertake this endeavor," Mrs. Jeffries said. They had been debating the issue for almost an hour now and it was almost noon.

"We've no guarantee we'll be successful on any of our cases," Mrs. Goodge pointed out. "So I don't see that we've anything to worry about with this one."

"But like Mrs. Jeffries says, the inspector won't be able to give us any bits and pieces on this one," Wiggins countered, "and that'll make a big difference. We might not find out anything."

"Of course we'll find out things," Mrs. Goodge argued. "People don't stop talking about a murder just because someone's been arrested and sentenced to hang. There's plenty of information out there, and there's no reason we can't find out every little detail of what happened that night."

"Maybe we can get a copy of the police file," Betsy mused.

"We've no reason to ask the inspector whether or not he even has access to the file," Mrs. Jeffries said. "It wasn't his case."

"Are you sayin' we shouldn't do this?" Smythe asked the housekeeper. He was amazed that it was Mrs. Goodge, who wasn't exactly a champion of the criminal classes, who was arguing so vehemently for their intervention. He'd have thought that with something like this, the chance to prove someone innocent, it would be Mrs. Jeffries wanting them to take it on.

She shook her head. "No, not at all. I'm merely trying to make sure that we all understand we might not succeed. I don't want anyone feeling disappointed or guilty if we can't prove Mr. Odell innocent. The task might be impossible."

"But why would it be so different?" Betsy asked. "As Mrs. Goodge pointed out, people will still be talking about the case. They'll still be clues for us to follow up."

"Yes, but without the inspector actively on the case, we'll need an enormous amount of evidence to get anyone to take notice." She didn't want to have to point out that on most of their previous cases, she'd used a deductive-reasoning method that relied half on instinct and half on evidence to catch the killer. She wasn't sure that would work on this murder. The trail was cold and she had a feeling that the timing of an investigation had a direct bearing on her own sense of urgency. Perhaps she wouldn't be able to pull it off this time.

"Then we'll get the evidence," Smythe promised.

"Even with evidence," she continued, "it'll have to be very compelling to get an execution stopped."

Smythe had had enough. They could go on arguing for hours, but they didn't have that much time. "This isn't like you, Mrs. J. What's really botherin' you?"

She hesitated before she answered. She was almost afraid that voicing her concern aloud would make it come to pass. It was silly, but she felt it nonetheless. "My worst fear is that we'll find enough to convince ourselves the man didn't commit the murder, but we won't get enough to convince the authorities not to hang him."

"Cor blimey, that'd be a terrible thing," Wiggins said softly.

"I'd not like trying to sleep at night knowing an innocent man had been hung because we weren't clever enough to save him," Betsy murmured.

"The police and the courts aren't quick to admit they've made a mistake," Smythe said.

"And that's why I'm hesitating," Mrs. Jeffries blurted. "It's not that I don't want to help; it's just that for us, the truth might be very hard to live with if we fail to stop the execution."

The cook looked around the table, her expression troubled. "I can't believe what I'm hearing. We can't turn our backs on someone who might be innocent just to protect our own feelings. If we find evidence Tommy Odell is innocent, we take it to the inspector. If that doesn't work, we find us a newspaper or a member of Parliament or someone in the Home Office who'll listen. But we don't hide our heads in the sand and pretend it's best not to do it at all rather than risk failin'."

Everyone stared at her in stunned silence.

"Cor blimey, Mrs. Goodge, you've missed yer callin'. They needs the likes of you in Parliament." Wiggins stared at her in admiration.

The cook nodded regally. "Thank you, Wiggins. Perhaps one of these days women will actually get the chance to run for public office. But as that's not likely to happen in my lifetime, I do hope I've at least changed the minds of those sitting around this table."

"You've changed mine," Betsy said quickly.

"And mine," Smythe added.

"Me, too," Wiggins nodded vigorously.

"Thank you, Mrs. Goodge, for reminding us where our duty actually lies." Mrs. Jeffries smiled softly. "You're right, of course. I just wanted everyone to be aware that we may face some sad consequences ourselves if we fail." She glanced at the clock. It was almost noon. "Let's put some food on the table. I'm sure Blimpey will be a bit hungry when he gets here."

Blimpey was delightfully surprised by the unexpected meal. "You didn't 'ave to go to this trouble," he said as he tucked into a plate of shepherd's pie.

"It's no trouble," Mrs. Jeffries replied politely. "Now, if you don't mind answering a few questions while you have your meal, we'll see what we can do to help."

Blimpey swallowed hastily. "Don't mind at all. Would it be easier if you asked me questions, or should I just tell ya what I know?"

"Why don't we try both," she replied. "We'll all ask questions, but if there's anything we don't ask that you think is pertinent, then by all means, speak up."

"When did the murders take place?" Mrs. Goodge asked. She had a vague idea from the newspapers, but as it hadn't been a very interesting case, she'd not paid much attention.

"It was the evenin' of January thirtieth," he said. "Mr. and Mrs. Muran were walkin' down Barrick Road, which is on the other side of the Waterloo Bridge, when it happened. Mr. Muran was hit over the head with something and Mrs. Muran was shot. That's how I know for sure Tommy didn't do it: he'd never hurt a woman. He'd never hurt anyone."

"I'm sure he wouldn't," Mrs. Jeffries muttered. "What time of night was it?"

"From what my sources tell me, it was almost eleven o'clock."

"Did they take a walk every evenin' at the same time?" Smythe asked.

Blimpey shoved another bite of pie into his mouth and shook his head. "As far as I can tell, they weren't takin' a walk at all. They'd been to a concert at St. James Hall, which is this side of the river and in the West End. On their way home, they'd had the hansom stop and let them off."

"Were they close to their house?" Betsy asked.

"The Muran house is in West Brompton. That's miles from where the murder happened."

"Why did they stop then?" Wiggins asked.

Blimpey shrugged. "That's a good question, and I'm not sure the police ever even asked it."

Mrs. Jeffries ignored that. "What sort of people were the victims?"

"Wealthy," Blimpey stated. "Mrs. Muran owns the Merriman Metal Works Factory in Clapham. They're rich people, not the sort to get out and go for a stroll in a commercial neighborhood on their way home from a concert."

"Perhaps it was because they were rich that they were picked as victims," Mrs. Jeffries speculated.

Blimpey shook his head. "Nah, Mrs. Muran dressed as plain as a pikestaff. She were raised Quaker, so she'd not have been sportin' fancy clothing. Her man would have been in a proper suit and hat, but that'd not have marked them as wealthy."

Smythe frowned thoughtfully. "So they just happened to be in the wrong place at the wrong time, is that it?"

"That's what the police would have you believe." Blimpey looked disgusted. "No disrespect meant to your inspector, but the police made a right old cockup of this case. They didn't ask the right questions, they didn't interview witnesses. They just found out that Tommy was the one who fenced that pocket watch and nabbed him for it."

"Do you know who was in charge of the case?" Betsy asked curiously. She hoped it wasn't one of the inspector's colleagues that they knew and liked.

"Course I do," Blimpey said. "It was Inspector Nigel Nivens."

CHAPTER 2

Mrs. Jeffries shot Wiggins a warning look and he managed to clamp his mouth shut. They loathed Nivens, but it wouldn't do their inspector any good if that information was known. "I take it Inspector Nivens was the one who arrested Tommy Odell?"

Blimpey nodded. "That's right. Nivens come across the pocket watch Tommy had lifted from Mr. Muran at a pawnshop. The watch was fairly distinctive, and since the murder, Nivens had been on the lookout for it."

"How was it distinctive?" Mrs. Goodge asked. Life had taught her it was important to get the details right.

"There was an engraving on the inside of the face plate. It read, 'To my beloved Keith from his adoring wife.' Keith is Mr. Muran's Christian name. Nivens put pressure on the pawnshop owner and they had poor old Tommy down at the nick in two shakes of a mare's tail."

"What's the name of the pawnshop?" Smythe asked. He thought it awfully peculiar that a pawnshop that was in the habit of receiving stolen goods would be easily intimidated by a police inspector.

"Murdoch's. It's on Albion Road in Soho. The owner's a nasty little toad named George Rumsfield. He rolled on Tommy pretty fast."

"Any idea why?" the coachman pressed.

"My sources tell me that Rumsfield didn't want to have anything to do with murder," Blimpey sighed. "But Tommy didn't kill anyone. He lifted that watch off Keith Muran earlier that evenin'. He used the old bump-and-run dodge."

"How do you know?" Betsy asked. "I mean, if Tommy had already been arrested when you returned from your holiday, how do you know any of these details? I'm not trying to be rude, but it's important for us to know how reliable our information is."

"And you can't see the police lettin' me into Tommy's cell for a little chat, is that it?" Blimpey grinned and looked at Smythe. "She's not just pretty; she's smart, too. You'd best hang onto this one, Smythe."

"You don't 'ave to tell me that," the coachman replied. "She's got a good point."

"Course she does, and her askin' it makes me all the more glad I come to you. It shows ya all know what you're about." Blimpey sobered. "Tommy didn't tell me any of this directly. I got it from one of my sources who's managed to make contact with Tommy in the nick. He's a reliable fellow. Used to be a solicitor, so you've no worry about the details. They're correct."

"Yes, of course, I'm sure your man is quite dependable. Do go on," Mrs. Jeffries urged.

"Well, as I was sayin', Tommy lifted the watch, but Tommy's mother took sick when he got home that night so he didn't fence the goods till almost two weeks later."

"Which gave the police plenty of time to have a description of the stolen items circulated to every constable in the city," Mrs. Jeffries mused.

"That's right." Blimpey took a quick sip of tea. "And it led 'em straight to poor Tommy."

"What else have your sources told you about the case?" Mrs. Goodge asked.

Blimpey thought for a moment. "Are you wantin' details of the crime or the case in general?"

"Either," the cook replied.

"Caroline Muran was practically a saint; she treated the workers at her factory decently, her servants loved her, and no one seems to have had a reason to want her dead."

"Who inherits her estate?" Mrs. Jeffries wanted to get to the heart of the matter. In her experience, which was quite extensive, she'd discovered that people killed for money, love, or vengeance. Sometimes all three.

"Her husband," Blimpey replied.

"What about her children?" Betsy asked.

"They didn't have any. Caroline Muran was forty-two, but she only married about five years ago. He was a widower and he'd no children, either."

"So he's the sole heir?" the housekeeper pressed.

"There was a brother, but he was killed while traveling in America. He was a bit of ne'er-do-well, if you know what I mean."

"I don't understand how Mrs. Muran ended up shot and Mr. Muran only got a cosh on the head," Wiggins said. "That don't seem right."

"That's one of the things I'm hoping you lot will find out." Blimpey put his mug down on the table. "I take it this means you'll help."

"We'll do the best we can," Mrs. Jeffries replied softly. "But we're not making any promises."

"Fair enough." He grinned broadly. "I'll make it worth your while."

"There's no need for that," Mrs. Jeffries said. "As I said, your poor friend may face the gallows despite our best efforts. We've not long. The execution is scheduled for April ninth and it's already March twentieth. We'll have to work fast."

"I've every faith in ya." Blimpey took out his watch. "Now, unless you've something else to ask me, I'd best be off."

Mrs. Jeffries looked around the table. "Does anyone have any questions?"

"I'm sure I'll have some later," Wiggins said. "But right now, I can't think of anything."

No one else could, either, so Blimpey took his leave. Smythe walked him to the back door. "This was a bit of a surprise," he whispered.

"Sorry." Blimpey grinned apologetically. "But I was in a bit of a hurry, mate. I didn't mean to spring this on ya." He kept his voice low.

Smythe reached for the doorknob. "No 'arm done. I don't think the others suspect we're more than just casual acquaintances."

"More importantly, your lady doesn't know the truth. She's a right beauty, Smythe. How'd a 'ard old dog like you got a lovely like that is beyond me."

As Smythe frequently wondered the same thing, he shrugged. "Just lucky I guess." He opened the door and the two men stood in the hallway staring out at the downpour. "You're going to get soaked to the skin."

"Not to worry." Blimpey wound his scarf high around his throat. "Nell will have something nice and hot waiting for me when I get home. You come along and see me soon. I've a few bits and pieces I didn't share with the others."

"Why'd you do that?"

"You're one of my best customers. I had to save a few things for you. I can't have your mates thinkin' poorly of your detective skills. See ya tomorrow then." He stepped out into the rain and hurried off in the direction of the garden gate.

Smythe didn't know whether to be insulted or pleased.

They were waiting for him when he got back to the kitchen. "'E's gone," he said as he slipped into his spot next to Betsy. "What do we do now?"

"I'm not sure," Mrs. Jeffries mused. "This is so different from our usual case."

"Do you really think so," Mrs. Goodge said in a tone that was more of a comment than a question.

"Don't you?" the housekeeper replied.

"Not really. We know just about as much as we usually do when we start our investigatin'." The cook got to her feet and went to the pine sideboard. Opening the top drawer, she took out her writing paper and pencil. "We know when the crime took place; we know who was killed and where they lived. That's not much more than we generally know." She put the paper down on the table and sat back down. "Now, I've a lot to do, so let's get this part of the meeting done with quickly."

"Luty and Hatchet are going to be fit to be tied." Betsy giggled. "They hate missing out."

Luty Belle Crookshank and her butler Hatchet were friends of the household. Luty Belle, an elderly, eccentric, and rich American, had been a witness in one of their first cases. Being clever and observant, she'd figured out what they were up to as they asked questions and tried to help their inspector solve a particularly ugly murder of a Knightsbridge physician. After that case was over, she'd come along with a problem and asked for their help. She and her butler had helped solve that murder, and ever since they'd insisted on being included in all the inspector's cases.

"And Luty missed most of our last case," the housekeeper commented. "Oh well, it can't be helped. They're not due back for three weeks."

"They'll never leave again." Smythe grinned. "No matter how much her lawyers or her bankers press her."

Luty had gone back to her home country to attend several company board meetings and meet with her American lawyers and bankers.

"She'll never forgive her lawyers for making her go now that she's going to miss a murder." Betsy laughed. "But at least Hatchet's missing it, too. Not like last time when he got to help and she didn't."

"She did a few bits," Wiggins protested. "She might 'ave been ill, but she weren't at death's door. She gave us a bit of 'elp."

Mrs. Goodge looked up from the list she'd been writing and gave them a good frown. "Come along now, we've got to get cracking. Go on, Mrs. Jeffries, get us started."

"You're right, of course. We really ought to get on with it." She thought for a moment, wondering how one stopped an execution, providing of course one had evidence someone was innocent. But she decided to cross that bridge when she came to it. The first thing they ought to do was solve the actual crime. "Let's see, uh, Mrs. Goodge, you'll do your usual activity. Do you have many people coming along in the next few days?"

The cook did all her investigating right here in the cozy warmth of the kitchen. Delivery boys, tinkers, rag and bones sellers, mush fakers, and street vendors were all part of the small army of people who trooped through the back door on a regular basis. Additionally, she had a network of former colleagues in the form of cooks, maids, tweenies, and gardners that she wasn't above using for information.

"No. The laundry boy came this morning and the street vendors stay inside when it rains like this. But not to worry, I've plenty of my old colleagues I can invite around. We've plenty of supplies in the larders, so I can start baking right away. Nothing gets people talking like some nice buns or a good slice of seed cake."

"Excellent." The housekeeper turned her attention to Betsy.

"I'll start with the shopkeepers in the Muran neighborhood," the maid said quickly. Betsy had a positive genius for getting trades people to talk. It was amazing how much information about a victim or a suspect one could find out from a friendly chat with a grocer or a fishmonger. She glanced anxiously toward the window over the sink on the far wall. "Maybe I can start today if the rain lets up a bit."

"I'll nip over to the Muran neighborhood as well," Wiggins offered. "If Mrs. Muran owned a factory, she must 'ave 'ad lots of servants. One of them is bound to be out an' about."

"Not in this weather," Mrs. Jeffries said. "Look, none of us can do much until the rain stops. So I've a suggestion: let's get everything done around here that we possibly can so that when we do get a break in the weather, we can get out without delay."

The rain finally stopped, but by that time Inspector Witherspoon had come home. "Good evening Mrs. Jeffries," he said as he put his umbrella in the blue-and-white-flowered porcelain urn that served as an umbrella stand.

"Good evening, sir," she replied. "Did you have a good day?" She reached for his wet bowler hat.

"It was fine." He shrugged out of his overcoat and hung it on the coat tree. "Luckily, there isn't much going on. I spent the morning at the Yard and the afternoon doing paper work at Aldgate police station."

"Would you care for a sherry before dinner, sir?" she asked. She wanted to find out if he knew any details about the Muran murder.

"That would be lovely," he agreed. "But only if you'll join me."

The inspector had been raised in very modest circumstances. He'd inherited a fortune and his huge house from his aunt Euphemia Witherspoon, so consequently he tended to treat his servants as human beings. Smythe and Wiggins had both worked for the late Euphemia Witherspoon, and the inspector, even though he had very little need for a coachman or a footman, had kept them both. He'd no idea how to run a big house, so he'd hired Mrs. Jeffries, the widow of a

Yorkshire policeman, to be his housekeeper and Mrs. Goodge to be a cook. Betsy had arrived in the household by collapsing with a fever on their doorstep. When she'd recovered, she'd stayed on as a housemaid.

They went down the hall to the drawing room and Mrs. Jeffries poured both of them a glass of Harvey's Bristol Cream sherry. "I understand that they found Tommy Odell guilty of that woman's murder," she began. The inspector wouldn't think it in the least odd that she wanted to discuss criminal matters. It was one of their main topics of conversation.

"Yes." Witherspoon nodded his thanks as he took his drink. "Odd you should mention the fellow. Inspector Nivens spoke to me about the case today as well."

"It was Inspector Nivens' case?" She pretended surprise, as the papers hadn't mentioned Nivens' name in the article she'd read and she'd bet her quarterly housekeeping money that Nivens was furious over the ommision.

"It was indeed." The inspector took a quick sip from his glass. "He got the case because the victim's pocket watch turned up in a pawnshop after the murder. Apparently Odell was easy to trace from that point."

"According to the papers, it was Mrs. Muran that was killed," she said slowly. She tried to think about what details the paper had mentioned. She didn't want to give away a detail they might have heard from Blimpey.

"For once, the papers got it correct." He frowned and shook his head. "The poor woman was shot in the head at very close range. Frankly, Mrs. Jeffries, I'm glad I didn't get that one."

"It sounds awful."

"It was. The husband was hurt as well, but luckily he wasn't killed."

"He was only wounded?" she said, deliberately getting the facts wrongs. "I don't recall what the papers said about him."

"He was hit on the head and knocked unconscious."

"Gracious, that's unusual, isn't it?" Mrs. Jeffries exclaimed. "One would think it would have been the other way around."

"That's what Constable Barnes said today when we saw Inspector Nivens," Witherspoon said, his expression mildly surprised. "I must say, Nivens didn't like the constable's comments, but apparently several of the rank-and-file lads thought there was something . . ." he paused, searching for the right words, "not quite right about the case."

"What do you think, sir?" She watched him carefully, hoping to see a glimmer of interest about the case in his expression. If they found themselves with enough evidence to cast doubt on Odell's guilt, but not enough to absolutely prove him innocent, they'd need the inspector's help. It wouldn't hurt to try and coax him on board, so to speak, at this point.

"I think that the facts of the case were presented before a judge and jury. Tommy Odell was found guilty. I've great faith in our system of justice, Mrs. Jeffries." He drained the last of his sherry, rose to his feet, and took a deep breath. "I'm sure that whatever questions were raised about the case were adequately explained at Odell's trial. Something smells wonderful. I'm famished."

Betsy stood on the corner of Drayton Gardens and the Fulham Road. She surveyed the area carefully. On the far side of the street were a greengrocer, a butcher, a chemist, a draper, and a dressmaker. On the other was a large grocery shop, an estate agent, an ironmonger, and the local branch of the London and Southwest Bank. Betsy crossed the road and started down the pavement. She stared into the windows as she passed the shops, looking for the one that had the least number of customers. She was also looking for one that had young male clerks behind the counters. She'd had great success in the past in getting information out of young men. They loved to talk, especially if they thought they could impress her with their knowledge. At the green-grocers, she saw a sour-faced old man pouring potatoes from a burlap sack into a bin so she walked on past. She paused at the butcher shop. The place was full—there was a woman at the counter and three more lined up behind her waiting their turn to be served. She went on to the chemist's shop and peeked in the window, then she pulled open the door and stepped inside.

"May I help you, miss?" The young man behind the counter smiled eagerly.

Betsy gave him her most dazzling smile in return. Momentarily, she had a twinge of guilt, but she ruthlessly fought it back. She wasn't being untrue to Smythe; she was trying to make sure an innocent man didn't hang. "Have you any lavender water?" she asked.

He turned to one of the shelves behind him and took down a small glass container. "We've this kind. Will it do you?"

"That'll be fine," she replied.

"Anything else, miss?" he asked.

Betsy pretended to think, hoping that he'd fill the silence by speaking. She'd noticed that if she said nothing, people often would start to talk. It was as though the silence made them uncomfortable. She also had noticed that people tended to say more if they were the ones starting the conversation.

"We've some nice hand cream that's just come in from France," he said. "Some of our local ladies seem to like it very much."

"Why, how very clever of you," she cried. "You must be able to read minds. That's exactly what I need."

He looked enormously pleased with himself. "It's just over here," he gestured toward a display case on the end of the counter. "It's very popular. Excellent quality for the price."

"Do the posh ladies like it?" Betsy turned and looked where he pointed.

"Oh, yes. Mrs. Morecombe—her husband's an MP—uses it, as does Lady Eldon and Mrs. Muran—"

"Mrs. Muran?" Betsy interrupted. "Wasn't she the lady that got murdered?" She couldn't believe her luck. "Oh dear, I don't mean to be indelicate, but I do recall reading about a lady by that name who was killed. Was it the same one?"

"It was during a robbery," he replied. "It was a terrible tragedy. Mrs. Muran was the nicest person. She shopped here regularly and was always as pleasant as can be. She always paid her bill in full each month. She could have sent one of the maids to pick up her medicines, but she always came herself."

"She sounds a very nice person indeed," Betsy said softly. "And I'm sure she'll be missed."

"The whole neighborhood misses her," he said. "She was very active in the local area, always supported the various charity drives and fund-raising activities. Of course, it's most likely her employees at the factory that will miss her the most."

"She was a businesswoman?" Betsy picked up the white bottle of hand cream and placed it next to the lavender water. She didn't really need it, but as the fellow was being so talkative, she thought she might as well buy from him. "The papers didn't say anything about that."

"She owned Merriman's Metal Works. My sister-in-law's nephew works there and he was really upset at her death. All of the employees were. She was one of the best employers in the whole country. She was getting ready to renovate a lot of their housing—" He broke off as the bell over the door rang and a matronly woman wearing a long blue cloak and carrying a basket stepped into the shop. He smiled at her nervously. "Good day, Mrs. Morecombe. Mr. Callow is in the back. Shall I get him for you?"

"I don't need medicine, so you can serve me, Albert. But you must be quick about it; I've a long list of items and several more stops to make this afternoon," she replied, her glance moving quickly over Betsy, assessing her simple coat before dismissing her as no one of importance.

Albert smiled apologetically at Betsy. "Will there be anything else, miss?"

Betsy shook her head. She wasn't going to get any more out of him. "No, thank you, this is quite enough."

Wiggins walked slowly up the pavement in front of the Muran town house. The ground floor was made of cream stone with the upper four stories done in light brown brick. A black door with a highly polished brass knocker and two brass side lamps was on the lower left side of the property. Wiggins peered through the black wrought-iron fence that separated a tiny wedge of grass from the pavement to the lower ground floor of the house, but he couldn't see anything except that the stairs were neatly painted and the servants' door was in neat repair. The rest of the house was well kept and tidy, but it wasn't as grand as he'd expected.

He saw the curtains twitch in the second floor of the house next door so he moved along. He'd only just arrived in the neighborhood, so he didn't think anyone would notice him, but it never did to hang about too long in front of one spot.

He pulled his jacket tighter. Even though a weak spring sun shone through the hazy mist, it was cold. Wiggins didn't like that. If it was too chilly, people avoided going outside, which meant that he'd not be able to find anyone who'd talk to him. But he wasn't going to give up yet.

Still keeping his eye on the Muran house, he moved on down the street. Just as he reached the corner, a figure came up the servants' steps. He stopped, knelt down, and pretended he was searching the pavement for something he'd lost. A young woman with a wicker basket over her arm stepped onto the pavement and walked briskly up the road. She wore a short black jacket over a blue broadcloth dress and a gray wool cap. From the cut of her skirt and color, he was sure she was a housemaid. Cor blimey, he thought, today was his lucky day. He'd only been here for a little while.

By the time she was close to him, he pretended he'd found what he was looking for and leapt to his feet.

Surprised by his sudden movement, she stopped.

"Oh, sorry, miss, I didn't mean to startle you." He smiled in apology.

"That's all right." She ducked her head and stepped to one side to go around him.

"I didn't see you," he continued. "If I had, I'd not have jumped up the way I did. I didn't mean to be rude."

"You weren't rude," she mumbled as she quickened her pace.

"Excuse me," he said as he fell into step behind her, "I don't mean to be forward, but I was hoping you might be able to help me."

"I'm in a hurry." She cast him a swift, suspicious glance and moved even faster.

"If I could just speak to you for a moment," he said, doffing his cap respectfully. He was moving fast just to keep up with her.

"Leave me be," she mumbled. She gave him a quick, terrified look and increased her pace.

Wiggins suddenly realized he was frightening the poor girl, so he stopped. "I'm sorry, miss," he called. She was now almost running. "I've just lost my dog, that's all. I was wondering if you'd seen it."

She didn't bother to even look back at him. She simply dashed across the road and disappeared around the corner. Wiggins stared after her, wondering what could possibly make someone so frightened they wouldn't even stop on a public street in broad daylight.

Mrs. Jeffries peeked into the kitchen and saw that Mrs. Goodge was chatting with the butcher's delivery boy. Checking that Samson wasn't about to try and escape, she opened the back door and went outside. The small terrace was still damp from the morning mist, so Mrs. Jeffries kept to the paths as she crossed the communal gardens. There was no point in arriving at Lady Cannonberry's with wet shoes.

She had thought long and hard about the wisdom of her present course of action and had concluded that they really had no choice in the matter. Last night, the inspector's words had made it very clear that he'd no desire to go poking about in a murder that to his mind was already solved. Furthermore, she had the impression he wanted to avoid confrontations with Nigel Nivens.

She pursed her lips and took a deep breath. It was bad luck that the case had been handled by Nivens. She knew that he'd fight tooth and nail to make sure it was never re-opened. Nivens didn't care a whit about justice, and she thought him quite capable of letting an innocent man hang if it would serve his career.

She stepped off the path and onto the grass leading to her destination. A moment later, she went down a short flight of stairs leading to a small white stone terrace and boldly knocked on the back door.

A young scullery maid answered. "Hello, Mrs. Jeffries." The maid bobbed a quick, respectful curtsey.

"Hello, Molly." Mrs. Jeffries smiled kindly. "Is your mistress at home?" She had no doubt she'd be welcomed here.

"She is, ma'am. Please come inside." Molly held open the door. "The mistress is in the kitchen, ma'am, having a word with cook."

Mrs. Jeffries followed the girl down a hallway and into a large well-kept kitchen, which was laid out almost identically to the one she'd just left. The homes on this garden had been built at the same time and were very much of the same design. But this kitchen floor was tiled in black and white squares and the walls were painted a pale gray-green, not the cheerful yellow of the inspector's kitchen.

Lady Ruth Cannonberry was sitting at the kitchen table with another woman who was wearing a cook's apron and hat. A large brown recipe book was laying open in front of the two of them.

"Why, Hepzibah, this is a lovely surprise." Ruth smiled in delight at her visitor. "Do say you'll stay for some tea."

"That would be lovely," Mrs. Jeffries replied.

"We'll continue this later, Mrs. Folger."

"Very well, ma'am," the cook replied.

Ruth got to her feet and hurried to her guest. Taking Mrs. Jeffries' arm, she said to the maid, "Molly, bring tea to the morning room, please."

"Yes, ma'am," Molly replied.

A few minutes later, they were taking their seats in a cozy sitting room that faced east. Unfortunately, there wasn't much morning sunlight. But the walls were papered in a lovely pale yellow-and-white-flowered pattern, the curtains were delicate white lace, and there were beautiful pastoral oil paintings on the walls.

"I'm so delighted you came over," Ruth said excitedly. "Sometimes I feel quite guilty with the way I'm always dropping by to see all of you."

Ruth Cannonberry was an attractive middle-aged widow with blonde hair, blue eyes, and a lovely smile. She was the daughter of a country vicar who took the gospel message seriously and who had instilled in her a very active social conscience. She had definite ideas about the roots of poverty, women's suffrage, and the evils of a hereditary class system. But she was also a sweet-natured woman who'd very much loved her late aristocratic husband, so for his memory's sake, she did avoid chaining herself to railings in front of Parliament and actually getting arrested.

She and Inspector Witherspoon were very fond of each other, but their relationship was continually threatened by her sudden absences from London. Unfortunately, she'd inherited her late husband's relatives, most of whom were elderly, self-centered, and certain that every sniffle meant they were at death's door. She was continually being called out of town to sit with some cousin, uncle, or maiden aunt who was sure they were on their deathbed. Ruth did it gladly, as it was in her nature to give when people needed help.

"Nonsense, we enjoy your visits," Mrs. Jeffries assured her. "You are welcome any time."

Molly brought in the tea on a silver tray and put it on the small table in front of the two women. "Will there be anything else, ma'am?"

"No, thank you, Molly," Ruth replied. "How is Inspector Witherspoon today?" she asked Mrs. Jeffries as she reached for the silver teapot. She insisted that the household of Upper Edmonton Gardens call her by her Christian name, but she was sensitive to the fact that they might not be comfortable referring to their employer in such a manner.

"He's very well and looking forward to your coming to dinner this evening," she replied. "Mrs. Goodge has a special meal planned, one I'm sure you'll both enjoy."

"I'm sure we will." Ruth poured their tea. "Mrs. Goodge is an excellent cook."

"That she is," Mrs. Jeffries replied. "But I didn't come to talk to you about tonight. I came to ask for your help."

"You need my help!" Ruth cried in excitement. "But that's wonderful. Does the inspector have a new case?"

She dearly loved helping them with Inspector Witherspoon's murders, and, like them, she was committed to making sure he never found out he was being helped.

"That's the difficult part." Mrs. Jeffries added a lump of sugar to her tea. "He doesn't know he's actually got a case."

"He doesn't know?" Ruth's pale eyebrows rose in confusion. "I don't understand."

"Of course you don't," Mrs. Jeffries sighed. "I've not explained it very well. Let me tell you what happened, and then after you hear what I've got to say, you can make up your own mind as to whether or not you want to help us."

"I'll assist you in any way I can," she began.

But Mrs. Jeffries held up her hand. "Wait until you've heard the facts of the matter, then make up your mind."

She told her about their visit from Blimpey Groggins, explaining who he was and his assertion that Tommy Odell was innocent. Then she took a deep breath and confided her doubts about how effective they could be in this kind of a situation. "So you see, unless we come up with compelling evidence that the man didn't commit the murder, we can't go to the inspector. It wouldn't be fair."

"I see the dilemma," Ruth said softly. "You can't ask the inspector to risk his career unless you can prove absolutely the man is innocent, and you're afraid we'll find just enough evidence to convince ourselves Odell isn't guilty but not enough to convince the police or the Home Secretary."

Mrs. Jeffries picked up her teacup. "That's my biggest fear. If we determine to our own satisfaction that the man wasn't guilty, but we can't convince the authorities to stop the execution, it will haunt us for the rest of our lives. I'm loathe to admit this, even to myself, but there's a part of me that wishes we'd never heard of this case." She sighed and closed her eyes. "I don't mean that, of course. Working for justice is a privilege, not a burden. Of course we must find the truth, regardless of what it may do to the inspector's career."

"You're worried about Gerald?" Ruth frowned. "But surely he'd not be harmed by trying to do right."

"One would think that should be the case," she replied. "But the original case was handled by Inspector Nigel Nivens."

"Oh dear." Ruth looked disturbed. "That's not good news. He's not an honorable person." She thought for a moment. "Then there's only one thing to do."

"And what would that be?" Mrs. Jeffries asked curiously. She'd not been able to think of what to do about this situation.

"We'll have to make sure we have irrefutable evidence

that Tommy Odell is innocent." Ruth smiled brightly. "That shouldn't be in the least difficult."

Constable Barnes didn't know what made him do it. It generally wasn't in his nature to spy on his superiors or eavesdrop just to satisfy his curiosity, but nevertheless, he couldn't quite explain what had compelled him to hide against the stairwell.

He'd come to deliver a box of evidence from Aldgate police station to the Metropolitan Police Force's new premises at New Scotland Yard. It wasn't a large box, but it was heavy enough that he hoisted it onto his shoulder rather than carrying it in his arms, so if one was looking at him from his right, his face would be obscured. He followed three people through the front door and into the foyer—two women and a man.

Inside the heavy oak doors, Barnes veered to his right, intending to set the box down on the counter and ask the duty officer to send a constable to assist him. Then he heard Nivens' voice.

"Mr. Muran, I do hope you'll forgive this dreadful inconvenience. I'm afraid the move into our new premises has become a bit of an excuse for incompetence further down the ranks. Please be assured I've disciplined the men who are responsible for this. You shouldn't have had to go all over town to retrieve your belongings now that the trial is over."

Barnes slowed his steps.

"That's quite all right, Inspector Nivens," a cultured male voice with an upper-class accent replied. "As long as you've my watch, I don't mind coming along to fetch it."

Barnes moved to the counter and nodded to the constable on duty, an older copper who Barnes had once walked a beat with in Leicester Square. "Can I leave this here a moment?" he asked, deliberately keeping his voice low enough so that Nivens wouldn't recognize it.

"I'll look after it for you," the constable replied, keeping his voice down as well.

Barnes nodded and then nipped back around the other side of the counter and positioned himself against the side of the stairwell. He moved into a spot where he could see and hear everything.

"Thank you for being so understanding, sir," Nivens replied. He reached into his pocket and pulled out a flat package wrapped in brown paper. "Here you are, sir. I've got it all ready for you."

Barnes peeked out between the railings of the staircase, craning his neck to get a good look at Nivens' visitors. The man was obviously Keith Muran. He was a decent enough looking chap, dark hair with a sprinkling of gray at the temples. He was clean shaven with nice, even features. He had the sort of looks that Mrs. Barnes would probably call distinguished.

"Did they ever find the braclet?" one of the women asked. She was a tall, older woman with hair that was gray with a bit of brown left in it, deep set eyes with dark circles beneath them, and a thin, bony face. She was dressed in black.

"No ma'am," Nivens replied. "But we're still looking. It's on our missing list, and I'm sure it'll turn up soon. Eventually, most jewelry does."

"*Humph,*" she replied. "It's probably on the arm of some doxy. The shame of it. That bracelet was made by Giuilani and has been in our family for two hundred years."

"Mother, please," the younger woman interrupted. "This is no time to be concerned with such matters. Caroline was our dear cousin and now she's gone."

She wore black, too, but her stylish hat had a hint of blue in its feathers and her jacket was trimmed with gold braid on the high collar and cuffs. Her hair was as black as her attire, her eyes blue, and her complexion perfect. Yet Barnes thought her nose was a trife too long and her mouth a bit too wide for her to be beautiful. But nonetheless, she was very pretty.

She gave the older woman a worried frown. "You must apologize to dear Keith."

"No, no, Lucy, your mother has a right to speak her mind," Muran smiled indulgently. "I know she meant no harm, and she's perfectly correct. The bracelet is a precious family heirloom that should go to her once the police find it, providing of course, they do find it."

"We'll do our very best, sir," Nivens interjected. "I'll put more men on the Soho pawnshops and notify you immediately when it turns up."

"I'm dreadfully sorry. I'm not myself." The older woman pulled a black handkerchief out of her muff and dabbed at her eyes. "Do forgive me, Keith. I've been out of my mind with grief since she was taken from us."

"Edwina, dear, there's nothing to forgive. This has been a trying time for all of us."

"It's almost over," Nivens said helpfully. "Tommy Odell is set to hang in a few weeks. That ought to help."

Keith Muran said nothing for a long moment; he simply stared at Nivens. "I don't think it will, Inspector. It certainly won't bring her back to me, will it."

CHAPTER 3

"I don't like that cat of yours." Tom Briggs, the butcher's boy, helped himself to a slice of freshly made bread from the platter next to the teapot. He glared at Samson, who was perched on a stool next to the hallway licking his paws.

The cook eyed the lad speculatively. He was a bit cheeky, but sharp as a tack and observant to boot. Tom was only eleven or so, but those blue eyes of his saw lots more than most people. Plus, he loved to gossip. Not that she expected him to know anything about the Muran murder, but she liked the boy and it paid to keep him happy and chatty—you never knew when he'd learn a tidbit that might be useful in one of their future cases.

"What have you got against my Samson?" she asked as she reached for a mug and poured herself a cup of tea. "He's a sweet old boy."

"He is not," Tom replied. "He hisses at me every time I set foot in the back hall. This morning he swiped at my ankles when I carried the meat into the wet larder. He's a real terror, Mrs. Goodge. Look, he's sittin' there waitin' for me to leave so he can have another go at me when I go down the hall."

"Nonsense." The cook genuinely couldn't understand why everyone, even animal lovers, hated her pet. "Just stay out of his way when he's having one of his cranky moments and you'll be fine."

Tom smeared apricot jam on his bread. "Mam says cats steal yer breath."

"That's an old wives' tale," the cook replied. Samson slept on her bed every night and she was still breathing properly.

"What's an old wives' tale?" he asked curiously.

"It's something people say is true that actually isn't true at all," she replied. "Now look, you'd best be quick lad. I'd not see you get in trouble with your parents for bein' late."

Tom stuffed a piece of bread into his mouth. He liked it best when Mrs. Goodge had those nice buns, but the bread was good, too. "There's no rush. Mam's gone to help her sister and Dad's goin' to be so busy this morning; he'll not notice what time I get back."

Samson stopped licking his paw and stared at the boy out of cold, green eyes. Tom wanted to sit right where he was until that beast got off the stool. He knew the cat was just waiting to get him. The nasty old thing was sitting at such an angle that it would be impossible to slip past without being in range of one of those big, ugly paws of his. Besides, he liked Mrs. Goodge. She always talked to him like he was a grown-up.

"If your mother's gone, shouldn't you get back quickly to lend your father a hand?" Mrs. Goodge peered at him over the top of her spectacles.

Tom shook his head. "He's got help. Eldon—he's my cousin—just lost his position, so he's workin' for us until he finds something else."

Mrs. Goodge didn't want to run the boy off and she had no one else coming in until this afternoon so she decided to let him eat his fill before she showed him the door. She crossed the kitchen to the dish rack next to the sink and grabbed the brown bowl that she used for cake making. A nice seed cake and a madeira would do nicely for her sources.

As soon as Mrs. Goodge had her back to him, Tom stuck his tongue out at Samson. The cat blinked, narrowed his eyes, and twitched his tail. Tom thought he might have just made a mistake; maybe he should have tried being friends with the ugly beast.

"Where's Fred?" he asked. He looked at the empty brown rag rug where the dog was usually curled up asleep. Tom liked Fred.

"He's upstairs in Wiggins' room," she replied. "He and Samson don't get along."

"Poor Fred." Tom knew just how the dog felt. "Mam says Eldon will probably be with us for a long while. Mam says Eldon must be thick as two short planks to lose his position. It was dead easy. All he had to do was nail boxes shut."

Mrs. Goodge put the bowl down on her worktable, reached underneath, and got out her flour sifter. She was only half listening to the lad. "Is that so?"

"Oh yes. Mind you, in one sense she's glad. It was only because Eldon got the sack that she could go and help Aunt Helen. That's her sister."

"Where does your aunt Helen live?" She got the tin cup she used for measuring dry ingredients from the shelf and set it next to the flour. "In the country?"

"Oh no, she lives near Victoria Station. It's not far at all."

Mrs. Goodge looked up at him. "Is your mam's sister seriously ill?"

Tom shrugged. "She's not got the bad sick kind where you're vomitin' everythin' you eat and have to take to your bed. She's got the other kind."

"What other kind?"

"The nervous disposition sort," Tom explained. "Dad says she had a bad shock and Mam's got to go spend some time with her. But I wish she'd come home. Mrs. Cubb comes in and does meals for us, but her cooking is right greasy. I miss my Mam. She makes the best toad-in-the-hole."

Mrs. Goodge nodded in understanding. That would explain why Mrs. Briggs was away from home even though her sister's house was only a short omnibus or hansom ride away. "It's very good of your mam to go and help out."

"Dad says Aunt Helen ought to stiffen her spine and get over her troubles." He shoved the last of the bread between his lips just as Samson leapt down and strolled out into the hallway.

Tom wasn't going to waste this chance. He got to his feet, picked up his empty dishes, and hurried to the sink. "I'd best get going, Mrs. Goodge. Thanks ever so much for the food. That bread was really good." He brushed past the cook as he ran for the door.

"Here, just a minute." Mrs. Goodge started after him. "What's wrong with your aunt Helen?"

"She's got the melancholy," Tom called over his shoulder. He skidded to a halt at the doorway and stuck his head into the hall, making sure that miserable cat wasn't waiting to pounce on him as he rounded the corner. The hall was cat free.

"Oh dear," Mrs. Goodge clucked sympathetically. She was fairly sure she knew what the melancholy was and she also knew it happened to every woman of a certain age. "Eventually, even that goes away. Let's hope it doesn't last long for your poor auntie."

Tom shrugged. "Dad says she ought to be over it now."

Mrs. Goodge sighed inwardly. It wasn't her place to speak of such things, especially to a young lad, but you'd think a grown man would have more sense. "Sometimes it takes some women longer than others," she said gently as she joined him in the doorway.

He started down the hall. "Dad says it's been over a month now, so she ought to be over it."

"A month!" Mrs. Goodge yelped. "Why, that's no time at all." If men had to go through what nature forced women to endure, she thought she'd bet her last quarter wages Mr. Briggs would be a bit more patient. "No time at all, I tell you. These problems can take years before they run their course."

"But why should it last so long?" Tom called over his shoulder as he jerked open the back door. "Dad says they've caught the bloke that did it so there's nothing more for Aunt Helen to be scared about."

"What bloke?" Mrs. Goodge raced after the lad. "I mean, what are you talking about? What man?"

Tom flew out into the garden. "I don't know his last name, but he's got the same Christian name as me, exceptin' that people call him Tommy and I'm just Tom."

Smythe was so frustrated he could spit nails, but he forced himself to appear calm. He'd spoken to every hansom driver in the West End and it had taken him hours to track down the cabbie that had driven the Murans on the night of the murder. To top it off, he wasn't even sure he had the right one. He had a feeling the man might be having him on. But he couldn't be sure.

Smythe glanced around the small cabstand. Three drivers were taking their tea. Two were hunched over the camp stove and the third was sitting at the far end of a tiny table next to the stove with his feet propped straight out in front of him.

"You're sure it was the right people?" Smythe pressed, his question directed at the taller of the two drivers warming their hands by the stove. He was named Fletcher, and he was a burly, brown-haired fellow with a full beard. "The ones I need to know about."

"There were dozens of toffs wantin' a cab that night." Fletcher straightened up and stepped closer to the table. "I was workin' that area and I remember pickin' up a couple that matches your description."

"We all picked up people that matche his description," the other cabbie said. "It was a busy night. The traffic was so thick it took hours just to get out of the West End. Most people coulda walked 'ome in the time it took to get down Oxford Street."

Fletcher ignored the other cabbie. "I'm thinkin' you're interested in that couple where the wife ended up murdered." He stared speculatively at Smythe. "And they was the ones that I picked up that night."

"Get on with you, Fletcher, quit tellin' such tales," the driver sitting at the table said. "Stop pullin' the poor feller's leg."

"Mind yer own bloomin' business," Fletcher retorted good-naturedly.

"You're sure you're not just sayin' you know somethin' because I offered to pay for information?" Smythe asked.

He was annoyed at himself for making such a mistake. It was always better to make sure your informant actually knew something before you offered to reach into your pocket. But he'd jumped the gun and stupidly walked into the hansom stand and announced he needed information and was willing to cross their palms with silver if they had it.

Fletcher looked offended. "I'm not a liar."

"He's not," the driver sitting at the table added. "He's a good Presbyterian."

Fletcher sighed and put his mug in the white tin bowl on the table that served as a sink. "Look, I'll tell you what I told the copper that come 'round here afterwards, not that he seemed all that interested in what I was sayin'."

The cabbie who'd been warming his hands straightened up, pulled on his gloves, and moved to the open entrance. "You can trust what Fletcher tells ya," he said to Smythe. "I'm off, lads. I'll see ya tomorrow."

The second cabbie got to his feet. "I'd best be on my way as well." He looked at Smythe. "I like takin' the piss out of Fletcher, because he's such a serious soul, but he tells the truth. He's no liar."

"I didn't mean to offend ya," Smythe said to Fletcher as soon as the two of them were alone. "But I need to be certain of what you're sayin'. It's a right important. Was the copper a uniform or a detective?"

"Both," Fletcher replied. He pulled his gloves out of his coat pocket. "I spoke to the police constable first, then a day or two later a detective come around and asked a few questions."

"You remember his name?" Smythe was fairly sure he knew who it had been.

"Inspector . . . er Nivens, yes, that's it. Not a very nice fellow." He made a face. "Bit of a toff with his nose in the air, if you know what I mean."

"I know the type," Smythe replied.

"He was in and out of 'ere in two seconds flat."

"What did you tell 'im?"

"I told 'im I'd picked them up that night," he explained. "There's always a line of folks after the concerts at St. James Hall. That time of night the fares are good, people want to get home, and like Ricky said, there was no end of traffic. The man told me to take 'em to West Brompton and I started off in that direction. But we'd not gone more than a mile when he stuck his head out and told me to take him to Barrick Street on the other side of Waterloo Bridge. Corse that was a bit further than I'd expected to go, but I did what he wanted and took 'em across. Last I saw of them, they were walking down the road where I'd let 'em off."

Smythe wasn't sure what to ask next. For a brief moment, he wondered if he'd completely lost the ability to do his own sleuthing. But then the obvious one popped into his head. "When they were in the cab, did you hear them talking?"

The cabbie laughed. "Not likely. Between the horses hooves and rattle of the traffic, it's too noisy to hear what your fares are sayin' to each other."

"Do you remember how they were actin'?" he asked.

Fletcher frowned. "Ya mean how they acted towards each other?"

"That, and if you noticed anything unusual about either of them."

He thought for a moment. "Not really. They acted like any other couple that'd been out for an evenin'. He helped her in and out of the carriage. There wasn't anything odd about it exceptin' Barrick Street was as deserted a place as I've ever seen."

"So you saw no one about?" Smythe prodded. Blast, he was hoping the man might have seen someone hanging about.

"It's an industrial area," Fletcher explained. "Nothing but old warehouses and small factories. Most of those places don't even have night watchmen."

Smythe's mind had gone blank again. "Er, so you just let 'em off and that was the last you saw of 'em?" He felt like an idiot. He was almost repeating what the man had just told him.

"That's right." Fletcher pulled a pair of black gloves out of his coat pocket. They were old and worn.

"Do you remember anything else about them or about that night?" Smythe watched as the cabbie put on the gloves. There were holes in two fingers of one glove and the thumb of the other was split down the side.

Fletcher picked his hat up off a stool and slapped it on his head. "Not really. No, I tell a lie: when I picked them up, they was talking to another couple, standing all together in a group like."

"Would you recognize this couple if you saw them again?" he asked.

"No." He smiled apologetically. "I weren't paying that much attention. Look, I've got to be off now."

"Wait," Smythe said as Fletcher headed for the open entrance. "I've not paid for the information."

The cabbie shook his head and grinned. "Keep yer coin, mate. What little I know wasn't worth much now, was it."

"That's all a matter of opinion." Smythe realized he'd offended the man's pride and was suddenly, deeply ashamed.

He'd handled this badly from the beginning, and he was determined to make up for it. Reaching into his coat pocket, he grabbed some coins and handed them to Fletcher. "You've saved me a lot of work."

The cabbie looked at the coins. "By crickety, this is three florins!"

"Take it. You earned it. Like I said, you've saved me a lot of trouble."

"Thanks, mate, this is right good of ya." Fletcher walked to the entrance, then stopped and turned. "I did see that other couple get into the hansom just ahead of mine. I don't know if that'll do ya any good."

Mrs. Jeffries was the last one to arrive for their afternoon meeting. "I'm so sorry to be late," she said as she hurried toward the coat tree, "but the traffic was dreadful today. The omnibus was held up for ages because of a crash between a hansom cab and a water cart."

"Not to worry, Mrs. Jeffries." Mrs. Goodge poured the housekeeper a cup of tea. "We've only just sat down ourselves."

"Excellent." She slipped into her chair, took a deep breath, and then looked around the table at the others. "I'd like to go first, if I may." She waited for a moment and then plunged ahead. "I've asked Ruth Cannonberry to give us some assistance on this case. Perhaps I ought to have spoken to all of you before I took such an action, but I honestly believe she could be a great deal of help to us."

"Does she know that our inspector doesn't have this case?" Betsy asked.

"I told her everything," she explained. "It didn't seem fair not to tell her the whole story."

"And she's not alarmed by the prospect of workin' behind the inspector's back, so to speak?" Mrs. Goodge asked.

"Not in the least." Mrs. Jeffries relaxed a bit. "I know it was a bit of a risk, my asking her for help, but frankly,

I really didn't see that we'd any other choice. She has some very powerful connections and we might very well need them."

"If we're lucky, maybe her connections will keep us from 'aving to put this on the inspector's plate," Smythe mused. "That'd be right useful."

"My thoughts exactly," Mrs. Jeffries replied. "I had another run of good luck by bringing her into it. She actually knew the victim. Caroline Muran occasionally came to her women's suffrage meetings. They weren't close friends nor did they move in the same social circles, but she was acquainted with her."

"Did she like her?" Betsy asked softly. Somehow, one of their own knowing the victim made it more real, more personal.

Mrs. Jeffries smiled sadly. "Ruth says she was a very nice woman—very kind and very intelligent. She was a strong financial supporter of the society and gave them a good contribution every year."

"I expect they'll miss that," Mrs. Goodge muttered. She wasn't sure how she felt about some of Ruth's radical ideas. She used to be dead set against all of them. She'd always believed that the British class system was right and proper and that the lower classes should know their places. But over the past few years, she'd changed her thinking on such matters.

"Did Lady Cannonberry know of anyone who had a reason to dislike Mrs. Muran?" Betsy asked. "Was there anyone in the society she'd had a quarrel with or anything like that?"

"No, she was a member, but she wasn't actively involved enough in the group to have made any enemies."

"I suppose that would have been too simple," Betsy replied glumly. "Finding out who hated Caroline Muran enough to murder her isn't going to be easy."

"Why wasn't she involved?" Mrs. Goodge reached for her tea cup. "She ought to have been if she believed in their cause. She had money and she had time—"

"But that's just it," Mrs. Jeffries interrupted. "She didn't have time. She was actively involved in running the metal works factory."

"You mean she was the manager?" Wiggins looked quite horrified by the idea.

"Why shouldn't she be the manager?" Mrs. Goodge said tartly. "She owned the place, she ought to have been able to run it as she saw fit. Women can manage factories as well as men."

"I didn't say they couldn't," Wiggins insisted. "But it couldn't have been a very nice place, with all them nasty chemicals about. I'll bet the place stank to high heaven."

"She had a manager," Mrs. Jeffries interjected quickly. "But she had to sack him." That had been the pertinent point she'd wanted to make. "She sacked him about a week before she was killed. So we know that she had at least one person in her life that couldn't have been too pleased with her."

"Why'd she fire 'im?" Smythe asked eagerly.

"Ruth didn't know any details." Mrs. Jeffries picked up her mug. "She heard the information secondhand after she found out about the murder. But she thought nothing of it, of course. Like everyone else, because Tommy was arrested so quickly, she assumed Mrs. Muran's death was simply a robbery gone wrong."

"That's what everyone seems to think," Smythe muttered. "We need to find out the name of her factory manager, the one she sacked. I can have a go at that tomorrow."

Mrs. Jeffries nodded in agreement. "We definitely should find out the man's name. But that's not all I have to tell you. After I saw Ruth, I went to St. Thomas's Hospital to have a quick word with Dr. Bosworth."

Dr. Bosworth was another friend who'd helped them on several of their earlier cases. He had some very interesting ideas about dead bodies, and his theories had often helped them when they were on the hunt.

He'd spent several years in San Francisco and had seen

a rather large number of homicide victims, virtually all of whom had been shot. Apparently, there was no shortage of either guns or bodies in California.

Dr. Bosworth had come to the conclusion that you could tell a great deal about how a person was murdered simply by a careful examination of the death wounds. He also believed that a thorough study of the murder victim could reveal more than the mechanics of the cause of death; he believed it could often give clues as to who had been the killer. Like the household, Dr. Bosworth was quite discreet about his help with Inspector Witherspoon's cases.

"Did he do the postmortem?" Mrs. Goodge asked. "That would make it nice and handy for us."

"Unfortunately, he didn't. But he promised he'd take a look at the attending doctor's report and get back to us. I don't know that it'll help much," she warned.

"It might," Wiggins mused. "Dr. Bosworth knows a lot about gunshot holes in a body. He might see something that'd be good for us to know. He might be able to guess what kind of gun it was. That'd narrow it down just a bit."

Mrs. Jeffries stared at him for a moment. "Why, Wiggins, you're absolutely right. We need to have some idea of what kind of weapon was used."

"I'll see if I can find out what kind of guns our suspects own," he offered eagerly.

"But we don't even know who our suspects are," the cook pointed out.

"That doesn't matter," Wiggins explained. "I'll just try to find out if anyone in Mrs. Muran's circle owned a weapon. That ought to be useful." He looked at Smythe. "And you ought to find out if the fellow that was sacked has a gun."

"I'd already thought of that," Smythe replied. "It might take a day or two, though."

"That would be most helpful." Mrs. Jeffries looked around the table. "Who would like to go next?"

"Let me," Betsy entreated. "It'll not take long. I walked my feet off but I didn't hear all that much. Mainly, it was just a repeat of what you've already told us. Mrs. Muran was very nice and well liked by her servants. Her factory workers are going to miss her, as she was getting ready to have their housing redone properly. The local merchants are going to miss her as well. She apparently settled her accounts promptly at the end of each month." She shrugged. "It's not much, I know, but I'll be out again tomorrow to see what I can find out."

"Don't be so hard on yourself; you've learned a lot." Smythe patted her shoulder. "Not as much as me, but enough so that you can hold your head up."

She laughed and cuffed him playfully on the arm. "You just wait. I'll find out lots more than you do tomorrow."

"I hope I find out who owns a gun tomorrow," Wiggins muttered. "I didn't find out anything at all today."

"No one would talk to you?" Smythe asked, his voice sympathetic.

"The only person I met was a housemaid, but she wasn't much of a talker. I hung about the area for ages, but I didn't see anyone else that seemed likely to speak to me. It was all posh ladies goin' to tea and gentlemen comin' home from work. All in all it wasn't a good day." He wondered if he ought to tell the others about how scared the poor girl had been. No, they might think he'd been silly and incompetent; best to leave it alone and make his own amends. The girl was probably fresh in from the country and he needed to be careful in how he approached her. If she saw him skulking about it would likely frighten her more.

"Not to worry, Wiggins, you'll do better tomorrow. We both will," Betsy said cheerfully.

"Of course you will," Mrs. Goodge said quickly. She was bursting to tell them her news. "Now, I'd like to have a go if no one minds."

"You must of found out somethin' excitin'." Wiggins grinned. "I can always tell; your cheeks go all pink."

Mrs. Goodge laughed. "Really? I'd no idea. You're right, though, I did find out something exciting and it was almost by accident, but that's neither here nor there. It seems the housekeeper for Mr. and Mrs. Muran has melancholia and has taken to her bed. She's had it ever since she heard about Mrs. Muran's murder."

"Melancholia?" Wiggins frowned. "Is that the sad sickness?"

"It's generally more of a mental or nervous condition," Mrs. Jeffries replied. "At least that's what I've always heard. Sorry, Mrs. Goodge, I didn't mean to interrupt. Do go on."

The cook told them about her visit from young Tom Briggs. She left out the part where she had to chase him clear across the communal garden with promises of seed cake and sticky buns in order to get him to come back. "According to what Tom overheard his mother tellin' his father, his aunt Helen hasn't set foot back in the Muran household since she heard about the murder."

"Where does she live?" Smythe asked.

"Number Eighteen Cedar Road, near the Waltham Green railway station."

"She wasn't a live-in housekeeper?" Mrs. Jeffries queried.

"No, she used to come in before breakfast and then leave as soon as the dinner was served."

"That's an odd way to run a 'ousehold, isn't it?" Wiggins asked curiously.

"It's actually becoming more and more common," Mrs. Jeffries replied. "I wonder if the other staff lived out as well."

"I don't know," Mrs. Goodge frowned. "That isn't the sort of detail I'd expect Tom to know."

"We can find out easily enough," Betsy said. She reached for the teapot and poured herself a second cup.

"I'll go along tomorrow and see what's what," Wiggins offered. "I was plannin' on goin' back anyway, you know to suss out who's got a gun or not. Or would you rather I go along to where the housekeeper lives and see what I can find out there?"

Mrs. Jeffries thought for a moment. "Go back to the Muran neighborhood. We've learned a bit about the victim, but I think we need to learn something about the rest of the household as well."

"I can go along to Cedar Road," Betsy offered. "The shopkeepers can wait for another day."

"Good." the housekeeper looked at Smythe. "How did you do today?"

"Not as well as Mrs. Goodge, but a bit better than Wiggins," he grinned. "I found the cabbie that dropped the Murans off on the night of the murder. Accordin' to 'im, when they first got in the hansom, Mr. Muran told the driver to take them home. But then he suddenly sticks his head out and tells the driver to take them across the river to Barrick Street. Last he saw of them, they were walking down the road."

"Did he see anyone else in the area?" Mrs. Goodge helped herself to another slice of bread.

"No, he said the place was deserted. It's one of them areas that's full of little factories and warehouses. Once the workday ends, there's no one about. The cabbie, who seems to know the neighborhood, claims most of those businesses don't even have watchmen at night." He told them the rest of the information he'd gotten that day, taking care to tell them every little detail, including the comments of the other two cabbies about the night of the murder. Previous cases had taught them that sometimes it was the unimportant detail that solved the case.

"Some businesses are so cheap," Mrs. Goodge muttered darkly. "You'd think they'd pay for a watchman or two. A deserted street in the middle of the night isn't exactly going to have many witnesses about."

Smythe sat back in his chair. "I thought I'd go around and have a good look at the road where they got let off. It'd be 'elpful if we knew exactly where the murder happened, you know, the exact spot."

"Will you have enough time?" Mrs. Jeffries asked. "It

might take hours for you to find out the name of the sacked manager and track him down."

"And you'll 'ave to find out if he's got a gun," Wiggins added. "That'll not be easy, either."

Smythe realized he also had to go see Blimpey, but he wasn't going to share that information with the rest of them. "We've got a bit of time," he replied. "I'll put goin' to the murder scene at the bottom of the list and if I can't get to it tomorrow, I'll go the day after."

"That's an excellent idea," Mrs. Jeffries said. She put her mug down. "If everyone agrees, I'd like to have a quick word with Constable Barnes tomorrow. He might be able to get us a copy of the original police report."

"That would be very useful," the cook said. "But we'd not want to put the constable in any sort of awkward position."

"He's a clever man," Betsy said. "He'd be very able to help us out a little without putting his own position as a police officer in any sort of . . ." she couldn't think what the proper word might be.

"We won't let him compromise himself," Mrs. Jeffries said quickly. "I'll be very discreet. As I've mentioned before, there are times when I think the good constable is very aware of what we're doing." Actually, she knew for a fact that Constable Barnes knew exactly what they did, but she couldn't recall if she'd told the others that fact. Sometimes she wished her memory was a little better than it was, or perhaps it was a sign she was getting older.

"You have a chat with him, Mrs. Jeffries. Right now we need his help," Mrs. Goodge said.

"Let's just 'ope he can get his hands on that report," Smythe said earnestly.

Wiggins got to Drayton Gardens just in time to see two well-dressed women come out the front door. He hesitated for a moment and then decided to follow them. He might as well find out what he could; it wasn't as if he could see anyone else about the area.

The women turned in the direction of the Fulham Road. The older one was dressed in black, the somber color relieved only by a touch of gray lace peeking out from the neck of her jacket. The younger one wore black as well, but there was gold braid along her cuffs, a white lace collar was visible over her the top of her wool jacket, and she carried a gold fur muff. When she'd turned, he'd seen a flash of silver earrings dangling from her ears. Wiggins, who'd only caught a glimpse of the young one's face, thought her one of the prettiest women he'd ever seen.

He fell into step behind the women, taking care not to get close enough to rouse their suspicion. The area was dead quiet, the only sound being the click of their shoes against the pavement. Wiggins lightened his footsteps and moved a bit closer. The older lady had turned her head and was speaking to the younger one.

"Do you have money for a hansom? I don't fancy walking all the way home."

He could hear her clearly, as she had a loud, nasally voice.

The younger one didn't reply. Wiggins frowned. Maybe she spoke so softly he'd not heard her. He eased just a little closer.

"Don't be absurd," the older one said. "Why would I have any money? Didn't Keith give you any? Surely we're not expected to walk all the way. For God's sake, we're doing this for him."

This time, he heard the younger one speak, but as he'd feared, her voice was so soft he couldn't hear what she said. He thought the older lady might be a bit deaf. His grandfather was losing his hearing. When he'd visited the family, he'd noticed his granddad spoke very loudly. Maybe that's why this lady's voice was loud enough to wake the dead. Truth was he could have heard her even if he'd been standing on the other side of the street.

"Walking all the way home is out of the question. It's too far and I'm an old woman."

The younger woman murmured something, which, of course, Wiggins couldn't hear.

"Then I want to stop and have tea at Lyons," she replied tartly. "I want one of those little lemon cakes. They do them so much better than cook. Speaking of which, when are you going to take care of Mrs. Black? Her puddings are dreadful, and she's impertinent as well. She actually asked me to leave the kitchen yesterday afternoon! Can you credit it?"

Instead of answering, the young woman looked over her shoulder straight at Wiggins. He smiled slightly and looked away, trying to act as though he just happened to be walking behind them.

She turned her attention forward again and he breathed a sigh of relief. Wiggins was now very interested in these two women. The nearest Lyons Tea Shop was on the Fulham Road. He increased his pace, crossed the street, and turned the opposite way on the next corner. He was bound and determined to find out what, if anything, they had to say.

Wiggins made it to the tea shop a few moments before the two women rounded the corner onto the Fulham Road. He ducked into the newsagent's across the street from Lyons, bought a paper, and then hurried back to the tea shop. He'd taken his cap off and tucked it under the paper, assuming that without the cap, the younger woman would be less likely to recognize him as the one who'd been walking behind them.

The women had taken seats at a table near the front window and were giving their order to the waiter. The room was very crowded. Wiggins went to the counter, ordered a cup of tea, and then made his way to an empty chair at a table behind his quarry. Two other people were already sitting there. One was an middle-aged man reading an *Illustrated London News* and the other was an elderly woman drinking a cup of tea. Wiggins nodded at the empty seat, and when neither of them objected he eased himself onto the chair. He whipped open his own paper and held it in front of his face.

The tables were very close together, but even so, hearing anything might be difficult. But he wasn't going to give up. He knew he had sharp ears and he wasn't going to be defeated by a bit of chatter and the clink of silverware.

The waiter brought the women their tea and a tray of cakes. Wiggins eased his chair a tad closer to them.

"This is almost as expensive as a hansom would have been," a familiar voice complained. "I don't see why we couldn't have had a cab."

"The exercise is good for both of us," a soft voice said in reply.

"Are you going to do something about that cook?" the older woman asked. "I'll not have someone of that class being impudent to me. She practically accused me of stealing food."

"Don't be absurd, Mama. You're imagining things again."

"It's true I tell you. When I went into the kitchen this morning to ask them to send up more bacon, cook asked me if I knew what had happened to the apple turnovers that were left over from yesterday's tea."

"Had you eaten them?" the younger woman asked.

"Certainly not!"

"Are you sure, Mama? Sometimes you do things and then you forget that you did them. You must try to do better at remembering things. I don't want this opportunity ruined by you doing something silly. Remember what happened the last time. If you hadn't forgotten she was coming to dinner that night, I'd have been married to him instead of her."

CHAPTER 4

Smythe pushed open the door of the Dirty Duck Pub and stepped inside. It was just after opening, but the place was already crowded. Day laborers, counting clerks, and dock workers stood two deep at the bar.

Blimpey was sitting in his usual spot near the fireplace; he saw Smythe and waved him over. "It took ya long enough to get here," he said by way of greeting.

"Sorry, I meant to come by yesterday, but I ran out of time." Smythe pulled a stool out and sat down. He was afraid the same thing was going to happen today. Despite getting up at the crack of dawn, he was already behind the schedule he'd set for himself.

"Doin' a bit of looking into things on yer own, were ya?" Blimpey nodded in understanding. "Your usual?" He signaled the barmaid as he asked the question.

"That'll do me." Smythe grinned apologetically. He didn't want Blimpey to think he'd been deliberately avoiding him. "Yesterday I started lookin' into this mess of yours, and, well, one thing led to another. I wasn't deliberately puttin' you off. I know you've got information for me."

"Two pints, please." Blimpey gave the woman their order and turned back to Smythe. "Stop explainin'. I know you'd a been here if you could. Look, I hope my comin' round to the inspector's house didn't land you in the drink. But I'm a bit desperate 'ere. The lad's innocent and they're fixin' to stretch his neck."

"We'll do what we can," Smythe replied. "But like Mrs. Jeffries told ya, we can't make any promises."

Blimpey sighed. "I know. Anyways, let's get on with it. Like I told ya the other day, there's a few bits and pieces about the case I didn't tell the others." He broke off as their beer arrived, nodding his thanks at the barmaid as she set their glasses on the table.

"What kind of bits and pieces?" Smythe picked up his beer and took a sip. It was a bit early in the day for him, but he didn't want to offend Blimpey.

"Despite what I said to the others about Mrs. Muran be-ing raised Quaker and not having enemies, there was more than a few who benefited from her death."

"Like who?" Smythe asked.

"Like Addison's Brass Works. They were wantin' to buy out Merriman's, but Mrs. Muran wouldn't sell. I've got it on good authority that now that she's dead, her husband has already started talking to Addison's again." Blimpey smiled cynically. "So much for him waitin' a decent inter-val and respectin' her wishes or her way of doin' things."

Smythe raised his eyebrow. "That is a bit quick."

"The poor woman wasn't even cold before Addison's had sent their man over to have a chat with the widower. Seems to me that when a company acts that fast, there's more to it than meets the eye."

"You're not seriously suggestin' that the owners of Addi-son's Brass Works actually murdered Mrs. Muran in order to buy her factory?" Smythe stared at Blimpey incredu-lously. "It's one thing for the widower to rush into sellin' the place, but quite another to suggest that a respectable business would stoop to murder to obtain someone else's factory."

"Don't be daft, man. Remember who you're talkin' to." Blimpey put his beer down and leaned closer, his expression dead serious. "It's my business to know what goes on in this city, and take my word for it, there's been more than one murder done to acquire something as profitable as Merriman's. It's a gold mine. They make high-quality product and there's a waiting list to get their goods. Even Her Majesty's government has to take their turn in the queue to get their orders filled. Addison's needs Merriman's."

"Why?" Smythe wondered if Blimpey was exaggerating. "If Addison's wants another factory so badly, why not build their own?"

"They can't. They've not got the money nor the brains to do it properly," Blimpey declared. "Addison's is on the verge of bankruptcy. What's more, I know for a fact that John Addison was in London the night Mrs. Muran was murdered."

Smythe stared at him. He couldn't quite believe Blimpey was right, but on the other hand, as he'd pointed out, he was in a position to know such things. Besides, if he'd learned anything in the last few years it was that people murdered one another for the strangest of reasons. "John Addison is the owner?"

"That's right. The company is in Birmingham. But he came to London a couple of days before Mrs. Muran was murdered and took rooms at the Fortune Hotel in Knightsbridge. He's been there ever since."

"If his company is almost bankrupt, how could he afford to buy Merriman's?" Smythe took another sip of his drink.

"He can't, but on the strength of the acquisition, the Birmingham and London Bank has agreed to give him a loan. As I said, Merriman's is a gold mine—plenty of cash in the bank and no outstanding debts. Now that Mrs. Muran is dead, they'll probably be dozens of hands reaching for that prize."

"Was she the sole owner?" Smythe asked.

Blimpey nodded. "That she was, and she refused to sell because she felt the company had a responsibility to its workers. Once someone else acquires the company, I've no doubt that will change as well."

"You're sure Mr. Muran is going to sell?"

Blimpey shrugged. "Why wouldn't he? It isn't his company, and he's not a businessman."

"So he didn't 'ave anything to do with the business?" Smythe said.

"No, it was hers and she was the one that had all the say so in how it was run."

"What did Keith Muran do before he married?" Smythe asked curiously.

"He didn't do much of anything." Blimpey grinned. "In other words, he was an English gentleman. His family was old money, but they lost most of it. He inherited a bit of lolly from his mother's people—not enough to make much of a splash in society, but enough to live comfortably without havin' to rely on the sweat of 'is brow. Muran was married before. His first wife died and he probably got a bit from her."

"So he's got two dead wives," Smythe muttered. "And both of them had money."

"Lots of people have been married more than once and lots of people inherit from their spouses. It's actually quite common, Smythe. Besides, I've got it on good authority that he loved both women."

Smythe snorted. "Despite your colorful occupation, Blimpey, you're a bit of a romantic. In my experience, there are plenty of people that have helped put their nearest and dearest into an early grave."

"That's true as well," Blimpey said. "But in my view, Keith Muran's no better or worse than anyone else of his class. He's spent most of his days being a gentleman of leisure. Goes to his club, sails, and spends his evenings making the social rounds. God knows how he ended up with

Caroline Merriman. She's not his sort at all, but by all accounts, the marriage was happy and both of them were certainly old enough to know their minds."

"Not all of us marry when we're young." Smythe spoke carefully to avoid stepping on any toes; Blimpey was no spring chicken and he'd been wed for just a year now.

"No, some of us have the good sense to wait until we find the right woman." Blimpey drained his glass. "If I were you, I'd take a look at John Addison. Seems to me his comin' to London when he did was a bit too coincidental."

"Is there anyone else I ought to look at?" Smythe finished his own beer.

Blimpey thought for a moment. "Not as yet. But I've got my ears out and about so when I get more information, I'll get word to you."

Smythe wondered why Blimpey hadn't heard about the sacked factory manager. In one sense, it made him feel good. It meant that Blimpey didn't know everything that went on in London. But he was certain that he'd find out soon enough, especially as he had his people actively scrounging for more information. He got to his feet. "We'll do our best to get this solved. I promise you."

Blimpey's eyes watered. He blinked rapidly and turned his head. "Blast, it's smoky in here. You'd think people would be decent enough to do their tobacco outside. It's not as if there's any decent air movin' about."

"The least they could do is open the windows," Smythe said. There was only one person smoking and he and his pipe were on the far side of the room. "I'll leave you to it, then, and be in touch."

"Smythe, thanks for takin' this on. Tommy's a nice lad, and well, I owe his mum a great deal. I've got to do what I can to make sure the lad doesn't hang."

"There's no word on whether or not Mrs. Muran's bracelet has ever turned up? Have your sources 'eard anything?"

Blimpey shook his head. "They've 'eard nothing."

"The reason could be that the killer knew the police were lookin' for it and so he's keepin' it till it's safe to sell." Smythe was talking off the top of his head, and he wasn't even sure if he was making sense. The only thing he knew about how stolen goods were sold was what he'd picked up on the street or heard from the inspector.

"Or it could be that it was never fenced in the first place, because Mrs. Muran's murder didn't have anything to do with robbery," Blimpey declared. "It were just made to look that way. Tommy lifted that watch hours before Mrs. Muran was killed. Keith Muran probably didn't even know it was gone, so when the police asked him what was missing, he told 'em his watch was gone and her bracelet. But the bracelet was taken to make the murder look like a robbery and that was the killer's big mistake. Mark my words, Smythe, you find that bracelet and you'll find your killer."

"We'll do our best," Smythe replied softly. He'd wondered why Blimpey had taken on this case. He was a decent bloke, but he was no bleeding heart taking on the woes of the world. But he was a man who paid his debts and he obviously owed a fairly big one to Tommy Odell's mother. "Don't worry; we're actually pretty good at this sort of thing."

Mrs. Jeffries waylaid Constable Barnes as he came out of the Shepherds Bush station.

Constable Barnes didn't look at all surprised to see her. "Good day, Mrs. Jeffries. It's nice to see you."

"It's good to see you, too, Constable," she replied politely. "If you've got a moment, I'd like to have a word with you."

"Of course." He took her elbow. "There's a café across he road. Let's have a quick cup of tea."

"Thank you, that would be very nice," she replied.

They maneuvered their way through the heavy traffic and into the café. Mrs. Jeffries went to an empty table by the window while the constable went to the counter for their tea. While she waited for him, she composed her thoughts.

"Here you are," he said as he put a cup in front of her and slipped into his chair. "Now, what's on your mind?"

"I've come to speak with you about something that you might consider a bit unpleasant," she said. "I want to discuss a case that's already been solved."

Barnes raised an eyebrow but made no comment.

"Oh dear, this is more difficult than I anticipated." She took a deep breath. "We've reason to believe an innocent man is going to be hanged."

"What man?" The constable's expression didn't change.

"Tommy Odell. He was convicted of murdering a woman named Caroline Muran, but he may not have done it. If he's executed, there might be a huge miscarriage of justice."

"I'm familiar with the case," Barnes replied. "Why do you think he's innocent?"

She hesitated, not sure precisely how many details she ought to share. After all, Blimpey Groggins might not want his name bandied about to policemen. "Someone came to us, someone I'm unfortunately not at liberty to reveal, but I assure you, his credentials are good and his reasons for believing in Odell's innocence are quite compelling." Taking care not to reveal Blimpey's name, she told Barnes what she knew. When she was finished, she picked up her tea and took a quick sip.

Barnes said nothing for a long moment. "I take it you'd like my help." It was a statement, not a question.

She nodded. "I know there's not really much you can do, but I was hoping you might at least be able to give us some guidance on what to do if we come across evidence that Tommy is innocent." She was a bit surprised at how easy this was going. After her rather disappointing conversation with Inspector Witherspoon, she'd been afraid the constable would share his convictions that justice had already been served.

Barnes grinned. "Come on, now, Mrs. Jeffries. You're wantin' more than just a bit of advice."

She smiled sheepishly. "You're right, of course. I do want more. But I'm not sure it's even right for me to ask it of you."

"Let me be the judge of that," he replied. "I know that Tommy Odell isn't pure as driven snow, but I don't think being a pickpocket is the same as murder." As the words came out of his mouth, Barnes was actually a bit surprised. He'd always considered himself a decent man who did his job and earned a reasonable living. He'd become a police-man because he'd needed work and the Metropolitan Po-lice had been hiring. He'd never worried overmuch about the pursuit of justice; he'd simply concentrated on doing the best he could. But something had changed in the past few years. He wasn't sure if it was because he'd been working exclusively with the inspector or whether it had happened because he was getting older and closer to meet-ing his maker, but justice had become important.

"You'll help us?" she asked.

"I'll do what I can," he replied. "But that's probably not near as much as your lot can do. I can't go about asking too many questions on a case that's closed. But I can pass on any bits and pieces I might pick up, and I've got a few sources I can tap. As a matter of fact, I saw something yesterday that might be of interest to you."

"What was it?" she asked.

"The victim's husband came to the Yard yesterday to col-lect his pocket watch," Barnes replied. "Apparently, it had been kept in evidence and was only just returned." He took care to give her all the details of the encounter, except, of course, for the fact that he'd been blatantly eavesdropping.

After he'd finished, she said nothing for a moment. "You were already suspicious about this case." It was a comment, not a question.

"This case was handled badly from the start," he replied softly. "But there was naught I could do about it."

"Maybe there is now, Constable," she said. "And thank you for the information." She'd no idea what, if anything, it might mean.

"You'd best be careful with the inspector," Barnes warned. "He's a good man, but he doesn't want to believe there's been a mistake in this case. Especially as it would mean he'd have to go up against Inspector Nivens."

"I'll make sure we're discreet," she promised.

"I'll try and have a quick look at the case file," he said. "See if there's anything there that might be of help. If I find anything, I'll send a street Arab along with a message, but it might take me a day or two to get my hands on the report."

"Don't do anything that might get you into trouble," she said quickly. "We don't want you taking any risks."

"Don't worry." He grinned. "I'm a sly old dog. I can manage it without raising so much as an eyebrow."

"Please be careful."

"No one will think anything of it if they see me with a case file. Policemen read files all the time, Mrs. Jeffries. It's our job. Don't worry, I'm not going to go borrowing trouble. I'll make sure neither of the inspectors are around when I'm having a gander at the murder file."

Betsy strolled up Cedar Road for the third time. How on earth did Wiggins ever learn anything by just hanging about a neighborhood and hoping someone would pop out so you could have a chat? She'd walked the length of the road three times now and hadn't gotten so much as a smile from anyone. So far she'd seen two women sweeping their front door stoops, three boys playing a game of tag, and a cat sitting in a front window licking its paws. Though the train station was less than a quarter mile away, there weren't any shops or businesses here. Her estimation of Wiggins' investigative methods went up quite a bit. He must be a blooming genius.

It wasn't a particularly pretty area, either. The street was narrow, badly paved, and it curved around in a half circle.

Both sides of the road were lined with identical redbrick row houses that had tiny patches of earth for front gardens.

She reached the end of the street and stopped. She didn't think she ought to go up and back again; someone was bound to notice. She glanced over her shoulder at number 18, but the door remained firmly closed.

Betsy stepped off the pavement. She might as well go back to the Muran neighborhood and see what she could learn. She started to cross, when suddenly a woman appeared. She was wearing a short brown jacket with a matching brown hat and carrying a shopping basket over her arm.

Betsy stared at the woman as she came closer. It took Betsy a moment to place her, but as her features became clear, she realized it was Mrs. Briggs, Tommy's mum. She'd seen her dozens of times behind the counter at the butcher shop.

Betsy hurried across the road, meeting her quarry squarely on the opposite corner. "Hello, aren't you Mrs. Briggs?"

Mrs. Briggs gaped at her. "Well, yes I am. Do I know you?"

"We've never been introduced," Betsy replied, "but I've seen you many times. I work for Inspector Witherspoon."

"On Upper Edmonton Gardens." Her face broadened into a smile. "Of course, of course. The inspector's a good customer. Fancy meeting you in this neighborhood. Are you visiting someone?"

"No, I've just come from seeing a friend off at the station and I thought I was taking a short cut to a Lyons Tea Shop." Betsy laughed. "But I think I'm a bit lost. I am surprised to see you here. I thought your family lived near your shop."

"We do." Mrs. Briggs sighed heavily. "But my sister lives just over there and I'm here helping her out."

"Oh dear, is she ill?" Betsy asked sympathetically.

"Well . . ." Mrs. Briggs glanced at the closed door of number 18 and then back at Betsy. "She's not really *ill*, she's just had a terrible shock is all."

"How dreadful for her," Betsy said quickly. "I do hope she's getting over it." She was careful not to say anything else. In her experience, you didn't need to ask a lot of specific questions to get people to talk. Being a willing listener was often enough to get even the quietest person to tell you their troubles. Judging by the eager look on Mrs. Briggs' face, she was dying for a sympathetic listener.

"If you ask me, she's letting it affect her much more than it needs to, but she's my sister, and well, I've got to come if she needs me, don't I."

"Of course you do. I'm sure you've been a great comfort to her," Betsy agreed. "I don't suppose you know where that tea shop is, do you?"

"I don't know of any Lyons around here, but there's a nice café just around the corner." She pointed back the way she'd just come.

"I'll try that way then," Betsy said. "You look like you could do with a cup yourself. Would you care to join me?"

Mrs. Briggs looked doubtful and Betsy was sure she'd lost the woman, but then she said, "That sounds heavenly. There's no reason to rush back; Helen's probably still asleep. Come along, then, the café's just this way. It'll be nice to have a good natter. You can catch me up on all the neighborhood gossip." She took Betsy's arm and tugged her across the road. They went around the corner, down another street, and onto a road lined with shops. As far as Betsy could tell, Mrs. Briggs didn't stop talking long enough to even draw a breath.

"The inspector is one of our best customers. He always pays his bill and never sends anything back." She pulled open the door of the café. "But then again, we use only the best meat."

"You go and have a seat," Betsy interjected quickly. "I'll get us tea."

"Thank you, dear. It'll be nice to be waited on for once. I've run myself ragged these past few weeks," Mrs. Briggs muttered, her voice fading as she maneuvered her plump frame between the closely spaced tables. She settled at a spot by the far wall.

Betsy ordered their tea and went to the table. "It was very kind of you to accompany me, Mrs. Briggs. I was dying for something to drink, but I don't really like coming to a café on my own. I don't mind a Lyons Tea Shop because there's always lots of ladies in those places. Sometimes cafes can be a bit frightening."

"I know what you mean, dear." Mrs. Briggs picked up her cup and took a sip. "It's always much better for us ladies to have company, isn't it. Actually, I'm beginning to think that's why Helen, that's my sister, is clinging onto me for so long. If you ask me, she's simply lonely. Well, she's used to being in a house full of people, isn't she, and now she's rattling around all alone in her own place, day after day. Her husband's a salesman and most of his customers are up in the midlands so he's gone for weeks at a time. My husband is getting rather put out. Luckily, though, we've a relation that was in need of a position, so he's filling in at the shop for me, but my Harry is getting lonely as well, not to mention what that scamp Tom's been up to. Tom's my lad. Oh, but then you know that, don't you? He delivers to the inspector. He quite likes your Mrs. Goodge, says she's always giving him treats and tea. I don't want to be unkind, but I've got to get home."

"You've been a saint to your sister," Betsy interrupted. She had to do something drastic. Mrs. Briggs could talk the paint off a post if given the chance. "Most people would count themselves lucky to have family as devoted as you. Is your sister getting any better at all?"

"I think she's on the mend," Mrs. Briggs replied. "But honestly, like I said, it's more loneliness than anything else. She used to have a day housekeeper position over in West Brompton, but her employer . . ." she stopped for a brief second, "actually, her employer was murdered and that's what has got her so upset that she quit her position and took to her bed."

"Murdered?" Betsy repeated. Finally, they were getting somewhere. "That's dreadful."

"Oh yes, it's quite affected poor Helen, but then again, I expect you know about such things, working for Inspector Witherspoon. Mind you, they caught the man who did it, but that's not helped Helen at all."

"How sad that she gave up her position," Betsy said. "She must have been very fond of her employer."

"Oh, she was. Mrs. Muran was a saint. It's awful that someone like her should be murdered like that, especially as there are so many nasty people still walking about as free as a lark. Not that I think people ought to be murdered just because they're nasty, but it does cause one to wonder, doesn't it."

"How did it happen?" Betsy asked, realizing that it was going to be difficult to keep Mrs. Briggs on the subject at hand.

"She was shot late one night when they were coming home from a concert or the theatre. It was a robbery. Terrible thing it was."

"Was she alone?"

"Oh no, she was with Mr. Muran. He was hurt, coshed over the head and left for dead."

Betsy looked down at her teacup. She needed to tread carefully here. "Mrs. Muran was shot and Mr. Muran was only hit over the head? That's a bit odd."

Mrs. Briggs stared at her with a strange expression. "That's exactly what my sister says," she stated bluntly. "I told her there could be any number of reasons why one was shot and the other coshed on the head. Perhaps the killer only had one bullet or perhaps Mr. Muran leapt at the fellow after he'd shot Mrs. Muran. Why there's any number of reasons why only one of them was shot."

"You're right, of course." Betsy smiled quickly. "It just struck me as peculiar. I can see why your sister was upset. That must have been dreadful for her and for the others in the household. Did Mrs. Muran have a large staff?"

"Not really," Mrs. Briggs replied. "That's why Helen liked working for her. Running the household was quite simple. There was a cook, a kitchen maid, a housemaid, and two day girls that came in to do the cleaning. They sent out the laundry and hired all the heavy work done every quarter. Mrs. Muran owned a factory, you see, a very prosperous one. She could easily have afforded a much grander house, but she wasn't one to be overly concerned with such things. At least that's what Helen said about her."

"Fancy that," Betsy murmured as she sipped her tea.

"Mrs. Muran spent a lot of her time at the factory," Mrs. Briggs explained. "Funny, isn't it, how some women seem to be happier when they've something to do other than take care of a home and children. Take me, for instance. I can honestly say I prefer working in the shop over doin' housekeepin'." She took another quick sip of tea, but before Betsy could think of anything useful ask, Mrs. Briggs continued speaking. "Cleaning and cooking and washing clothes is hard work and dead boring if you ask me. I used to think there was something wrong with me for feeling that way, and I felt ever so much better when Helen mentioned that Mrs. Muran was like that, too. More interested in running her business and bein' out and about the world, she was. Of course, some would say she was like that because she had no children, but I don't think that's true. I've children but I'd much rather be behind the counter than at home rolling out pie crusts or scrubbing floors."

Betsy started to ask another question, but her mind suddenly went blank. Perhaps it was the rapid pace of Mrs. Briggs' speech or maybe she simply couldn't think of what to ask.

"Mind you," Mrs. Briggs continued, "Helen's problem is only going to get worse if she doesn't take herself out and about."

"Is she afraid of being murdered?" Betsy interrupted, relieved that something had popped into her head.

"Funny you should say that," Mrs. Briggs replied. "I

think that might be the case. She keeps sayin' she's upset over Mrs. Muran's death, but I don't think I believe her. She liked the woman, but she'd only worked for her for since she'd married Mr. Muran. He was the one who decided that Mrs. Muran needed help running the household if she was out everyday—"

· "Why is my saying that funny?" Betsy interrupted again. "I should think being afraid of a killer would be normal."

"But they caught her killer."

"Maybe your sister doesn't think they caught the right person," Betsy said.

Mrs. Briggs stared hard at her. "How on earth did you know that? I've told Helen the police don't make that sort of mistake and that of course they've caught the right person, but she won't listen. She's sure that they've got the wrong man."

"How can she be sure?" Betsy asked softly. Her head hurt and she'd be lucky if she remembered half of what Mrs. Briggs had said.

"Well, I'm not one to be telling tales out of school, but Helen thinks that Mrs. Muran was afraid of something. She said that on the day that Mrs. Muran was murdered the poor woman was as jumpy as a cat. Why, she was so nervous she had Helen tell Miss Turner—that was her cousin— that she wasn't at home. Mrs. Muran was never one to do something like that. Helen says it was almost like she knew something awful was going to happen. Mind you, Helen's got a good imagination."

"Would you care for more tea?" Ruth asked her guest, Olga Spreckles.

Ruth was working her way through the membership of their women's group. She'd already had tea with two other women today, but they'd known nothing about Caroline Muran except that she'd been murdered.

"Thank you, that would be nice." Olga handed Ruth her delicate china cup. "I was so glad to get your note. It's been ages since we've seen one another. I thought you were out of town."

Olga was a chubby woman in her late fifties. She wore a pale yellow day dress festooned with lace at the collar and overlaid with a brown-and-green-striped jacket. A huge hat adorned with feathers, flowers, and a trailing veil sat atop her iron gray hair.

"I arrived home a few days ago," Ruth murmured. "I was concerned about you. You weren't well the last time I saw you."

Olga beamed in delight. "How kind of you; but it was only a cold. I'm quite over it."

"Good, I'm relieved you're well." Ruth frowned slightly. "Wasn't it awful about Caroline Muran. You knew her, didn't you? Sometimes she came to our group." She held her breath, praying that Olga would know something about the case.

"We were well acquainted. It was because of our acquaintance that she started coming to our lectures. She was practically my neighbor." Olga shook her head sadly. "Poor woman, I'm so glad they caught the blackguard that murdered her. She was the sweetest soul. Very simple and plain in her tastes, though she could afford anything she fancied."

"Olga, I'm so sorry. I shouldn't have brought it up," Ruth apologized.

Olga waved her hand impatiently. "Don't be silly. Of course you'd be curious. It's only human nature to want to know things about people. Not that most of us admit it, of course. But that's simply the way we're made."

"You're very understanding," Ruth replied. She liked Olga Spreckles. Despite her wealth and position, she was quite an intelligent, compassionate woman. "I'm sorry you lost your friend."

"We weren't terribly close, but I did like and respect Caroline very much. She was a rather private person, very orderly and predictable in her habits. At least that's what we all thought before she married Keith Muran. Most of us hadn't a clue she was even seeing him. Then one day I see the announcement of the marriage in the *Times*."

"You hadn't met him before they were married?" Ruth asked casually.

"No one had," Olga exclaimed. "Everyone in our neighborhood was wildly curious when it happened. No one had any idea she was contemplating such a thing." She broke off and grinned. "Oh I shouldn't say such things, but that marriage set tongues wagging."

"Gracious, why was that?" Ruth asked easily.

"Because Caroline wasn't the sort one ever thought of as being in the least interested in a husband. Then one day she up and marries the very handsome Keith Muran. From the gossip I heard, even her brother was surprised, and I shouldn't have thought that, considering Russell's life, there would be anything in this world to surprise him." She sighed. "Oh well, poor Russell was at least spared knowing his sister was murdered. Perhaps the two of them have met in heaven. At least one hopes so."

"When did her brother die?" Ruth fiddled with the linen serviette on her lap.

"I'm not sure of the exact date." Olga frowned. "But it was sometime last year."

"What happened to him?" Ruth had no idea if this was a useful question or not, but as she couldn't think of anything else, it would have to do.

"He died when he was in America. I'm not very clear on the details, and it wasn't the sort of thing one could mention, but his obituary suddenly appeared in the *Times* and that's how everyone found out he'd died. It was a very simple announcement as well. Odd isn't it, how the same family can produce two such different people."

"I expect it happens more often than we realize," Ruth murmured.

"It was such a tragedy." Olga put her cup down on the table and leaned back. "They were raised very plainly. I believe their mother was a Quaker. Caroline was studious and serious while Russell wasn't very serious about anything at all, especially his duty to take over the family business. He was a terrible disappointment to their father."

"How sad that both of them are dead," Ruth said. She had no idea if she was learning anything useful.

"The gossip had it that that's why Caroline was left control of the factory instead of her brother. Their father's will gave Caroline a majority interest in the business. But to be fair, he left Russell the house. Rumor had it that Caroline actually bought Russell's share of the company several years back, but if that's true, I'll warrant that he'd not much left of that money by the time he died."

"I take it he wasn't very good with money," Ruth said softly.

"It slipped through his fingers like water." Olga shrugged. "It was the usual vices—liquor and gambling. Apparently he wasn't much good at either activity. But the poor fellow's dead now, may he rest in peace."

"Did Russell Merriman and Keith Muran get along?" Ruth asked, unsure of why this particular question had popped into her head. Investigating murder was actually much more difficult than she'd imagined. On the previous cases she'd helped with, Mrs. Jeffries had usually given her some suggestions as to what information she ought to obtain. But her only instruction this time was to find out what she could. She didn't think she was doing very well.

"I never heard that there was any problem between the two men, but Russell did move out shortly after the marriage. Perhaps he felt awkward living with two newlyweds."

"So Caroline and Russell lived together before she married Keith?" Ruth picked up her teacup.

"Oh yes, despite the differences in their characters, they were very close. Caroline was quite upset when Russell left the country."

"As you said, let's hope brother and sister have reunited in heaven," Ruth said quietly.

"Oh, I do hope so. I know it broke Caroline's heart when she got the telegram telling her about Russell's death."

"And you've no idea how he died?"

Olga shook her head. "No. But I do know his death was very painful to Caroline. But she never spoke of the matter."

"I wonder exactly where it was he died?" Ruth took a sip of her now cold tea.

"It was in one of those western states." Olga's brows furrowed as she concentrated. "Oh dear, what's the name of that big state at the very end of the country?"

"California."

"That's it." Olga nodded. "That's right, I remember now. My tweeny told me that the telegram came from a place called Los Angeles. Russell died while he was in jail there."

CHAPTER 5

Constable Barnes stood in front of the huge redbrick building that was New Scotland Yard and took a deep breath. The day was overcast and the damp from the river had seeped into his bones. He hoped he wasn't here on a fool's errand. More importantly, he hoped he wasn't doing something that would ruin his career and the inspector's. Not that he ought to be terribly concerned about the matter; after all, he was getting close to his pension, and Witherspoon had plenty of money, so neither of them would starve. Besides, what could happen? He was simply going to have a look at a file. If anyone asked what he wanted with it, he'd simply tell them he thought it might relate to one of their current cases.

The mournful bleat of a boat horn sliced through the noisy traffic of the embankment, startling him out of his reverie. He straightened his shoulders and started across the paving stones to the door. He'd best get this over with. For goodness' sakes, it was only a file. It wasn't like he was out to pinch the queen's jewels. He climbed the short flight of stairs and stepped inside the building.

"Good day, Constable Barnes," the constable on duty behind front counter said.

"Morning," he replied. "Miserable day out, isn't it? Looks like it's going to rain soon." Barnes didn't know the constable's name, but he wasn't surprised the fellow knew him. He'd become quite well known since he'd been working with the inspector. Usually, he enjoyed the extra bit of attention, but today he hoped he didn't run into too many people who recognized him.

"Are you here to meet Inspector Witherspoon?" the constable asked. "He's not come past me, and I've been on duty for an hour."

"Oh no, I'm just here to have a gander at one of your files." He hurried toward the staircase.

"You'll want the records room, then," the constable continued. "Good luck finding it. Since we've moved into this building they can't find a ruddy thing. It wouldn't surprise me in the least if a whole room went missing."

Barnes laughed and kept on going. He climbed the stairs to the first floor but didn't stop there. The records room was all the way at the top of the building. Whether the file was properly stored there or not remained to be seen, but he had to start somewhere. He passed several constables but none that knew him personally. By the time he reached the top floor, he had to stop on the landing to catch his breath. He was huffing and puffing like a train engine. Then he started down the hallway toward a large room at the very end.

Barnes reached the doorway, grasped the knob, and took a quick look behind him to make sure no one was watching. But the corridor was empty, so he stepped inside.

Rows of wooden cabinets were lined up across the room like soldiers standing at attention. Along the walls shelves were filled with boxes, files, stacks of paper, and metal lock boxes. Opposite the door was a tall, narrow window that let in the gray morning light. He crossed the green linoleum floor and looked out at the view. For a moment, he was almost dizzy; he wasn't used to being up so high. From this height, the boats and barges plying the Thames seemed almost like toys. But he didn't have time to stand here gawking; he had to find that file. Barnes turned and surveyed the room, wondering where on earth he ought to start. Just then the door opened and Inspector Witherspoon stuck his head into the room.

Barnes gaped at him. "Good morning, sir." He'd no idea what the inspector was doing here. Blast, that stupid constable on the front desk must have mentioned he'd come up here.

"Hello, Barnes," Witherspoon said, stepping into the room. "The duty constable said you'd come up here."

"Uh, yes, sir." Barnes silently vowed to stop being so chatty.

Witherspoon stared at him expectantly. "I thought we were meeting at Ladbrook Grove."

Barnes cleared his throat. "Well, sir, as I was coming in this morning, it suddenly struck me that there was something about that Lamotte case we're working on that seems awfully similiar to some other cases I've heard about. So I thought I'd come along and have a quick look at the files before I met up with you. Was there any particular reason you came here today?"

Witherspoon stared at him, his expression incredulous. Barnes was sure he was doomed. But then the inspector said, "Why, that's remarkable; I had the exact same thought. That's what brought me here today. Gracious, Constable, we've worked together so long now that we're even starting to think in the same manner as one another."

Barnes hid his relief behind a weak smile.

"I thought I'd have a look at the Compton case file." Witherspoon headed for a shelf at the far end of the room. "Is that the file you were after?"

"Yes, sir, that's the one."

"The items taken from the Compton premises were very much like the things stolen from the Lamotte offices."

"That's what I thought, sir," Barnes replied. They were currently working on a case of theft. Several typewriters had been stolen from the offices of Lamotte and Lamotte, Insurance Brokers. Barnes wasn't in the least interested in the Compton case, yet he had to tread carefully. It wouldn't do to arouse the inspector's suspicions about what he was really doing here today. "There were a couple of typewriters stolen from the Compton offices. I wanted to see if they were ever recovered or if the name of the fence was in the file."

"They were recovered," Witherspoon said brightly. "Gracious, Barnes, we're onto something here, I can feel it. Come along, then. Let's have a good look."

"Wouldn't it be in one of the cabinets, sir?" Barnes asked.

"The most recent files are always stored on the shelves," Witherspoon replied. "The Compton case was less than six months ago, so I'll warrant that we'll find the file just about here." He pulled down a file box, flipped it open, and then grinned triumphantly. "Ah, here it is."

"That was fast, sir," Barnes said.

Witherspoon laughed. "You forget, I used to run the records room. I rather enjoyed it, and I must admit, I was actually quite good at it."

"I'm sure you were, sir, but you're better at solving murders." Barnes didn't want his inspector getting any silly ideas about running back to the records room.

"He's not the only one who can solve murders around here." Nigel Nivens, who'd entered the room so silently neither man had heard the door open, stepped farther into the room. "What are you two doing here? You'd better not be looking for the Odell file; you'll not find it. It's still on my desk."

"Gracious, Inspector Nivens, why would you think we were interested in that case?" Witherspoon held up the file he'd just taken out of the box. "This is the Compton case file. We're not the least concerned with your case; it's closed."

"And it had better stay that way," Nivens snapped. "I'm warning you, Witherspoon, keep your nose out of the Muran case. I got Tommy Odell dead to rights and he's going to hang."

Witherspoon, ever the gentleman, tried again. "I assure you, I'm not in the least interested in Tommy Odell."

"Perhaps we should be, sir," Barnes said softly. He glanced at Nivens and noted, with some satisfaction, that his face was turning red. "It seems to me that Inspector Nivens is going to a great deal of trouble to try and scare us off. It makes you wonder, doesn't it?"

"How dare you." Nivens glared at the Constable. "Just what are you implying?"

"I'm sure the constable wasn't implying anything untoward," Witherspoon said hastily. Confused, he looked at his constable and then back at Nivens. "Er, uh . . ."

Barnes knew he was playing a dangerous game. It could all blow up in his face and if things went horribly wrong, and he could end up spending his last few years on the force making the rounds in Whitechapel or Brixton. On the other hand, if he played his cards right, he might just be able to actually pull the inspector onto the case. Nivens might have just made a really bad mistake.

"I was only curious, sir," he said to Witherspoon. "I mean, even if we were looking for the Odell case file, why should Inspector Nivens get so het up? You never get upset when other policemen look at your cases, sir."

"Well, uh . . ." Witherspoon wasn't quite sure what to say. The constable had a point. He always had to track his old case files down from someone's desk, but he'd been flattered that his fellow officers were interested in his methods. Still, he didn't wish to aggravate Inspector Nivens needlessly—but it was odd that the man was so upset about the matter. Very odd indeed. "Perhaps uh . . ."

"This is outrageous. Are you accusing me of having something to hide?" Nivens cried, but his tone was now slightly defensive. "I'll have you know there was nothing wrong with my handling of that case, nothing at all. It was good detective work on my part."

"I'm sure it was, Inspector," Witherspoon said calmly, but his tone was slightly less mollifying than before.

"And you got a quick conviction," Barnes goaded. He'd heard the new note in his inspector's voice. He also knew that by virtue of Witherspoon's past successes, if he took the matter to the chief inspector, they'd have to listen to him.

Nivens glared at the constable and then turned his attention back to Witherspoon. "I'm warning you. Stay out of this case. Let me make this perfectly clear: if I hear you've been interfering in this matter, there will be dire consequences."

Witherspoon said nothing. He simply stared at Nivens.

"Well, I'm glad that you understand." Nivens dropped his gaze and began backing toward the door. "There's no reason we can't be civil about this matter. After all, I don't go snooping about in your cases."

Barnes snorted faintly, but Nivens didn't notice. His attention was on the inspector, who still hadn't said a word.

"I'm glad we were able to get this issue resolved," Nivens muttered as he reached the door. He turned on his heel and left.

For a long moment, the inspector said nothing, and Barnes was sure he'd pushed too hard.

"Constable, I do believe you and I ought to have a word with the chief inspector."

"Are you going to complain about Inspector Nivens, sir?" Barnes wasn't sure that was the best idea. Perhaps it would be better to wait until they had evidence of some sort before they went to the chief. Nivens was an incompetent fool, but he was a fool with good political connections.

"Complaining about Nivens wouldn't do the least bit of good. He's too well protected."

Amazed, Barnes stared at Witherspoon. Maybe the inspector wasn't quite as naïve as he'd thought. "Then why do you want to see the chief inspector, sir?"

"I want his permission to have a look at the Odell case. I've a feeling that something is terribly wrong about the matter. What's more, Nivens knows there's something wrong but he was so desperate for a conviction on his books that he overlooked it. We can't have that, Barnes. We must be sure. A man's life is at stake."

Just across the river, Mrs. Jeffries hurried down a corridor at St. Thomas's Hospital. As she came around the corner, her quarry stepped out of a door and into view. He spotted Mrs. Jeffries and a wide smile spread across his bony face. He was a tall man with dark red hair, pale skin, and deep-set hazel eyes. "Good morning, Mrs. Jeffries. I had a feeling you'd be along soon. I'm just on my way to my office. Would you care to join me? I expect we could get a cup of tea along the way somewhere."

"Thank you, that would be lovely," she replied as she fell into step with him. She really didn't want anything to drink, but it felt churlish to refuse.

They stopped at the nursing station and he got both of them a hot mug of tea and told the nursing sister he'd be in his office.

"Come along, then. I've changed offices since you were last here," he explained as he led her down a short flight of stairs and along the corridor. "This one actually has a window." He opened the door and nodded for her to step inside.

Mrs. Jeffries couldn't see that this office was much of an improvement over his old one, but she kept that opinion to herself. Despite the pale light seeping in through the narrow window, the room was small and rather dim. The air was filled with the scent of dampness mingled with soap and disinfectant. The room was as cluttered as she remembered— with books, medical magazines, and papers covering every inch of the desktop and most of the shelves along the wall.

Dr. Bosworth put his cup on the edge of his desk and picked up the pile of books that had been sitting on the chair opposite his desk. "Do have a seat, please."

"Thank you," she said, sitting down. On the cabinet behind his desk, she could see a glass jar with a grayish pear-shaped object in it. It appeared to be suspended in some sort of liquid. She wasn't sure she wanted to know what it might be. She forced herself to look away.

Bosworth took his seat. "I had a chance to read the postmortem report," he began.

"Was the report detailed enough to give you any idea of the kind of gun that was used to murder Mrs. Muran?" Her gaze flicked back to the object in the glass jar.

"Based on the details in the report, my guess is that it was a fairly large pistol. The entry wound was over half an inch wide."

"Did the doctor doing the autopsy measure the wound?" She forced her gaze away from the jar and back to him. "Are your methods becoming well known?"

Bosworth laughed. "I'd like to think so, but the truth is, the postmortem was done by a friend of mine, and he's quite familiar with my theories. I don't think he believes them to the same extent that I do, but he was curious enough to measure the wound." His smile faded. "The poor woman never had a hope of surviving. She was shot in the head and the heart."

"There were two shots?" Mrs. Jeffries prompted.

Bosworth nodded. "Whoever did it wanted to make sure she was dead."

"But surely a shot to the head would have done that," she pressed.

"Not necessarily," Bosworth replied. "Quite a number of people have survived head wounds. You can walk around quite easily with one or even more bullets in your brain. I once treated a gambler in San Francisco who had two bullets lodged in his head. I was treating him for the gout. No, whoever shot Mrs. Muran wanted to make sure she was dead, and the only way to do that was to make sure you hit both the brain and the heart. By the way, that sort of knowledge isn't generally known by the public."

"What are you saying, Dr. Bosworth?" she asked. She wanted to make sure she understood precisely what this evidence might mean. "Are you implying the killer must have medical training?"

"Not exactly." Bosworth leaned forward. "Anyone who'd ever been on a battlefield or around a hospital could have such knowledge, as could anyone who has studied anatomy or physiology. It doesn't mean your killer is a physician or a nurse. But whoever the murderer is, he must have known that the only way to be sure of certain death is to go after both organs. Either that or he was just someone who liked shooting and happened to hit just the right spots." Bosworth leaned back in his chair and shrugged. "I can't prove any of this, Mrs. Jeffries, but as you know, I've seen a number of shootings in my time, and frankly, most people are such awful shots that one is just as likely to be wounded or maimed rather than killed. But Mrs. Muran was killed, and from what the postmortem reveals, she was killed quickly and cleanly."

"Could it be a coincidence?" she asked. "I mean, could it just be that the killer got lucky?"

"Anything is possible," he replied. "I wish I knew more, but I'm afraid that's really all I was able to understand from the report."

"You've been very helpful, and we're very grateful. I know you're busy, so I'll not keep you further." She rose to her feet and he started to get up as well, but she waved him back to his chair. "I can find my own way out."

"But Mrs. Jeffries, I wasn't finished." He grinned. "I did find out something else, something you might find quite useful."

She sank back down. "But you said there was nothing else in the report."

"That's true, but I had a chat with the fellow who treated Mr. Muran's head wound."

"How very clever of you." She stared at him in genuine admiration. "How did you manage that?"

"London may be a large city, but the medical community isn't that extensive," he explained. "Mr. Muran was treated here."

"Gracious, that's a lucky coincidence."

"Not really. The murder scene was just across the bridge. We were the closest hospital, so the constables brought him here. I found out who was on duty that night and made some discreet inquiries. Keith Muran was seen by Dr. Matthew McHenry. McHenry and I went to medical school in Edinburgh together."

"What did you find out?" she asked eagerly.

"Muran's injuries were genuine. He had a severe concussion and spent several days in hospital. Whoever hit him, hit him very hard. Unfortunately, Dr. McHenry isn't particularly interested in my theories, so he didn't examine the injury closely, he only treated the man. He'd not taken any measurements nor had he paid attention to the actual shape of the wound."

Mrs. Jeffries wasn't sure what he meant. "Is that important?"

Bosworth sighed. "I think so, but not everyone seems to agree. McHenry looked at me as if I were quite mad when I inquired about the particulars of the wound. But Mrs. Jeffries, if he had paid attention to the shape and specific size of the injury, it might give us some idea of what kind of weapon was used on Keith Muran."

"Knowing the weapon might make a difference," she murmured.

"Of course it would," Bosworth insisted eagerly. "First of all, it would give you some idea of whether or not your assailant used the pistol handle, brought another weapon with him, or whether he simply used a handy brick or a stone to cosh Muran over the head."

Mrs. Jeffries wasn't certain how one could use this sort of information, but she suspected it might mean a great deal in the overall scope of an investigation. "Yes, I can see how that might be helpful."

"Secondly," Bosworth continued. "If the sides of the wound were a nice, even shape with straight, square edges, you'd know that the fellow was probably coshed with a brick or a small paving stone, but if it were rounded and irregular, you'd have to consider other possibilities."

"But what if the victim had been hit more than once?" she speculated. "Wouldn't that change the shape of the wound?"

"Of course, but Mr. Muran was only hit once or possibly twice, and even if he'd been struck multiple times, there would still be evidence on some of the wounds as to the kind of weapon that had been used." He smiled self-consciously. "Don't get me started, Mrs. Jeffries. I shall take advantage of you. You're one of the few people I know who actually appreciate my interest in this subject."

"And your interest in this subject has been very instrumental on more than one occasion in catching the right killer," she assured him. "Don't doubt that for a minute, Doctor. That's one of the reasons we keep coming to you for help."

"You're very kind. Let's hope that one day people will understand the importance of looking at every detail in a murder. Mark my words, Mrs. Jeffries, in the future, there will be an entire field of study devoted to the examination of both the victim and the murder scene."

"You know, Dr. Bosworth, I do believe you're absolutely right."

Wiggins walked along Barrick Street and thought it a right miserable place. He'd gone back to the Muran neighborhood after he'd followed the two women to the tea shop, but his luck had apparently run out. He'd seen no one nor had he caught so much as a glimpse of that scared young maid, either. There were only so many times you could walk up and down a street without someone noticing, so he'd decided to come along here and have a firsthand look at the murder scene. Fat lot of good that had done him.

He'd been hoping to run into Smythe and get his advice on what to do next, but so far he'd not seen hide nor hair of the coachman. Wiggins stopped and folded his arms over his chest. This was just about the silliest idea he'd ever had in his life. What had he thought he'd find here? In the light of day, the street was just another ugly commercial neighborhood without people or color or anything to recommend it.

He started walking again, taking his time and trying to get a sense of the place, trying to see what would make someone come here late at night. But for the life of him he couldn't see any attraction to the place. He trailed his fingers against the dull brown bricks of a large, windowless building that was built right up to the edge of the narrow pavement. The building was like all the others on the road. At the far end of the road was a solid wall of another, taller building.

Wiggins shook his head in wonder. Maybe he'd got his facts wrong. Why would anyone come here? He noticed that at the dead end there was a narrow passageway, and he hurried towards it. But when he got there, he saw it only led to a set of double doors set back a bit from the street proper.

"You lookin' for somethin', lad?"

Wiggins whirled around and stumbled backwards. An apparition was standing less than three feet from him. It took a moment before he realized that the fellow wasn't a demon from hell, simply one of the city's many walking advertisements—a boardman. *Love's Lost Lies,* a pantomime playing nightly in Soho, was splashed across the square wooden board slung over the old man's torso in bold red and green letters. A fool's cap of the same bright colors sat on his head.

"You oughtn't to come sneakin' up on people like that," Wiggins cried. He was embarrassed to have been so startled. Cor blimey, it was just an old man trying to earn a living, and a hard living it was at that.

"Sorry, lad." The man grinned showing off a full set of brown-stained teeth. "But I thought you was trying to get in that back door, and I only wanted to say the entrance is on the other side of the building. They keep the back locked up good and tight. Mind you, you're a bit late. They're full up for today, but I heard the gov say they'd need more of us tomorrow to advertise a new pantomine that's starting on Friday evening."

It took a moment before Wiggins understood. "I'm not lookin' for work," he said. He was wearing his good black jacket and cap, his second best blue shirt, and a new pair of gray trousers. Why would anyone think he was looking for a position?

The old fellow drew back. "Then what are you doing back here?"

"That's not any of your business."

"It's my business if you're up to mischief."

"I'm not up to any mischief," Wiggins snapped, suddenly angry.

"You must be," the man insisted. "I already told ya, there's nuthin' here but the back doors to them empty buildings or the work hall."

"I don't 'ave to be explainin' myself to the likes of you," Wiggins yelled.

"Likes of me," the boardman repeated. "The likes of me can go fetch a copper right quick if yer up to no good."

Wiggins forced himself to calm down. "It's a public street, and I'm not doin' anything but walkin' about."

"Course it's a public street," the fellow replied, his tone a bit more civil. "Look, I was just tryin' to be helpful, that's all." He turned and walked away, muttering to himself.

"Wait, I'm sorry, I didn't mean to be rude." Wiggins hurried after him.

The boardman stopped. "Then watch how you talk to your elders, lad. I might be poor and I might be a bit down on my luck, but you'd no call to speak to me like I was lower than the dirt on your shoes. Do you think I like doin' this kind of thing?" He punched the center of the board with a chapped, dirty finger. "Course I don't. No one would. It's a miserable life. The omnibus drivers play their nasty tricks on us, street lads throw stones every chance they get—knowing that with this stupid thing across my chest I can't chase 'em off—and the pay is rotten. But I thought you might be lookin' for work, and I was only tryin' to help. Believe it or not, some of us poor folks try to help one another."

Wiggins whipped off his cap. "Please accept my apologies, sir. I shouldn't have spoken to you in such a manner, and I appreciate the fact you were trying to do me a good turn. May I buy you a cup of tea, sir?" He was ashamed of himself on two counts. One, that he'd lost his temper so easily, and two, that he'd looked down on the man in the first place. Wiggins knew what it was like to be poor.

The boardman eyed him skeptically for a moment, trying to assess if the offer was genuine, then he shrugged. "There's a pub around the corner. I could do with a pint; would that do ya?"

Wiggins didn't much care for beer; he would rather have had a cup of tea. But as he'd already offended the old man, and it wouldn't hurt him to stand him a quick pint. "Lead on, sir, and we'll have a beer together."

Smythe stood in the small service road just outside of Merriman's Metal Works and stared through a crack in the wooden gate into the cobblestone courtyard. The factory was a long, two-story building set back from the street. From his vantage point, he watched as a wagon filled with barrels pulled into the yard and a set of huge double doors opened, giving him a glimpse of the factory proper. A half a dozen men came out and began the task of unloading the wagon.

He frowned slightly. Keith Muran was an English gentleman who didn't know anything about operating a business, and this place didn't have a manager. Mrs. Muran had sacked him a week before she was murdered. So who was running the business?

Smythe knew enough to understand that businesses didn't just run themselves. Someone had to be there to order supplies, sign contracts, and generally make the day-to-day decisions that cropped up in any enterprise.

"Wonder how long this is gonna last," he heard a red-haired man say to the other workers.

"Let's not go borrowin' trouble," a dark-haired fellow with a handlebar mustache replied. "Even if it happens, they'll still need workers." He untied the ropes holding the barrels in place.

"Yeah, but we'll not have it like we did before," a third man with a pockmarked face interjected. He shoved a wide piece of wood up against the edge of the wagon. "They'll not give a toss whether or not we've got decent housin', let alone a decent wage."

The red-haired man climbed onto the wagon, grabbed a barrel, and rolled it down the makeshift ramp. "It's not right, I tell ya. She meant for us to live right."

"We could talk to Mr. Muran," the dark-haired man said. He looked over his shoulder toward the open door. "Maybe he'd listen." He rolled the barrel across the yard and into the open doors.

The man with the pockmarked face snorted. "He's not much interested in the likes of this place or the likes of us. Besides, we've already tried to talk to him. Fat lot of good it did us." He jerked his head toward the doors. "What do you think he's doin' right this minute? He's sellin' this place out from under us as quick as he can."

"We don't know that," the red-haired fellow said.

"Don't be daft," Pockmark replied. "Why do you think Addison is here? He's not applying for a position, I can tell ya that."

"Shh . . ." the dark-haired man hissed. "They're coming."

Two men speaking quietly to one another stepped into view. The taller of the two men was dressed in a heavy black overcoat and the other wore a gray coat and a black top hat.

"Mr. Muran, do you have a moment?" the dark-haired man asked.

"I'm afraid I don't," Muran replied. "But if there's a problem, you can see Mr. Digby about it."

"Nah, there's naught Mr. Digby could do to help us," he said softly. He glanced at the other workers, his expression troubled.

Muran nodded absently and turned back to his companion.

Smythe couldn't hear what the two men were saying, but he knew that the man with Muran was John Addison. He waited until they'd gone through the front gate and then he hurried after them, coming up behind them just outside the factory.

He knew he didn't have much time, as he'd no doubt they'd hail a cab as soon as they reached the main road. Smythe quickened his pace, trying to get close enough to eavesdrop. He managed to get within twenty feet of his quarry, but he could hear nothing except snatches of words. Their blooming footsteps were simply too loud.

He cursed silently as they rounded the corner onto the main road and a hansom pulled up. Just his blooming luck! You could never find one of the ruddy things when you wanted one.

Muran and Addison had stopped and were waiting for the fare to get out. Smythe had no choice; he had to keep right on walking. He went past the two men and on down the road, trying to step as softly as possible so he could hear their destination. Luck, it seemed, had taken pity on him, because he heard one of them call out to the hansom driver: "The Fortune Hotel in Knightsbridge, please."

All of them were a bit late for their afternoon meeting, but for once Mrs. Goodge didn't care. Having just shoved her last source out of the kitchen, she was running behind as well and had gotten the kettle on only seconds before Betsy arrived.

"Sorry I'm late." Betsy took off her cloak and hat as she hurried toward the coat tree.

"It's all right, dear, none of the others are back yet. Would you mind buttering the bread for me?"

"It's been ever such a busy day," Betsy exclaimed as she went to the counter and picked up the butter pot. "My feet are wore out, and believe it or not, my ears are sore."

Alarmed, Mrs. Goodge stared at the maid. "You've got an earache? You best sit yourself down, girl, and let me put a warm cloth—"

"Oh no, Mrs. Goodge," Betsy replied. "I'm sorry, I didn't mean to say it that way, I meant to say that my ears are sore because I ran into Mrs. Briggs—"

"Tom's mum?" the cook interrupted.

Betsy nodded.

"It's no wonder your ears hurt; Mrs. Briggs is a good talker. I've seen her hold conversations with three different customers at once." Mrs. Goodge relaxed a bit. She turned back to the teapot and reached for the tin. She smiled to herself, realizing how much of a mother hen she'd become in her old age.

By the time the tea was on the table, all of the others had arrived. Smythe, who'd come in last, slipped into his seat and said, "I hope this won't take too long; I've got to get back out." Under the table, he grabbed Betsy's hand and gave it a squeeze.

"Where've you got to go?" she asked with a frown.

"The Fortune Hotel," he replied. "One of our suspects is stayin' there."

"Who?" Wiggins asked.

"John Addison." Smythe reached for his tea.

"Why don't you go first then," Mrs. Jeffries suggested. "That way, if you must leave, you can go and Betsy can tell you the rest of our information when you come home."

"That'll be 'elpful," he said, giving Betsy a quick grin. "John Addison has been hangin' about since just before Mrs. Muran was murdered."

"I don't understand," Mrs. Goodge complained. "Why is he important?"

"Cor blimey, I'm not makin' much sense, am I?" Smythe apologized. "Sorry, let me start at the beginnin'." He gave them the information he'd gotten from Blimpey, being sure not to mention that Blimpey was his source. He took his time and spoke carefully, making certain he gave them every little detail he'd heard about Keith Muran and John Addison. He finished by telling them about his trip to Merriman's Metal Works and what he'd overheard from the workers in the courtyard. "So that's why I want to go back out tonight. There's bound to be a bellboy or footman from the hotel that can tell us more about Addison."

"And you think Addison is a likely suspect?" Mrs. Jeffries asked.

"Addison 'as been tryin' to get his hands on Merriman's since before Mrs. Muran was murdered, and now that she's dead, he's got his chance," Smythe explained. "Keith Muran is probably goin' to sell to him. I think the workers resent Muran. He wouldn't even stop to talk to 'em today."

"I shouldn't wonder," Ruth said softly. "Caroline Muran was a wonderful employer and very much loved by her workers. She thought their welfare was just as important as her profits."

"Maybe you can find out if John Addison has a gun," Wiggins suggested. "Mind you, that's actually 'arder to find out than it might sound. I didn't 'ave much luck with it today."

"Well it doesn't sound like Mr. Muran is followin' in his late wife's footsteps," Mrs. Goodge commented.

"When someone is murdered, one of the questions you have to ask yourself is who benefits from the victim's death." Smythe took a quick sip of tea. "It seems to me that John Addison is right at the top of the list. Buyin' Merriman's will keep him from goin' bankrupt."

Mrs. Jeffries shook her head in disbelief. "I find it hard to believe that someone would commit murder to get their hands on a business."

"So do I," Betsy agreed.

"I don't," Wiggins said. "Goin' bankrupt is a pretty powerful motive, and what's more, we don't have us that many suspects, so we ought to 'ang onto the few we've got. Cor blimey, that didn't come out right."

"I think we all understand what you mean, Wiggins," Mrs. Goodge said. "But after you hear what I've learned, we may have a few more people we can put on our suspect list. Mind you, though, John Addison does seem to have benefited nicely from Mrs. Muran's murder."

"But perhaps others have as well." Mrs. Jeffries pushed the bread and butter toward Smythe.

"Come on, Mrs. Jeffries, we've seen people killed for the strangest of reasons," Smythe argued. "It seems to me that wantin' someone's factory isn't much different than wantin' someone's money."

"But a murder would involve so many risks," she replied. "John Addison would have to be sure that even with Mrs. Muran dead, Mr. Muran was prepared to sell to him."

"Maybe he was sure," Ruth said.

"Murder is a risky business," Mrs. Goodge pointed out, "and most killers think it's a risk worth taking."

CHAPTER 6

"True." Mrs. Jeffries nodded in agreement. "Let's hope the risks this particular killer took will lead us straight to him or her." Despite all they'd learned, she'd still not come up with any reasonable ideas about this case, and that worried her. Then again, perhaps she was expecting too much—they had only just begun their investigation. "Were you able to find out the name of the sacked factory manager?"

Smythe shook his head and got to his feet. "I ran out of time. I'll have a go at that tomorrow and at taking a gander at the murder scene."

"Don't bother. There's nothing to see exceptin' a work hall and a fat lot of empty buildings," Wiggins said. "I wasted the whole afternoon there and didn't find out anything worth knowin'."

Betsy got up. "I thought you were going to snoop about the Muran neighborhood today."

Wiggins grinned broadly. "I did, and I think I might 'ave found out somethin' interestin'. But by the time I got finished followin' the ladies to Chelsea and got back to Drayton Gardens, there was no one about."

"What ladies?" Mrs. Goodge demanded.

"It's a bit complicated," Wiggins replied.

"And it sounds like it'll take more time to tell than I've got." Smythe grabbed Betsy's hand and pulled her toward the hall. "You can tell me everything later," he told her.

"Mind you don't stay out too long," Betsy murmured as soon as they were out of earshot of the others. "I'm going to wait up for you."

"Don't. You need your rest, lass, and I might be hours. Anything you hear tonight can keep until tomorrow morning." He gave her a quick kiss and stepped out into the night.

Betsy closed the door and leaned against it for a moment. She hated it when he went out alone at night. Smythe could take care of himself, of that she was sure, but nonetheless, once the darkness set in, she'd rather have him safely home.

Mrs. Jeffries waited until Betsy took her chair before asking, "Who would like to go next? Or should we let Wiggins do his explaining before we go any further?"

"His information certainly sounds intriguing," Ruth said.

Wiggins smiled self-consciously. "It might be nothing, but then again, you never know. When I got to Drayton Gardens this morning, two ladies come strollin' out the front door of the Muran house like they owned the place. So I followed them." He took a quick sip of tea and told them how he'd had a feeling the women might be important so he'd trailed them to the tea shop. "I got lucky enough to get a table close to 'em so I heard everything they was sayin'." He repeated the conversation he'd overheard. "Then I followed 'em to a little house in Chelsea."

"What if they were just visiting the Muran house?" Betsy speculated.

"They might be Caroline Muran's cousins," Mrs. Goodge

added. "My sources mentioned that she had cousins living in Chelsea. It's probably these two."

Mrs. Jeffries said nothing for a moment. "I expect you're right. Constable Barnes said there were two women with Keith Muran when he came and collected his watch from the Yard."

"You've spoken to Constable Barnes?" Mrs. Goodge asked.

"Yes. I'll tell you all about it in a few minutes." She glanced at Wiggins. "Are you finished?"

"That's all I found out." Wiggins decided not to talk about the boardman he'd taken to the pub. The old fellow hadn't known anything, and he didn't want the others to think he'd been larking about in a tavern instead of snooping for clues.

"You've done well today," Mrs. Jeffries said. She turned her attention to Lady Cannonberry. "Ruth, you go next. Did you have any luck today?"

"As a matter of fact, I think I did," she said, smiling eagerly. "But I'm not certain it has anything to do with the murder."

"Tell us anyway," Mrs. Goodge instructed. "We never know what's useful and what isn't until after the case has been solved."

"It's about Caroline Muran's brother. It's so sad, really. He also came to a tragic end." She told them the gossip she'd gotten from Olga Spreckles. When Ruth was finished, she leaned back in her chair and waited to see what the others thought. When several moments passed without any of the others making any comments, she feared the worst. "Oh dear, I was afraid it wasn't going to be very useful."

"Nonsense," Mrs. Jeffries said briskly. "You've given us an enormous amount of good information. It is strange that both brother and sister should die like that."

"And now we know that the marriage was a surprise to all of Caroline Merriman's friends," Betsy commented. "That could be significant."

"Why'd she want to get married at her age?" Wiggins asked curiously. "Sounds like she were a bit of a spinster, what with her running the factory and giving money to them ladies that chain themselves to fences."

"They don't only chain themselves to fences," Ruth said defensively. "The women's sufferage movement is dedicated to giving women the same rights under the law as men. That's very important."

"Oh, I weren't sayin' it were wrong," Wiggins said hastily. "I quite admire 'em. I think everyone should be able to vote and have a decent position. Bein' poor is awful and it's been my observation that woman seem to be more poor than men. Leastways there seems to be more of 'em, especially in the more miserable parts of the city. I didn't mean any offense."

"None taken," Ruth replied with a smile.

"I quite agree with Wiggins," Mrs. Goodge said stoutly, "and one of these days, we'll have a nice old natter about the rights of everyone, but right now, let's get back to the matter at hand." She glanced at the carriage clock on the pine sideboard. "Time marches on and I don't want to be late getting the inspector's chicken in the oven."

"I wonder how Mr. Muran's first wife died," Betsy said.

"I think that might be something worth pursuing," Mrs. Jeffries muttered. "Do you happen to know the lady's Christian name?" she asked Ruth.

"I can find out." Ruth's pale brows drew together. "I've heard something about her, but I can't recall what it might have been. I believe she might have been ill for quite some time before she died. It should be easy enough to find out the details."

"That would be most helpful," Mrs. Jeffries replied.

"There's a hint of scandal in that direction." Mrs. Goodge wrinkled her face as she concentrated. "I heard that Lucy Turner, that's Caroline Muran's cousin and probably the younger of the two women Wiggins followed today, had set her cap for Keith Muran."

"The older one was her mama," Wiggins added. "What's her name?"

"Edwina Turner," Mrs. Goodge replied. "She and her daughter apparently live off a small pension from her late husband. He was an army officer in India. When he died, Edwina and Lucy came back to London to live."

"They might have wanted Mrs. Muran dead," Wiggins suggested. "Maybe Miss Turner wants to marry him now that he's a widower."

"It's possible," Mrs. Goodge replied. "But I don't think so. The gossip I heard is that Miss Turner's pride took a beating when Muran married her cousin. Besides, the house they're living in belonged to Caroline. It now belongs to the estate, and they may or may not be allowed to go on living there."

"This is all very interesting," the housekeeper murmured. She wondered what, if anything, it all meant. They seemed to be learning a great number of facts, but were they facts that would actually solve this case before poor Tommy Odell was hanged? "Why don't you let me go next. My information dovetails nicely with what we've heard so far." She told them of her meeting with Constable Barnes and the little bit of eavesdropping he'd done.

"Was the constable suspicious of this case as well?" Ruth asked.

"Apparently so, but that's not all I found out." She gave them the details of her meeting with Dr. Bosworth, emphasizing Bosworth's conviction that the weapon in the case was a pistol. She glanced at Wiggins. "Perhaps your idea about finding out what sort of weapons our suspects have isn't so far-fetched."

"I'll keep tryin'," he promised. "But first I've got to find a servant that'll talk to me."

"This case is a bit of a mess," Betsy said, sighing. "I don't understand anything yet. It's so sad: first her brother dies and then poor Caroline gets murdered."

"Not to worry, we'll sort it out eventually, and one of them at least will have justice," Mrs. Jeffries replied.

"Can I finish?" Mrs. Goodge asked.

"Oh dear, I am sorry, you should have said something." The housekeeper smiled apologetically at the cook. "I didn't realize you still had more to report."

"No harm done." The cook made sure she had everyone's attention before she resumed speaking. "I'd not waste too much time worrying about Caroline's brother."

"But the poor bloke died in a foreign country," Wiggins protested.

"No he didn't." She smiled smugly. "Russell Merriman isn't dead."

"Not dead?" Wiggins repeated.

"But Olga was certain," Ruth exclaimed. "She went to his memorial service."

"I've no doubt that they had a service for him," Mrs. Goodge continued, quite enjoying herself. Today she'd struck gold. Her old friend, Ida Leacock had popped in for morning coffee, and when Mrs. Goodge had mentioned Caroline Merriman's murder, Ida supplied her with the information that Caroline's supposedly dead brother had turned up very much alive. "But he didn't die in America. It was some sort of mistake. He got put in jail."

"Your source was sure of this?" Mrs. Jeffries asked. Dozens of question were now whirling about in her head.

"Absolutely." Mrs. Goodge reached for her tea cup. "Ida's niece works as a housekeeper to a Mr. John Brandon—he's Russell Merriman's solicitor. Helen, that's the niece, gave Ida all the details about his return from the dead."

"Cor blimey, that's about the strangest thing I ever 'eard. I think we ought to keep our eye on this bloke," Wiggins said. "You don't see dead people popping back up alive very often."

"Wiggins is right," Mrs. Jeffries murmured with a frown. "We need to find out all that we can about the situation." If

Inspector Witherspoon were on the case, it would be fairly simple. She'd have come up with some story about someone having seen the late Mr. Merriman and put him on the hunt, so to speak. "But without the inspector's help, I'm not sure where to begin."

"We could begin with Mr. Groggins," Betsy suggested. "Doesn't he deal in knowing things that go on in London? Shouldn't he be able to get us at least enough information to get started?"

"Wouldn't Russell Merriman be staying with Mr. Muran?" Ruth asked. "After all, it is his house."

"But neither of the Turner women mentioned it when Wiggins was eavesdropping today. If Merriman was at the Muran house, they'd likely have mentioned it," the cook pointed out.

"I agree," Mrs. Jeffries replied. "That sort of news has the whole neighborhood taking notice, but from what Wiggins said when he went back there today, it was very quiet. But that's not all we have to find out about him. We need to know when he arrived back in England."

"I'll see if any of my acquaintances know anything," Ruth offered.

"And we'll ask Smythe to go along and have a word with Mr. Groggins tomorrow," Mrs. Jeffries added. She grinned at the cook. "You've quite enjoyed this, haven't you."

Mrs. Goodge took another sip of tea before answering. "Indeed I have. It's not often that I get the goods, so to speak, on the rest of you. Most of my information is generally just background gossip."

"You did well, Mrs. Goodge," Betsy said. "I'm afraid my information won't hold a candle to this." But she didn't begrudge the cook her moment of glory. She deserved it.

Mrs. Goodge laughed and then said, "I'm afraid I've not learned much of anything else."

"Shall I go next, then?" Betsy asked. "Seems to me we've all had us quite a day and we've lots to tell before it gets too late. We don't want the inspector coming home early and not finding his dinner ready."

Betsy needn't have worried about Witherspoon getting home earlier than usual. Today the inspector was going to be very late indeed.

At the new offices of Scotland Yard, Constable Barnes and Inspector Witherspoon were sitting in two straight-backed chairs outside of Chief Inspector Barrows' office.

"Nivens has many powerful friends, sir. Are you certain about this?" Barnes asked. He was still in shock over Witherspoon's decision to take the matter to their superior. Barnes had been hoping for some sort of involvement, but he hadn't been expecting the mild-mannered Witherspoon to make a full-frontal assault.

"I'm quite sure, Constable," the inspector replied. "Frankly, this case has been worrying me since we had that encounter with Inspector Nivens in the canteen." He pursed his lips and shook his head. "I understand Inspector Nivens' desire to solve a homicide. He's an ambitious man, and that is one of the routes to advancement." An image of the brand-new records room popped into his head and he sighed wistfully. It was a lovely room. He wouldn't have minded being in charge of it. Filing was really very important.

"Wanting advancement is understandable, sir," Barnes said.

"But not at the expense of justice." The inspector was glad that he'd made it very clear to his superiors that he wasn't interested in moving up any further. Gracious, it was difficult enough solving the murders that cropped up with incredible regularity on his patch. He'd no desire to be in a position where he had to take on even more.

"What made you change your mind about Nivens, sir?"

"His manner," Witherspoon replied. "He was so defensive about a few simple comments. Well, it did make me wonder. Mind you, I had managed to put the incident out of my mind until today. Gracious, all we were doing was looking for a file. Yet he was so worried we might be looking for the Odell file that he climbed all the way to the top of the building to see what we were doing?"

"You think he might have fiddled with the evidence, sir?" Barnes cast a quick glance at the closed office door and wondered who was inside with the chief. As far as Barnes knew, there weren't any major cases going on right now.

Witherspoon spoke carefully. "I wouldn't go so far as to say he did anything of that nature, but I suspect he didn't conduct as thorough an investigation as he ought to have done. I want to make sure that the chief inspector is satisfied that the investigation was conducted properly."

The inspector had tried his best to stay out of this case, but he couldn't ignore his own conscience. Constable Barnes comments that day in the canteen *had* bothered him, and his conversation that evening with Mrs. Jeffries hadn't help put his fears to rest, either. After today's strange behavior, well, he couldn't turn his back on the matter. He pulled out his pocket watch and noted the time. "I wonder how long the chief is going to be?"

Just then the door opened and Barrows stuck his head out. "Ah, Witherspoon, goodness, this is a coincidence. Either that or you must be one of those clairvoyants they have at the music halls. I was getting ready to send a constable to fetch you. Do come into my office. You, too, Constable. I'd like a word with both of you."

Barnes heart sank as he followed his inspector into the office. Nivens had beaten them to the chief. He must have had already made his complaint.

Barrows went behind his desk and sat down. Sitting opposite the chief was another man. He stared at them curiously out of a pair of deep-set blue eyes.

"Inspector Witherspoon, Constable Barnes, this is Russell Merriman." Barrows waved Witherspoon into the only other empty chair in the room. Barnes took up a position next to him.

Russell Merriman appeared to be in his forties, with thinning dark blond hair that was going gray at the temples. He was clean shaven and well groomed, but there were dark circles under his eyes. He wore a beautifully cut black suit with a gray waistcoat, black and gray cravat, and a pristine white shirt. But despite the expensive clothes and the manicured fingernails, Barnes noted the faint pallor of Merriman's pale skin. "Prison pallor" is what coppers generally called it.

"How do you do, sir," Witherspoon said respectfully. Constable Barnes nodded.

Russell Merriman rose to his feet and held out his hand. "I'm pleased to make your acquaintance, sir," he said softly as the two men shook hands, "and I'm hoping you can help me."

"I'll certainly try, sir," Witherspoon replied, his expression a bit confused. He didn't have a clue who Russell Merriman might be.

To Barnes' surprise, Merriman extended a hand toward him as well, nodded in acknowledgement of the introduction as they shook hands, and then sank back into his chair.

"I expect you're wondering what this is all about," Barrows said to the inspector.

"I am a bit curious, sir."

"Mr. Merriman has come to us about his late sister," Barrows explained. "I'm sure you recall the case, Inspector. Mrs. Muran and her husband were accosted by a robber on their way home. Unfortunately, she was killed during the course of the crime."

"I'm familiar with the case, sir," Witherspoon said, turning to Merriman, "and I'm terribly sorry for your loss."

"The man responsible for Mrs. Muran's death is sentenced to hang," Barrows continued. "But Mr. Merriman isn't sure that all the facts of the matter have been brought to light. He'd like us to have another look into the case."

Barnes wondered if heaven had actually intervened in this case. First the inspector had come around and now this. He knew that getting the police to even admit the possibility of a mistake meant that Merriman had some serious political connections.

"I've no wish to embarrass the police, but I don't feel there was a sufficient investigation," Merriman said. "And I'll not rest until I know what really happened that night."

"I assume that you think her death wasn't the result of the robbery," Witherspoon said.

"You assume correctly," Merriman replied. "My sister was no fool. If someone waving a gun around had accosted them, she'd have given them anything they wanted. Things didn't mean much to her: people did. She would never have risked her life or her husband's life for a pocket watch and a piece of jewelry."

"So if you don't believe it was simply a robbery gone bad, do you have reason to believe there was someone who wished to harm your sister?" Witherspon pressed. He wished he'd read more about the case when it was actually happening, but he'd been busy himself at the time.

Merriman smiled bitterly. "There were any number of people who might have wished her harm. Caroline was a good woman. She was kind and gentle, but if she thought something was right, she wouldn't let anyone move her from her course. I'm not explaining this very well, but I know what she was like. She'd help anyone who needed assistance, but at the same time, she wouldn't let anything or anyone stop her from doing what she thought was morally right." He sighed heavily. "I suspect she had ruffled quite a few feathers with some of her social ideas. She believed in things like employer responsibility and that the welfare of the workers was as important as profits."

"Why have you waited so long to come forward with your suspicions, sir?" Barnes asked.

Barrows looked at the Constable sharply but said nothing.

"I was out of the country when she was murdered," Merriman replied. "Specifically, I was in jail in Los Angeles. That's a rat hole of a town in California. It's a miserable place, gentleman, and I rue the day I ended up there."

"You were incarcerated?" Barrows asked in surprise. "On what charge?"

"Being drunk and disorderly." Merriman closed his eyes briefly. "My sister and I were very different. She was industrious, hardworking, and thrifty. She began helping our father run the family business when she was in her late teens. I've always been a bit too free with the drink, and before I knew it, it had me in its grip and showed no signs of letting go. When our parents died, my father left control of the estate to Caroline. He knew I wasn't responsible enough to handle money or the company. I'd just drink it away." He paused and looked at the floor for a brief moment. "Even though Father tried to let me save a bit of my pride by leaving me the family home, it was still humiliating. Caroline gave me a generous allowance and did her best not to nag me over my dissolute ways. Then she married Keith Muran and I felt a bit awkward staying on in what had now become their household. So I left."

"Your sister provided you the funds to go?" Barnes asked again. He knew that Barrows was probably more than a bit shocked he was asking questions in the presence of senior officers, but that was one of the reasons Witherspoon was so successful: he didn't rigidly adhere to old-fashioned ways of doing things. Besides, Barnes knew that with the trail this cold, they were going to need all the information they could get. Every fact, even background facts, could be important.

"Everyone thought she did," Merriman smiled grimly. "As a matter of fact, Caroline insisted that we tell everyone that she had bought out my share of the estate. But she didn't. She loaned me a few thousand pounds and I left."

"Why did she want people to think she'd bought your part of the estate?" Witherspoon asked.

"I don't know," he admitted. "But she insisted that's what we do. At the time, I was so intent on getting away that I didn't care enough to ask any questions. I simply took the letter of credit and left. I knew I'd let her down. I knew I'd let the whole family down with my behavior, but Caroline still loved me."

"So you went to America," Barrows prompted. He glanced at the clock on the wall.

"I went to Paris first," Merriman explained. "My luck was very good to begin with and I made a lot of money. But that never lasts. So I took a ship to New York and from there I went west. I thought I was having a great adventure, but I wasn't; I was simply drinking and gambling my way across that great continent. By the time I got to Los Angeles I was almost broke. On my first night in town, I tried to get into a card game but before I even sat down at the table, things went bad. Before I knew it, a fight had broken out and two men were shot, one of them fatally. I ended up in jail. The local authorities thought the dead man was me, so they notified the British authorities in Washington who then notified my sister. That's why everyone thought I was dead."

"Why did they think the dead man was you?" Barrows interjected.

"During the scuffle, he managed to get hold of my purse. It had my money and my identification in it. The sheriff in Los Angeles thought the purse was his, not mine."

"It must have been a very odd sort of fisticuffs," Barnes murmured.

"There was nothing odd about it all, Constable," Merriman smiled ruefully. "I wasn't really involved except that I happened to have the bad luck to pick that moment to try and get in the game. I'd taken my purse out to see how many dollars I had left when one player accused another one of cheating. A moment later, everyone was on their feet and someone slammed into me. We both ended up on the floor. By that time, shots were being fired in my direction . . ."

"Fired at you?" Witherspoon asked. "But why?"

"Not at me; at the other man. But as he was lying across me, I realized I was likely to be hit, so I shoved away from him as quickly as I could, managing in the process to get clipped on the head by someone's boot as they ran for cover. When I came to, I was in jail, my purse was gone, and the card cheater was dead."

"Why didn't you clarify the error when you realized what had happened?" The inspector regarded him curiously.

"Because I didn't realize exactly what had happened for several days. Then it took me ages to convince the American authorities that I was me and that I'd done nothing more than just reach for my purse to try and get into a card game."

"Then you came home?" Barnes pressed. Somehow, the time wasn't right.

"No." Merriman shook his head. "I had to earn the money for my passage. That took almost two months."

"And exactly how did you earn the money, sir?" Barrows asked curiously. "By gambling?"

"Certainly not." Merriman seemed offended. "I haven't had a drink nor played at cards since that dreadful experience. Let me tell you, sir—a few weeks in a Los Angeles jail is enough to keep anyone on the path of righteousness, no matter how boring it might be. Oh no, I earned the money to get home by giving piano lessons." He shrugged. "I'm not a particularly gifted pianist, but that didn't seem to matter greatly. I still had more students than I could possibly accommodate."

"When did you arrive back in England?" Witherspoon flicked a quick glance at Barnes as he asked the question.

"Three days ago," Merriman replied. "I came in on the *Atlantis Star.* I'd telegraphed our family solicitor about my circumstances—I wanted him to let my sister know I was still alive. Somehow, just walking up to her front door didn't seem right. No one deserves that sort of surprise." His eyes filled with tears again. "But as it turned out, I needn't have worried. My poor sister was already dead and buried."

"Let me buy you a quick pint to show there's no 'ard feelings," Smythe said to the man he now knew as Charlie

Tully. He'd gone to the Fortune Hotel, and by crossing a bellboy's palm with silver he'd managed to run into the desk clerk just when the man was getting off the late shift. "I almost ran you down, and you've been bloomin' decent about it."

"There's no need for that. We've all been in a rush at one time or another." Charlie Tully brushed a bit of dust off his jacket sleeve. He was a tall, rangy man with smooth hands, dark hair, and a strong jawline. "When you first banged into me, I thought you might be a rough wanting my pay packet."

"There's roughs in this neighborhood?"

"Sometimes. They come to the hotel wanting casual work, but you can't rely on them so we don't use them very often." Tully put his bowler on. "Well, I'd best be going."

"Let me buy you a drink." Smythe gestured toward a small pub on the corner. "Please, I'd feel better. I knocked you into a wall."

Tully hesitated and then grinned. "All right then."

They went to the pub and Smythe pushed through the crowd to the bar. "A pint do you?"

Tully nodded and pointed to a nearby table whose occupants were getting up. As soon as they'd left, he slid onto the small stool and put his foot on the one opposite to save it.

Smythe, holding a beer in each hand, maneuvered his way to the table and put their drinks down. He slipped into his seat and lifted his glass. "Cheers."

Tully nodded, lifted his glass, and took a long drink. "Ah . . . that's good."

For the next ten minutes, Smythe made sure they chatted about everything except John Addison. He found out that Tully was single and lived with an aged uncle off the Edgeware Road, that his uncle worked nights as a watchman, and that Tully was thinking about immigrating to New Zealand.

"There's a lot of opportunity for a hardworking man in New Zealand. I've always wanted my own business, and I've lots of experience in hotels," Tully exclaimed. "Mind you, I've got my fare saved and enough to live on for a good while, but I really can't go until Uncle Len dies. It wouldn't be right to leave him on his own."

"Maybe he could go with you," Smythe suggested. "Sounds like he's a right strong man if he's still working nights."

"Nah, he'd not leave," Tully replied. "He likes his house and his neighbors. He'd not leave my aunt Letty's grave, either. They were married for thirty years before she passed on." He took another drink.

"Sounds like you know what you're about," Smythe said. "Do you like workin' in hotels? Don't you get a lot of complainin' customers?"

"Not really. Well, there's always a few that complain, but part of the job is making sure you do things right. Take tonight for instance. We had a lady complaining that she'd not gotten her messages delivered to her room."

"How did you handle that?" Smythe took another sip of beer.

"I assured her that she'd not had any messages, which she hadn't," he broke off, frowning. "Mind you, that actually seemed to make her angrier. I think she was expecting something that didn't come."

"That's not your fault," Smythe said quickly. "Women aren't easy to understand at the best of times, are they? I expect you're better at handling men—you know, business travelers. As a matter fact, I thought I recognized my old gov comin' out your door. That's one of the reasons I almost ran you down. I thought I saw Mr. Addison and I wanted to catch him."

"You worked for Mr. Addison?" Tully asked. "Mr. John Addison from Birmingham?"

"That's right. I worked there for two years," Smythe said. "Was that him then?"

"It was," Tully frowned. "You've not got a Birmingham accent."

Witherspoon was very late getting home. But Mrs. Jeffries was waiting for him when he came through the front door. "Good evening, sir," she said as she reached for his bowler. She noticed he had a thick brown file under his arm.

"Good evening, Mrs. Jeffries. I do hope my tardiness hasn't ruined one of Mrs. Goodge's delectable suppers." He shrugged out of one sleeve of his coat and transferred the file to his other hand while he slipped out of other one.

"It's herbed chicken sir, Mrs. Goodge has it in the warming oven. I can serve it whenever you're ready." She tried to read the name on the file as she reached for his garment, but the printing was too small.

"Actually, I'd like a sherry before I have my meal. I've had the most extraordinary day." He tucked the file back under his arm and started down hall.

"Certainly, sir." She tossed the coat on the coat tree and hurried after him.

When they reached his study, she went to the cabinet and pulled out a bottle of Harvey's Bristol Cream, his favorite sherry.

"Pour yourself one as well," he instructed. "I need to talk to you."

Her hand stilled on the cork as a dozen different possibilities, all of them awful, leapt into her mind. She told herself not to be silly—he frequently asked her to join him in a small drink before dinner, especially after he'd had a terrible day. "Thank you, sir. I'd enjoy a glass. Is something troubling you, sir?"

"I'm afraid there is, and I really must speak with you about it. I quite simply don't know what to do. It's very troubling, when one stumbles onto something like this and then to have one's suspicions confirmed . . ." He broke off and shook his head.

Mrs. Jeffries' heart sank to her toes. They'd been found out. Somehow, someone had gotten to the inspector and told him of their involvement in his cases. Blast. She'd known that one day they might face this situation, but she'd not really believed it would happen so quickly and with so little warning. "Well, sir, before you jump to any conclusions, perhaps you ought to have a nice long think about it and make sure you've all the facts."

She handed him his drink, sat down on the settee, and knocked her own back with all the grace of a convict on his first day out.

"That's precisely what I told Constable Barnes." Witherspoon gaped at her. Gracious, she was putting that drink down like a sailor. "Mrs. Jeffries, is there something wrong?"

"Wrong, sir?" She smiled sadly. "That all depends. Why don't you tell me what it is you've found out and we'll have a good talk about it." Maybe if she offered to resign, he'd let the others stay on in the house. No, of course he'd let them stay, but she was determined to be the one to take the blame.

"Well, er, that's exactly what I wanted to do. I mean, unless something is bothering you . . . Oh, Mrs. Jeffries, I do hope everything is all right with you and the rest of the staff. It's selfish of me, I know, but right now I genuinely need your good advice. Chief Inspector Barrows called me in today and now I've got a case that's already been solved."

It dawned on Mrs. Jeffries that perhaps her portents of doom had been a bit premature. "There's nothing wrong here, sir," she said quickly. "I simply was making a comment about the world at large. Do tell me what happened, sir. Which case did you get?"

"Are you sure everything is all right here?" He stared at her, his expression anxious.

"Everything is fine, sir," she assured him. "Now, sir, what on earth happened?"

Witherspoon nodded at the file he'd laid on the table next to his chair. "That's the case file for the Muran murder," he said, taking another sip of his drink. "Chief Inspector Barrows wants me to have a look at it tonight."

"But that case has been solved." She sent up a silent, heartfelt prayer of thanks. "Why does he want you to look at it? Is it being reopened?"

"Oh, it's a long story, and the truth is, even without him calling me into his office I was going to have a look at the case."

"Really, sir, why is that?"

"Several reasons, actually." He told her about his and Barnes encounter with Inspector Nivens in the records room and his suspicion that something was wrong.

For a moment, she was silent, then she said, "If you were going to have a good snoop on your own, sir, then why are you so downhearted because the chief inspector has officially given you the case?"

"But don't you see? Now that's it's official, now that the chief has his doubts as well, it puts a great deal of pressure on me."

"What made Chief Inspector Barrows get involved in the matter?" she asked curiously.

Witherspoon told her about the meeting with Russell Merriman. As she listened to his recitation of the day's events, her mind raced with possibilities.

"Now I'm to find the killer, providing, of course, it isn't actually the man who's going to hang for the crime."

"You're sure Tommy Odell isn't guilty," she pressed.

"No one can be absolutely sure," he admitted. "But ever since he was convicted there were rumors and hints from the rank-and-file lads that something was wrong. To my shame, I looked the other way." He shook his head. "Mrs. Jeffries, the trail has gone cold, the verdict is already in, and what's more, I have a feeling that finding the real killer is going to be difficult if not impossible."

"Of course it's not impossible," she said briskly. She could tell he needed reassurance. Sometimes he had very little faith in his own abilities. "If it were, then the Lord wouldn't have put it on your plate."

"One doesn't wish to be arrogant or appear to question the will of the Lord," he said, smiling faintly. "But I do think it would have been better if the Almighty had given me this assignment a bit earlier. Tommy Odell's scheduled to hang in a few weeks."

CHAPTER 7

—

The minute she could decently get away, Mrs. Jeffries left the inspector eating his dinner and hurried down to tell the others the good news.

Wiggins and Fred were at the foot of the staircase, the dog's tail wagging madly and the lad putting on his jacket.

"Oh good, I've caught you in time," she said. "Don't be long on your walk. I've news. The inspector is on the case."

"Cor blimey, that's a bit of a surprise." Wiggins grinned broadly. "'Ow'd that 'appen?

"It's a long story, and I might as well tell everyone at once. We'l have a quick meeting as soon as you get back. Go along to Lady Cannonberry's and tell her the news. It would be best if she were here as well."

Fred suddenly lunged forward and charged across the hall and through the kitchen door. "Fred!" Wiggins grabbed for the dog, missed, and almost slammed headfirst into the newel post. "Cor blimey, Fred, what's got into you?"

They heard a shriek, followed by a loud crash and the sound of breaking crockery. "You wretched beast; leave my darling alone," Mrs. Goodge shouted.

Wiggins and Mrs. Jeffries rushed into the kitchen. Samson was standing in the center of the table, his fur on end, his tail twitching, and his ears pinned back. Fred was on his hind legs with his forepaws on the table's edge, trying his hardest to get at the cat.

The dog was growling and the cat was hissing like a steam engine. Mrs. Goodge was ineffectually waving a tea towel at the two combatants. An overturned chair and a broken tea mug were on the floor. "You silly mutt," the cook cried. "Leave my Samson alone!"

"No Fred," Wiggins said, grabbing the animal's collar and pulling him away from the table. Fred didn't come willingly but kept making lunging motions toward the cat. Samson hissed, leapt onto the pine sideboard, jumped down to the floor, and then ran lickety split into the hallway where he turned and ran toward the safety of Mrs. Goodge's room.

"Oh, Mrs. Goodge, I'm awfully sorry. Please don't be mad at Fred. He's usually a good dog." Wiggins kept one hand on Fred's collar and used the other to lift up the overturned chair. Mrs. Jeffries picked up the broken pieces of crockery and laid them on the counter.

"Not to worry, lad," Mrs. Goodge said, laughing. "I've been waiting for this to happen. It was only a matter of time before Fred put Samson in his place. Mark my words: from now on Samson will give him a wide berth. It's all for the best; we couldn't have the dog slinking around here all the time being scared of my little darling." She looked at the housekeeper. "Is the inspector ready for his pudding?"

She nodded. "I'll take it up when I go. But that's not why I came down. We're going to have another meeting tonight. The inspector is on the case."

It was well past midnight before Mrs. Jeffries went to her rooms. She changed into her bed clothes, turned off the lamp, and sat down in her chair by the window. The rest of the household was asleep and the house was silent.

Everyone, even Ruth and Smythe, had been able to attend their impromptu meeting. When Mrs. Jeffries had told them about Witherspoon getting the case, the relief on all their faces had been almost comical. Despite their brave words and their determination to solve this murder, having the inspector on board made their investigation much easier.

She looked out into the dark night and pulled her wool housecoat tighter against the chill. A heavy fog had drifted in from the river, obscuring the faint glow of the gas lamp across the road. Staring at the tiny dot of light, Mrs. Jeffries relaxed and let her mind go blank.

She didn't try to think about the case, and she didn't try to come up with any theories or see any patterns. She simply let the bits and pieces play about in her mind.

Caroline Muran was shot twice, and what was she doing in that area in the first place? Why hadn't they gone straight home? Why was she nervous that day? Had someone threatened her? Keith Muran was an English gentleman and was already selling the factory. What was the name of the sacked factory manager? Could he have been following them that night?

Mrs. Jeffries sat there for a long time, letting her mind go where it would. Caroline's cousins were poor relations and living on a small pension. Maybe they resented their wealthy cousin. Was Russell Merriman telling the truth, and had he really been in jail in California? Or maybe he'd been living in London under an assumed identity. As the last idea popped into her head, Mrs. Jeffries straightened up and blinked in surprise. Gracious, where did that notion come from? On their previous cases, she'd learned it was dangerous to ignore ideas that seemingly came out of nowhere. She decided she'd best mention the possibility that Merriman had been in London to the inspector over breakfast. She heard the downstairs clock strike the hour. She eased out of her chair and made her way to her bed.

But even though it was very late and she was very tired, it was almost dawn before she drifted off to sleep.

"This isn't going to be very pleasant," Witherspoon muttered to Barnes as they climbed the short flight of stairs to the Muran house. "I imagine Mr. Muran thought all of this was over and done with."

"A bit of inconvenience won't kill him, sir," Barnes said as he lifted the brass knocker and let it fall. "If it was me, I'd want to know the truth about what happened that night."

"Let's hope he's in a cooperative mood," Witherspoon said.

A young maid opened the door. She drew back in surprise as she saw Barnes.

"May we see Mr. Muran, please?" Witherspoon said quickly.

The girl looked flustered. "I'll see if he's receiving." She edged back, leaving the door open.

"This isn't a social call," Barnes said.

But by then the girl had gone.

From inside the hallway they heard the sound of muffled voices, and then a moment later the maid stuck her head back out. "Come this way, please. The master will see you in his study." She ushered them down the hallway and into an elegantly furnished sitting room.

Keith Muran was standing by a fireplace at the other end of the room. He didn't look pleased to see them. "Good morning," he said curtly.

"Good morning, sir. I'm Inspector Gerald Witherspoon, and this is Constable Barnes. We're sorry to disturb you, but we've come on some rather urgent business."

"What business?" He sat down in one of the cream-colored side chairs by the fireplace. "I've already retrieved my pocket watch from your premises. I can't see what business you could possibly have to discuss with me."

"It's not about your watch, sir," Witherspoon said softly. "It's about the murder of your wife."

"Inspector Nivens assured me this was all over and done with," Muran replied. "My wife's murderer is going to be hanged very shortly."

"There are some questions, sir." Witherspoon didn't think it was going well, but he wasn't about to give up and go away.

"What questions?" Muran sighed heavily. "Inspector, I've no idea what is going on, but I assure you, I've told the police everything I can recall about that awful night."

"I know this must be painful, but, well, there are a few loose ends we must clear up."

"Loose ends?" he repeated. "This has something to do with Russell coming back, doesn't it?"

"That's true, sir," Witherspoon admitted. Chief Inspector Barrows hadn't said anything about keeping Mr. Merriman's involvement a secret. "I'm sure Mr. Merriman's return from the dead, so to speak, must have been a shock to you."

"Most certainly," Muran replied. "When Mr. Brandon told me the news, it was difficult to comprehend. Frankly, I didn't really believe it till I saw him with my own eyes yesterday afternoon."

"As I said, Mr. Merriman isn't satisfied that all the questions surrounding his sister's death have been answered," Witherspoon said.

"Russell and Caroline were very close. She was devastated when she thought him dead," Muran murmured. "I'm forgetting my manners. Please do sit down and make yourselves comfortable."

"Thank you." Witherspoon took a seat in an overstuffed easy chair and Barnes perched on the edge of an empire-style love seat.

Muran waited until the two men had settled themselves and then he turned his attention to the inspector. "What is it you want to know?"

"I've read your statement regarding what happened that night, and there's a couple of questions that need clearing up." Witherspoon cleared his throat and tried to recall exactly what those questions might be.

"But I've already told you," Muran replied. "I told the police everything I can remember. Surely it was all in the police report."

"The report didn't say why you went to Barrick Street in the first place instead of going home," Barnes said bluntly.

"But I explained to Inspector Nivens why we'd gone there that night." Muran looked confused.

"He didn't put it in his report," Witherspoon said.

"My wife wanted to have a quick look at a building we were thinking of acquiring. She was considering buying another building and expanding the business," Muran explained.

"Wasn't it rather late to be looking at a building?" Witherspoon asked.

"Of course it was," Muran replied. "But she wanted to have a look at the neighborhood. She was a very busy woman, Inspector, but once she had an idea in her head, it was difficult to sway her. She could be very stubborn. I told her it was a foolish idea, that she couldn't get a decent look at a piece of property in the middle of the night, but she was adamant."

"I'm sure that's true, sir," Witherspoon said sympathetically. "I'm sorry to distress you, but it is important we ask these questions."

"Why is it important?" he asked. "Caroline's killer has already been tried and convicted. I've answered questions and testified in court. Frankly, sir, this is most distressing. I understand that Russell is upset, but for God's sake, he shouldn't try to alleviate his guilt that he wasn't here when she died by dredging all this up."

"Do you think that's what he is doing?" Witherspoon queried. It didn't really matter why Merriman had brought the matter up again; they were duty bound to continue the inquiry.

"Of course he felt guilty. Russell had always turned his back on his responsibilities so he could enjoy himself. He left everything to Caroline—all the work, all the worry, and all the decisions—while he rode off to have a grand time. He was in jail, Inspector," Muran added. "In California. Caroline thought he was dead. We'd been told he was dead."

"Well he isn't dead, sir, and he isn't happy with the way this case was handled, either," Barnes said. "Would you mind telling us what happened once you left the hansom cab?"

"We got out and started walking toward the building," he replied. "Frankly, that's really all I remember. The next thing I knew I was in the hospital and there were two policemen next to my bed."

"So you were knocked unconscious before your wife was shot?" Witherspoon clarified.

"That's correct," Muran replied. "It was late, cold, and dark, Inspector. I hadn't wanted to stop in the first place, so I was hustling Caroline along so we could get it over with and get home. It's all very vague, but I recall someone suddenly just being there and then I don't remember anything at all until I came to in the hospital."

"So you never really saw your assailant?" Witherspoon pressed.

"That's what I've just said," he muttered.

"How were you planning on getting home?" Barnes asked.

"What?" Muran looked surprised by the question.

"How were you planning on getting home?" the constable repeated. "You said it was cold and dark and you were in a hurry. You were in the middle of an industrial neighborhood and you'd not find a cab easily in that neighborhood. Yet you didn't ask the hansom cab to wait for you."

"But I did, Inspector," he said quickly. "I do remember that. I specifically told him to wait for us. But as soon as I'd paid him and we'd gone up the street a bit, he drove off.

I remember being annoyed, but Caroline said not to worry, that we'd find another one near the bridge. The building was close to Waterloo Bridge." He sighed again. "Not that it mattered all that much; traffic was so awful that night we could have walked home faster than the hansoms were moving."

"I see," Barnes said.

"Do you know of anyone who might have wanted to harm your wife?" the inspector asked. "Did she have any enemies?"

"Enemies?" Muran looked down at the carpet. "She was a kind and decent woman. No one would want to hurt her. It was a robbery, Inspector. We were stupidly at the wrong place at the wrong time and that's all there was to it. It's my fault. I should have put my foot down and insisted we go home. But it was hard for me to deny Caroline anything. I loved her very much."

"You weren't to know there was danger about, sir," Witherspoon said kindly.

Muran looked up. "Wait. Now that I've thought about it, there is someone who was very angry at Caroline."

"And who would that be, sir?" Barnes asked, relieved that they might actually be making progress.

"I'm not saying a word against my wife," he replied. "But Caroline could be very hard when she considered a principle was at stake."

"Meaning what, sir?" Witherspoon prompted.

"Meaning she sacked her factory manager just a few days before she was murdered. His name is Roderick Sutter. Yee Gods, that's right. I'd quite forgotten. Caroline had sacked the fellow, and as I recall, he'd not taken it very well at all."

"Russell Merriman must have plenty of influence to get the police to have another look," Blimpey Groggins said to Smythe. "Looks like we caught us a bit of luck on that one."

"What do you know about him?" Smythe asked. He took a quick sip of his beer and tried not to make a face. It was a bit early in the day for him, but after their meeting this morning, it had become important they learn what they could about Merriman. The Dirty Duck was closed, but as Blimpey was probably the owner of the establishment, they were having a quick pint anyway.

"Don't you worry, old mate, I've already got my sources on it," Blimpey replied. "What I know so far is that he's a bit of a ne'er-do-well, bit of a drinker and a gambler. He's not much good at holdin' the liquor or handlin' the cards."

"We know that much," Smythe retorted. "What we need to know now is whether or not he might have 'ad anything to do with his sister's murder."

"You're wantin' to know if he was in London at the time of the murder and livin' under another identity," Blimpey said shrewdly. "He wasn't."

"You know that for a fact?"

"If he'd been 'ere, he'd have let Tommy Odell hang, and as 'e's the one stirring it up at the Home Office, I think you can safely say he'd nothin' to do with it."

"That's what we thought as well." Smythe sighed, remembering the rather heated discussion they'd had on the subject at breakfast. "But it doesn't hurt to make sure about the fellow. There's a chance that even if he didn't do it, he might have put one of his mates up to doin' the deed for him."

Blimpey shook his head. "I'm one step ahead of ya. Russell Merriman didn't have the sort of mates that'd do murder for him. He and his kind are usually gutless, upper-class toffs that don't get their hands dirty. Besides, ever since I come back to London and found out Tommy was in the nick, I've had my sources out gatherin' information, and I've not heard any hints that Merriman was back in England or that he had anything to do with his sister's death. By all accounts, the two of 'em were right fond of each other."

"Exceptin' for the fact that he was a drunk," Smythe retorted.

"So what?" Blimpey shrugged. "Just because someone drinks don't mean their kin stops carin' about 'em."

"Have you found out anything else that might be useful?" Smythe looked down at his beer glass, a bit embarrassed to be asking this kind of question. But though it pleased his vanity to tell himself he'd do all his own investigating from now on, the truth was, Blimpey did have incredibly good sources of information and a man's life was at stake.

"Well, I'm a bit annoyed that I didn't catch this earlier, but about a week before she was killed, Mrs. Muran sacked her factory manager. Seems he'd been helpin' himself to her money. My sources tell me she was tryin' to decide whether or not to set the law on the man."

"I knew she'd sacked her manager," Smythe said. "But I haven't had time to find out his name yet."

"His name is Roderick Sutter. He lives at forty-two Landry Place in Fulham."

"What do you think, sir?" Barnes asked as they climbed into a hansom.

Witherspoon sighed. "I think we're in a bit of a mess," he said, grabbing the handhold as the cab lurched forward, "and I'm not in the least sure what to do about it. I suppose we'd best just carry on as if the trial hadn't already taken place and the verdict been given. But honestly, it does make getting information out of people a bit difficult. Did we get some police constables set up to do a round of the neighborhood?"

They'd asked Chief Inspector Barrows for a few men to go around to Barrick Street and see if they could find any witnesses. After reading the file, even Barrows had admitted the original investigation had been woefully incompetent.

"I've got several lads assigned to it, sir," Barnes replied. "But as you said earlier, the trail's gone cold and those streets are pretty empty once the businesses close. But we'll see if we can find something. What do you think we'll learn by speaking to Mrs. Muran's solicitor?" They were headed for the law offices of Brandon and Wells, just off Russell Square.

"I'm not sure," Witherspoon said, sighing again. "But maybe if we learn a bit more about the lady, we'll come up with something. Honestly, I was hoping Mr. Muran might have been a bit more helpful. But apparently, he can't remember anything."

"I expect getting coshed on the head could do that. But I still think it's odd, sir. Why wasn't he killed as well as Mrs. Muran?" Barnes was very mistrustful of situations that didn't make sense, and this murder didn't make sense at all. Even the information he'd gotten from Mrs. Jeffries in their meeting this morning wasn't particularly helpful. The inspector's household had learned a good number of facts, but none of them were shedding much light on the identity of the killer. Not yet anyway.

"Perhaps whoever did the killing only wanted her dead." Witherspoon cocked his head to one side as another idea popped into his mind. "Gracious, that's what we've got to do. That's the answer." His housekeeper was right, sometimes it paid to listen to his "inner voice."

Over breakfast this morning, she'd said, "You've simply got to trust yourself, sir. Listen to your instincts. That inner voice of yours hasn't failed you yet."

"What's the answer, sir?" Barnes stared at him curiously.

"Why, it's as plain as the nose on your face, Constable," Witherspoon said happily. "We've simply got to find the reason that someone would want her dead while having an equally compelling reason to keep him alive."

Barnes blinked in surprise, caught himself, and said, "You mean like someone thinking that he might be easier to deal with than she was. You know, in a business sense, sir. From what Mr. Merriman told us, his sister tended to be more concerned with principles than profits when it came to her business."

Witherspoon stared at him. "I'm not certain I understand what you mean."

"Uh . . ." Barnes struggled to think of the right way to say it. "Like you pointed out, sir, the killer wanted only her dead.

She controlled the business, and maybe the killer thought that with her gone, Mr. Muran, who isn't a businessman at all, would be easier to deal with." He held his breath, hoping he'd not gone too far. But he had to somehow introduce the idea that Witherspoon should have a look at John Addison.

"That's one possible motive," Witherspoon agreed. "I'm sure there are lots of others. After we see the solicitors, I want to see Roderick Sutter. Frankly, I'm surprised that Inspector Nivens never even bothered to interview the man."

"I'm not," Barnes muttered.

Wiggins hovered behind a post box on the Fulham Road watching as Constable Barnes and the inspector got into a hansom cab. As soon as the cab moved off, he came out from his hiding place and turned down Drayton Gardens. If he was lucky, he might find someone who'd talk to him. He slowed his pace and tried not to look directly at the Muran house.

Just then, a maid came up the ground floor steps and onto the street. She had a shopping basket over her arm.

Wiggins recognized her immediately; it was the girl he'd frightened. Without thinking, he moved to block her path, whipped off his cap, and blurted the first words that came into his head. "Excuse me, miss, but I've come to apologize."

"Apologize for what?" She came to a full stop.

"For scaring you the other day," he replied. "It's made me feel right terrible. I've come back here three times, hoping to see you so I could say how sorry I was."

She said nothing for a moment, and then she smiled faintly. "You've tried to find me?"

"Just to say I was sorry, miss. It's not nice to scare young ladies." He couldn't quite recall what he'd said to her on their first encounter, so he tried to avoid saying too much now.

She cast a quick look over her shoulder toward the house and then looked back at Wiggins. "Did you ever find your dog?"

He grinned. "Yes. He'd just run off ahead of me."

"Good," she said, starting toward the Fulham Road. "I like dogs."

"May I walk with you, miss?" He put his cap on and hurried to catch up with her. "I'd be pleased to carry your shopping basket."

"You can walk with me, but I'll hold onto the basket myself if you don't mind." She cast him a quick, sideways glance.

She wasn't a particularly pretty girl, but she wasn't homely, either. Her eyes and hair were brown and her complexion quite pretty. He wasn't quite sure what approach to take. "Are you a housekeeper, miss? You're awfully young and pretty to be in such a position."

She laughed in delight. "No, I'm just a housemaid. But Mrs. Turner hasn't the faintest idea of how a proper household should be run, so she sends me off to do the shopping."

"Is that your mistress, then?" he asked. They were nearing the Fulham Road and he wanted to make sure they were deeply engrossed in conversation before she went into the shops. "Mrs. Turner?"

The girl made a face. "No, my mistress passed away recently. Mrs. Turner and her daughter are simply family cousins. Poor relations, if you know what I mean. But they've barged in to try and take over everything. Not that it matters to me; I'm looking for a new position. I shan't be staying there much longer."

"You're looking for a new place, then?" He grinned broadly. "Perhaps I can be of 'elp. I know several households that might be needing more staff." This wasn't a lie, either. Mrs. Jeffries had commented that two of their neighbors were looking for servants.

"Really?" She looked at him, her expression hopeful. "I've got recommendations."

"That'd be good," he replied.

"And I can get another from our current housekeeper. She took ill right after the mistress died, but I know her address and can easily get a letter from her."

Wiggins felt a bit uncomfortable. But he ruthlessly pushed the feeling to one side. He would do his best to help the girl secure another job, but in the meantime, he'd find out what he could. "That would be most helpful, miss. My name is Wiggins, and I work in Holland Park."

"My name is Charlotte Brimmer." She smiled shyly.

"Would you have time for a cup of tea, Miss Brimmer?" he asked politely. "I'm just a footman, but I really think I can help you. There's a Lyons Tea Shop just up the road, and that's a right respectable place. They do a nice cuppa as well."

She hesitated for a brief moment and he thought he'd overplayed his hand. Then she shrugged. "Why not, it's not as if any of them are going to notice how long I've been gone, not with the police coming around this morning."

"You understand I had no choice but to ask the Home Office for help in this matter," John Brandon said as he ushered the two policemen into his office. "I hope that, as police officers, you'll do your best to find the truth."

"Of course we'll do our best," Witherspoon assured him. Brandon was a short, balding man with a circle of thick gray hair around his skull, a long nose, thin lips, and sharp blue eyes.

"Good. It's imperative the police put their resentments aside and get to the truth of this matter." Brandon sat down behind his mahogany desk and gestured for them to sit down.

"I assure you, sir, I've no resentments whatsoever," Witherspoon said as he took one of the two empty chairs and Barnes took the other one. "Our concern is the same as yours—finding the truth in this matter as quickly as possible."

"Good, then let's get on with this, sir." He stared at them expectantly.

"Uh, yes, of course." The inspector racked his brain for a useful question, but of course his mind refused to supply him with one.

"Was Mr. Muran the sole beneficiary?" Barnes asked softly.

Brandon raised his eyebrows, surprised that the constable had asked a question. "No, there were a number of people and charities that benefited from her death. Mr. Muran was her main beneficiary, but she left bequests to her cousins, her servants, and several of her factory employees. She also left funds for the establishment of a legal defense fund for the London Women's Suffrage Union. Of course, now that Mr. Merriman has risen from the dead"—he grinned at his own joke—"Mr. Muran won't get anything except a reasonable allowance."

"You mean Mr. Merriman inherits everything?" Witherspoon asked. This could put things in a very different light altogether.

"Correct." Brandon leaned back in his chair. "There was a rumor going about that Mrs. Muran had bought her brother's share of their joint estate, but that wasn't true. She loaned him some money so he could travel, but she never bought him out of his birthright."

"But everyone thought she had?" Barnes pressed. That was the gossip he'd heard, and he wanted to see how widespread it had become.

"I know, Caroline started the rumor deliberately. She wanted people to think that Russell was virtually destitute."

"But why?" Witherspoon leaned forward slightly.

"She thought it would keep a certain element from taking advantage of him." Brandon pursed his lips in disapproval. "Specifically, she hoped that people would stop loaning him money to drink and gamble with if they thought he had no prospects. She was trying to protect him. She was like that, always thinking of others. Even the well-being of her workers was important to her. Do you know, she was planning on spending virtually all the company's cash to buy decent housing for her employees."

"We heard she might have been planning on buying another factory." Witherspoon watched the solicitor, trying to gauge from the man's face if this information was a surprise.

But Brandon's expression didn't change. "She had thought about doing that as well," he replied. "She was very concerned with unemployment."

"There was enough capital to do both?" Barnes asked.

Brandon shook his head. "Not really. Caroline could have done both if she'd been willing to take a loan, but she was opposed to doing that. She didn't like banks. I think she'd made up her mind to spend the money on her workers' housing. She was certainly leaning that way the day she died."

"You saw her that day?" Witherspoon's head began to hurt. He'd been on the case for less than fourteen hours and it had already gotten complicated.

"Yes. I brought her the estimates for both the purchase of the properties and the cost of renovations."

"I see." The inspector was getting confused. "Is it a standard business practice to buy houses for workers?"

"It's not a standard practice, but she certainly isn't the first employer to do it. Housing in that area has become quite expensive, at least by the standards of most factory workers," Brandon explained. "Mrs. Muran was going to buy the row houses and then let them back to her workers at a reasonable cost. It was the only way they could afford to live close to where they worked."

"Who knew of Mrs. Muran's plans?" Barnes asked.

Brandon thought for a moment. "Mr. Muran knew, as did Roderick Sutter, her former manager. Sutter was pressing her to open the additional factory. I think he was hoping to be put in charge of both operations. But then she ended up sacking him, so his opinion hardly mattered. I'm not sure if her cousins knew or not. I don't think she ever discussed business with those two ladies, but she might have."

"Cousins?" Witherspoon repeated.

"Mrs. Edwina Turner and her daughter Lucy are Mrs.

Muran's cousins. They live in Chelsea. As a matter of fact, Mrs. Muran left them the house they currently occupy. They'd been letting it from her, at a very nominal rent, I might add. I believe it was Miss Turner that introduced Mrs. Muran to Mr. Muran."

The Turner women lived in a rust-colored brick town house on a long, narrow street off the Kings Road. "I wonder if the ladies are home, sir," Barnes murmured as he reached for the brass door knocker. "I think both of them were at Mr. Muran's this morning." He'd glimpsed a female figure staring at them out the upstairs window as they'd gotten out of a hansom.

"Let's hope they've come back," Witherspoon replied. "I've no idea what we ought to ask them, but as they were beneficiaries to Mrs. Muran's estate and her relations, I felt we ought to come around and have a quick word."

The door opened and an elderly woman peered out at them. "Yes?"

"May we speak with Mrs. Turner, please?" Witherspoon asked politely.

The woman's heavy eyebrows rose in surprise. "I'll see if she's receiving."

"This isn't a social call," Barnes said quickly. "We're police officers and we've come to speak to Mrs. Turner on police business." He was tired of people treating the police like they were inconvenient interruptions to their ruddy social life.

"Wait here." She shoved the door shut.

"Sorry, sir, I didn't mean to speak out of turn," Barnes said. "But it is tiresome the way some people seem to think they don't have to speak to the police at all. I mean, honestly, sir. I'm in uniform. Do they think we're leaving a calling card?"

Witherspoon chuckled. "I expect the sight of the two of us on the doorstep startles people, so they simply say the first thing that pops into their heads."

The door opened and the servant motioned them inside. "Mrs. Turner and Miss Turner will speak to you in the drawing room. It's just down there." She pointed to a door at the end of the short, dim hallway.

The two women were waiting for them when they stepped into the room. The older one, who Witherspoon assumed was Mrs. Edwina Turner, was sitting on a settee. She wore a brown bombazine day dress with a black mourning veil that trailed down her back. Standing by the fireplace was a much younger woman. She had black hair, blue eyes, and exquisite skin. Lucy Turner wasn't in the first flush of youth, yet she was so beautiful it didn't matter.

"Good day," Witherspoon said, taking off his bowler. "I'm Inspector Witherspoon, and this is Constable Barnes. We've a few questions we'd like to ask you concerning the murder of your late cousin."

"I see that Russell's been very busy. I didn't expect you quite this quickly. Do sit down. I'm Lucy Turner, and this is my mother, Mrs. Horace Turner." She gestured toward two matching parlor chairs.

"How do you do." The inspector nodded politely as he and Barnes sat where she'd indicated. Edwina Turner simply stared at them out of cold, hazel eyes.

Lucy Turner sat down at the far end of the settee. "Go ahead, Inspector, ask your questions. Though I've no idea how my mother or I can be of any help."

Once again, Witherspoon's mind went blank. Drat, this was getting ridiculous. For goodness sakes, he was a policeman who'd solved over twenty murders. What was wrong with him? "Er, can you tell us if there was anyone who might have wished to harm Mrs. Muran?"

Lucy Turner shook her head. "Not really."

"Had anyone been threatening her?" Barnes asked.

"Not that I know of," Miss Turner replied. She glanced at her mother. "Mama, had you heard anything?"

The old woman shook her head. "No, but I don't listen to gossip."

"How about Roderick Sutter?" Witherspoon blurted. "Hadn't she just sacked him?"

"You mean her factory manager," Miss Turned replied. "I suppose you could say he might have wished her harm, but honestly, Inspector, I hardly think getting sacked is a reason to commit murder."

"When was the last time you saw your cousin alive?" Witherspoon asked.

Her blue eyes widened in surprise at the sudden change in direction. "Let me see . . . it was a day or two before she died."

"It was the day she died," Edwina Turner interjected.

"Are you sure, Mama?" Lucy said gently. "I think it was the day before that we went to have tea."

"I know what day it was," Edwina insisted. "I occasionally get mixed up, but I recall that day very well, and you should, too. Don't you remember? Caroline was thinking about not going to the concert that night but you told her that she ought to go, that she'd been leaving poor Keith on his own because she'd been working so hard at the factory. You said it would do her good to get out and enjoy herself. Remember?"

CHAPTER 8

Betsy smiled at the young man behind the counter. "I'd like a tin of Cadbury's, please, and a bar of Pears soap."

"Yes, miss," he replied.

She'd ordered items that the household needed so her trip wouldn't be wasted if she didn't find out anything today. She was in a grocery store on the Kings Road, quite close to where the Turner women lived.

After their meeting this morning, it had been decided that even with the inspector on the case, Odell's date with the hangman was still getting closer with each passing day, so they had best find as much information as they could about anyone who might be a suspect.

The clerk put the cocoa and the soap on the counter. "Anything else, miss?" he asked. He was a tall, lanky lad with dark hair, deep-set brown eyes, and a very prominent Adam's apple.

"That's all, thank you," she replied. She decided on the direct approach. "I don't suppose you know of a family around here named Turner? They're from the same village as my mum, and she wanted me to give them her regards."

"You don't have the address?" he said, pushing a lock of hair off his forehead.

"That's the silly part. Mum sent me their address and I've managed to lose it. But I know it was somewhere around here." Betsy forced a giggle. "That's all right, then, I didn't expect you to actually know them."

"Who said I didn't know any Turners?" He grinned. "But I doubt the ones that come in here are from your village. They're both very posh and proper city ladies."

Betsy pretended to be disappointed. But she wasn't going home empty-handed. This case wasn't going well, they weren't getting information fast enough, and she was determined to find out something useful, even if she had to stand here all day. "I see. Then I expect it couldn't be them."

"Sorry, miss. This Mrs. Turner and her daughter are good customers. They come in all the time and I'm sure they're not from a village."

"They do their own shopping?" Betsy commented. "I thought you said they were posh and proper."

"They are," he said hastily. "You can tell from the way they act. The daughter, Miss Lucy, always wants the very best. Mrs. Turner insists on being served by the owner and not one of us clerks. Mind you, Mr. Winkles gets his back up a bit over them, especially as they're generally a bit behind on their bill."

"They don't pay their bill on time," she repeated. "That's not very proper."

"They've been payin' better recently," he said, casting a quick glance over his shoulder toward the curtained doorway that seperated the shop from the private areas of the establishment. "Mr. Winkles doesn't like me gossiping, but it gets right boring in here. The only reason the Turners are paying on time is because Mr. Muran sends along a check every month." He looked over his shoulder again. "And from what I've heard, we're not the only shop getting a check from him. Bertie, he's my friend who works at the greengrocers just up the road, he says that Mr. Muran pays up there every month, and Lorna—she works at the dressmakers on Tibbalt Street—told me that Mr. Muran had settled all of Miss Lucy's outstanding debts there as well. Miss Lucy owed them a lot of money. Mind you, she does wear the loveliest dresses."

"It sounds like your Mr. Muran must be very fond of these ladies," Betsy murmured.

The clerk smirked. "He's fond of Miss Lucy all right. Bertie's mum says they've known each other for years. Mrs. Turner helped nurse Mr. Muran's first wife when she was ill. Bertie's mum says she expects Miss Lucy thought she'd have a crack at marryin' Mr. Muran, when the first Mrs. Muran passed on, but then she made the mistake of introducin' him to her cousin. He went and married her instead, and then the last we heard, that poor lady had up and died as well."

"Some men don't seem to be able to hang onto their wives," Betsy said, giving him another flirtatious smile. "It's so nice to talk to someone who's aware of what's going on in his neighborhood. You know ever so much; I'll bet all the young ladies love to talk with you."

He blushed with pleasure. "Oh, it's nothing really. But I do like takin' an interest in what goes on around here, and believe me, I hear plenty."

Just then, the door opened and two women stepped inside the shop. A second later, the curtains behind the counter parted and a small, elderly man stuck his head out. "Jon, don't dawdle about gossiping; you've customers."

"Yes Mr. Winkles," Jon replied.

Betsy put her purchases in her basket, smiled at Jon, and hurried out of the shop. When she got outside, she stopped and looked up and down the busy road. But she couldn't see what she wanted.

"Excuse me," she said to a middle-aged woman with a

shopping basket over her arm. "But could you direct me to the greengrocers?"

Roderick Sutter lived in a two-story brick house near Putney Bridge. He was a tall, middle-aged man with thinning light brown hair, brown eyes, and a weak chin. He didn't look pleased to see the two policemen. "I've no idea why you're here, Inspector," he said as he led them into a sparsely furnished drawing room. "According to the newspapers, this case was solved and the miscreant responsible for Mrs. Muran's murder is going to hang."

"There are some questions concerning the case," Witherspoon replied.

"What do you mean?" Sutter flopped down on a gray threadbare settee. He did not invite the two policemen to take a seat. "How can there be questions? The man has already been tried and judgment passed. I believe he's going to hang in a few days."

"That's irrelevant, sir. There are still some important questions to be answered," Barnes said quickly. "The first of which is, Where were you on the night of January thirtieth?"

Sutter's jaw dropped. "I beg your pardon?"

"It's a very simple question, sir," Witherspoon added. Like Barnes, he was a tad put out to be kept standing. It was very rude. "Where were you on the night of January thirtieth? The night Mrs. Muran was murdered."

"You can't possibly think I had anything to do with it," Sutter blustered. "That's ridiculous."

"Could you please just answer the question, sir." Barnes watched the man carefully.

"I was here," Sutter replied. "And frankly, I resent this sort of question being asked in the first place."

"Why do you resent it, sir?" Witherspoon asked. "Surely you must realize the police would have questions for you. After all, Mrs. Muran did sack you only a few days before she was murdered."

"Some would say that was a powerful motive," Barnes said softly. "You and Mrs. Muran were overheard having a very loud argument the day she dismissed you." Barnes had heard this tidbit on his own.

Sutter had gone pale. "This is absurd. Surely you're not suggesting that I had anything to do with Mrs. Muran's murder. For God's sake, she was killed during a robbery!"

"That's what the killer may have wanted us to think," Witherspoon said. "Why don't you tell us in your own words about your last meeting with Mrs. Muran. That might go a long way to getting this matter cleared up nicely, don't you think?"

Sutter swallowed and then nodded. "It was a few days before she was killed. I was supposed to be the managing director, but my title was really just for show; she made all the decisions. I wish I'd known how involved she was going to be before I agreed to take the position."

"Who actually hired you?" Witherspoon asked.

"Mrs. Muran." He smiled bitterly. "To be fair, she told me she was involved with the business, but I foolishly didn't think that meant she'd be there eight or nine hours a day. For goodness' sakes, she was married. Why wasn't she home taking care of her husband like any decent woman should be?"

"Are you married, sir?" Barnes cast a quick, meaningful glance around the small, bare room. There were no pictures on the wall, the few pieces of furniture were old and faded, and a pair of limp green curtains hung at the window.

"No," Sutter snapped. "I've always been too busy to have a wife. I've always worked long hours in my positions and when I took this one, I assumed I'd do the same, but there was no need. She was always there, always making decisions and undermining my authority."

"It sounds as if you resented her," the constable said.

"Of course I resented her; she wouldn't let me do my job."

"Could you tell us about the argument, please," Witherspoon prompted.

Sutter got a hold of himself. "I was in the office. She came in and announced that I had to go, that I was sacked. I can't say that it was a surprise. We'd disagreed on a number of things. She thought I was too hard on the workers and I thought she was ridiculously easy. For goodness' sakes, she gave them a morning and an afternoon break plus a whole hour for lunch. It was ridiculous; she was coddling them like a bunch of babies. Every time I tried to instill some discipline amongst the workers, they'd go running to her and she'd overturn my decisions. That day, I'd finally had enough. When she sacked me I told her she was an unnatural woman and that if I'd had my way, the business could have doubled our profits for the year."

"How long had you worked for Mrs. Muran?" Barnes asked.

"Just a little over a year. Before that I worked at Anderson and Michaels in Leeds," Sutter replied. "If I'd known how peculiar her business ideas were, I'd never have accepted the job. She was going to take all the capital on hand and use it for buying up row houses for the workers. Can you believe it? I told her it was ridiculous, that she'd never recoup that money, that it was like pouring sand down a rat hole, but she insisted. I tried to get her to consider Addison's offer, but she refused to even meet with the man."

"What offer?" the inspector asked.

"John Addison, his family owns Addison's Brass Works, he was going to offer her a fortune for this company, but she bluntly refused to even consider meeting the man. I tried to talk sense into her, tell her to take the meeting and hear the man out, but she wouldn't. She kept saying she wasn't interested in selling."

"So you knew Addison?" the inspector asked. His lower back began to ache from standing so long in one spot. He shifted his weight a bit, hoping it would ease the pain.

"Yes," Sutter admitted. "Addison had paid me twenty pounds to arrange a meeting with her. He was going give me another twenty pounds when the meeting actually took place."

"Is that why she sacked you, because you disagreed with her opinion?" Barnes stared hard at Sutter.

"Oh no, she sacked me because I stole money," he replied bluntly. "It wasn't much, but I was angry, you see. When she refused to meet with Addison, I lost twenty quid, so I took it out of one of our suppliers' cash accounts. Of course she caught me, but I didn't care. I knew I couldn't stand working for that woman any longer. I didn't care if she sacked me. It was a bit of a relief when it finally happened."

Ruth Cannonberry arrived for their afternoon meeting just as the others were sitting down. "I do hope I'm not late," she apologized as she slipped into her chair. "But I was un-avoidably delayed. Honestly, some people simply haven't any idea of when to stop talking and it's dreadfully difficult to tell the vicar that one simply can't serve on another com-mittee."

"We've not really started," Mrs. Jeffries assured her. "The others have only arrived. Would you like to go first?"

"Only if no one else wishes to do so." She smiled self-consciously. "I've not much to report, but I did find out a little about Keith Muran's first wife."

"That's quick," Mrs. Goodge said, nodding in encourage-ment.

"Her Christian name was Emmaline, and she died of pneumonia. She and Mr. Muran were married for eleven years, and by all accounts it was a happy marriage. Less than a year after her death, Keith Muran met Caroline Mer-riman and they married fairly soon after."

"They didn't wait until Mr. Muran was out of mourn-ing?" Mrs. Goodge helped herself to a slice of seed cake.

"He was out of mourning, but only just," Ruth replied. "The first Mrs. Muran died in November and he married Caroline December of the following year."

"At least he waited a bit more than a year," Mrs. Jeffries muttered. "But we mustn't jump to conclusions. Perhaps the man was simply lonely. Some men are like that—they don't adjust well to living without a spouse."

"Especially if they've been happily married," the cook added.

"That's really all I managed to find out," Ruth admitted. "But I'll keep on digging about and see what I can learn."

"You've done very well." Mrs. Jeffries looked around the table. "Who'd like to go next?"

"As we've been talking about Mr. Muran's first wife," Betsy said, "I'll go next. I heard a bit that might be useful." She repeated what she'd found out from the lad at the grocers. "So after talking to him, I had to go along and see what I could find out from the greengrocer. I ran into a bit of luck there—Bertie's mum was a bit of a talker." She grinned. "Once the other customers had left, she couldn't wait to have a fresh ear. Apparently, Lucy Turner and Keith Muran had been close for a number of years. Bertie's mum says she's sure that Lucy Turner was Muran's mistress. Once Emmaline died, she fully expected Keith Muran to marry her, but instead, he up and marries her cousin."

"But if he was happily married, why'd he have a mistress?" Wiggins asked. He looked quickly around the table at their faces, wanting to make sure his blunt question hadn't offended any of the ladies present.

"We don't know for certain he did," Mrs. Jeffries said slowy. "And even in happy marriages, in some circles, such things happen."

"That don't seem very nice or very dignified." Wiggins made a disapproving face. He was quite a romantic at heart.

"Matters of the heart are often undignified," the cook said philosophically.

"So it would seem that Lucy Turner has been a part Keith Muran's life for a good number of years," Mrs. Jeffries said thoughtfully.

"And she's not about to stop," Wiggins interjected. "Accordin' to Charlotte, Lucy Turner and her mum have barged right in and taken over runnin' the 'ouse."

Betsy frowned at the footman.

"Oh, sorry, I'll wait my turn."

"Thank you," she said tartly. "I also found out that Mrs. Turner nursed Emmaline Muran during her illness. Bertie's mum told me that everyone in the neighborhood was surprised when she up and died. Apparently, she hadn't been that ill, and no one, not even her doctor, had thought death was that close."

"But she died anyway," Mrs. Jeffries said. "That's very interesting."

"But not very useful," Mrs. Goodge said. "Just because the woman died doesn't mean there was foul play. Doctors are wrong more often than they're right, and even big strong people can succumb to an illness."

"That's true," Mrs. Jeffries agreed. "We've learned from our past cases that we must keep an open mind and not make assumptions until all the facts are known." She looked at Betsy. "Anything else?"

Betsy shook her head. "Not really. But I'll keep at it."

"Can I go next?" Wiggins asked. "I've found out something as well."

"Go on, then," Smythe said. "We're waitin'."

Wiggins told them about his meeting with Charlotte Brimmer. "Like I was sayin', the Turners have barged in and taken over the Muran house. The servants don't like either of them, especially Mrs. Turner. Claims she don't know how to run a proper house."

"Why wouldn't she know how to run a household?" Mrs. Goodge asked. "She's a lady. Her husband was an army officer in India and she'd have run her own household out there."

"Maybe it's different in them foreign places," Wiggins replied. "Charlotte says Mrs. Turner can barely read or write, doesn't know how to order provisions properly, and has a nasty temper to boot. The servants hate her. Charlotte says she'll go along for days being decent and kind and then someone will drop a spoon or leave a smudge on the table and she'll go mad. The first time I saw Charlotte, she looked scared to death, and that was because that very morning Mrs. Turner threw the salt cellar at the scullery maid. Cut the poor girl on the head. Accordin' to Charlotte, that wasn't the first time Mrs. Turner had acted like a mad woman. When she loses her temper, she likes to throw things about the place."

"That's not so unusual," Mrs. Goodge said. "I once worked for a woman that got so angry over a dinner party that didn't go well she turned over the table in the butler's pantry and made us eat with our plates on our laps for a week. We hated her."

"Why didn't people leave and find other positions?" Betsy asked the cook.

Mrs. Goodge smiled sadly. "It's not like now. Back in those days there weren't many positions. Times were hard. You couldn't go off and get a job in a factory or a shop."

"Some people are just born mean and nasty," Wiggins continued. "Mrs. Turner is even horrible to her own daughter. Charlotte told me that right after the New Year she overheard the old woman tell Lucy Turner that she'd better quite larkin' about, that her beauty was startin' to fade and if she didn't grab herself a husband soon, she'd lose her chance."

"How awful," Betsy exclaimed.

"That's why Charlotte's lookin' for another position; she's afraid that once the mourning period is past, Mr. Muran is goin' to marry Miss Turner," Wiggins said. "They don't want to have to put up with Mrs. Turner."

"And they're certain Mrs. Turner would move into the Muran house as well?" Smythe asked.

"That's what Charlotte thinks," Wiggins replied.

"Did you find out if there's a gun in the Muran household?" Smythe helped himself to a second slice of cake.

"Charlotte's never seen one." Wiggins wondered if he ought to ask Mrs. Jeffries to help him find the maid another position.

"The Turners probably have a gun," Mrs. Goodge said.

Wiggins looked at the cook in admiration. "Cor blimey, Mrs. Goodge, 'ow'd you find that out so quick?"

"I'm only guessing, lad," she admitted ruefully. "But colonial families generally all have guns. My guess is that Mrs. Turner kept her husband's weapons when they returned from India and that they're somewhere in the Turner house."

"That's true," Mrs. Jeffries added. "You've done very well, Mrs. Goodge."

"Thank you." The cook sighed. "But as I said, I'm only guessing. The only other tidbit I heard today was from Maisie Dobson. I invited her for morning coffee because she used to housekeep for a gentleman that lives just up the road from the Murans. But she didn't really know anything." The cook frowned and shook her head. "All I got out of her was that Mr. Muran dearly loved his wife—the silly girl had seen them holding hands once and decided on that flimsy evidence that they were madly in love."

"Maybe they were," Wiggins said.

The cook ignored him. "That's really all I found out. I've got some more sources coming in tomorrow. Let's hope I find something useful."

"Everything's useful," Mrs. Jeffries said softly. "And you've certainly done better today than I have. I found out absolutely nothing."

"I learned a bit about Russell Merriman," Smythe said. "He wasn't in the country when his sister was killed, and more importantly, he loved her. He wouldn't have had her murdered."

"Besides, if he had, he wouldn't be the one kicking up a fuss and getting the case reopened," Betsy muttered. "He'd just let Tommy Odell hang."

Mrs. Jeffries nodded slowly. She still wasn't sure about Merriman. Devotion to a sibling could be faked, and there might be a goodly number of facts about the matter that they hadn't uncovered as yet. For the moment, Merriman was still on her list of suspects.

"What are we going to do next?" Wiggins asked. "If you don't mind my sayin' so, time's movin' right along and we're no closer to sussin' out who really murdered that poor woman."

"I know." Mrs. Jeffries hadn't learned anything new because she'd spent the afternoon thinking about the murder. She'd put all the facts together and tried to come up with some idea as to who truly benefited from Caroline Muran's death. But she'd not come up with any definite conclusions. Just before the others returned, she'd realized she might be approaching the problem from the wrong set of assumptions. Sometimes, murder indirectly benefited the killer. She needed time to think, but the truth was, she was afraid that time was the one commodity they didn't have. "It's a puzzle, isn't it."

"It's a puzzle we've got to solve if we're going to save Tommy Odell from the hangman," Smythe said. "And so far, we're not findin' out much that's useful. One of the first things we've got to do is start eliminatin' people from our suspect list."

"And how do you propose we do that?" Betsy asked.

"For starters, I'm goin' to find that hansom driver and see if he lied. Keith Muran told the inspector he'd asked the driver to wait for them that night, but that's not what the driver told me, so one of them is lying. If it's the driver, then I think that puts Muran off our list."

"I don't see how." the cook said.

"Because if Muran had asked the driver to wait, then that means he couldn't have killed her. He'd not do it in front of a witness." Betsy cuffed Smythe on the arm. "You clever man. No wonder I said I'd marry you."

"Eliminating people off our suspect list is a very good idea," Mrs. Jeffries said. "Does anyone have any other suggestions as to how we can go about it?"

"I think we ought to be very practical," Wiggins declared. "We need to know where all our suspects were that night. Whoever killed Mrs. Muran had to go to Barrick Street and do the evil deed, so he or she wouldn't be where they claimed to be, would they?"

"That's very practical," Ruth said. "But I think it might be difficult obtaining that information. The murder was weeks ago, so people might not recall where they'd been."

"Oh, but they would." Mrs. Jeffries' eyes gleamed with excitement. She had the sense that they were starting to move in the right direction. "Ruth, do you recall what you were doing on the day your father passed away?"

"I remember every single detail. I was in the garden helping Mama pick gooseberries when our housekeeper came running to tell us poor Papa had collapsed in the . . ." she broke off as understanding dawned. "Oh yes, now I see what you mean. When something awful happens to someone important in your life, you know exactly what you were doing."

"Caroline Muran was important to a good number of people." Mrs. Jeffries smiled triumphantly. "And I'll warrant every one of our suspects can recall exactly where they were on the night she died."

"I hate to admit this," Betsy said, looking confused. "Maybe it's me being thick, but exactly who are our suspects?"

At breakfast the next morning, Mrs. Jeffries told the others everything she'd learned from Witherspoon the night before. He'd come home tired and discouraged, but over a glass of sherry and a sympathetic ear, she'd found out about his interviews with Keith Muran, John Brandon, and the Turner women.

"I don't think having police constables huntin' about

Barrick Street for a witness is goin' to do much good," Smythe commented. He took a quick bite of toast. "Not at this late date."

"You never know," Betsy said brightly. "I'm always amazed at what tidbits people can remember."

"Should I pop over to Lady Cannonberry's?" Wiggins asked. There was one last fried egg on the platter in the center of the table, but he'd had three already and he didn't want to make a pig of himself.

"She's stopping by here on her way to her Ladies Missionary Society meeting at the church." Mrs. Goodge reached over, scooped the egg up, and dumped it on Wiggins' plate. "I'll tell her when she gets here. Eat this, lad; it'll just go to waste if you don't."

"Our inspector didn't learn very much yesterday," Smythe complained. "Leastways not as much as I'd 'ave liked."

"I wouldn't say that," Betsy stated. "He found out about Sutter getting sacked for stealing."

"But we already knew that, so it's not going to do us much good," he countered. "I was 'opin' our inspector had learned somethin' we didn't know."

"But he did." Mrs. Jeffries put her cup down. "He found out that Mrs. Muran hadn't wanted to go to the concert that night. She'd been thinking of staying home."

"And Lucy Turner talked her into going," Mrs. Goodge added.

"And that it was Mrs. Muran who insisted on going to see that empty building," Wiggins pointed out. "Leastways that's what Mr. Muran claims."

Mrs. Jeffries didn't say anything for a moment. She was thinking. "You know, I'm not sure I believe that."

"Why not?" the cook asked.

"Why would Mrs. Muran be looking at a new factory building when we know she had already gotten the estimates to purchase and renovate the row houses for the workers? John Brandon had taken them around to her house that very day."

"Maybe she hadn't made up her mind," Mrs. Goodge suggested. "Brandon only brought her estimates, not contracts. Maybe she wanted to have a look at the empty building before she made her final decision. Brandon told the inspector she was very concerned about unemployment."

"That's possible." Mrs. Jeffries got to her feet and reached for the empty platter. Betsy began clearing the breakfast plates.

"Leave that," Mrs. Goodge ordered. "All of you get on out and get cracking. See what you can learn. I'll clean up in here."

"But you must have time for your sources," the housekeeper protested.

The cook waved a hand dismissively. "My sources aren't coming by for a bit, and like you said, we're running out of time."

"We'd like to see Mr. John Addison," Constable Barnes told the man behind the desk.

The clerk stared at him for a long moment then raised his arm and gestured at a bellboy. "I'll see if Mr. Addison is receiving."

Barnes sighed inwardly. "This isn't a social call. Now, just tell us the fellow's room number and we'll see to it ourselves."

The clerk blinked, clearly taken aback by the constable's harsh tone in such a fine establishment. "It's 204," he said. "But I hardly think it wise . . ."

But the two policeman weren't really listening; they were on their way toward the staircase. They ignored the curious looks of the other guests as they climbed the carpeted stairs to the second floor. Room 204 was the second room down the hall.

Barnes rapped sharply on the door.

"Just a moment," said a hoarse, male voice. Then the door opened and a man with his collar undone stuck his head out. He started in surprise. "Gracious, you're the police."

"Are you John Addison?" Barnes asked politely.

"That's right." The man had curly gray hair, a florid complexion, and very bushy eyebrows. "What do you want?"

"May we come in, sir?" Witherspoon asked. "We've some questions we'd like to ask you."

Addison opened the door wider and stepped back. "Come in, then. I've an appointment shortly, but I can spare a few minutes. What's this about?"

The bed was still unmade and the wardrobe door was standing open, but the elegant room was tidy. There was a claw-foot table and two green silk upholstered chairs next to the open window. Addison motioned toward the chairs in an apparent invitation for the policemen to sit down. He took the only other seat in the room—an overstuffed easy chair next to the marble washbasin.

"We're making some inquiries into the murder of Mrs. Caroline Muran," Witherspoon said as he took a seat. "And we understand you were trying to buy her business."

"I still am, Inspector," Addison replied. "But that's neither here nor there. I thought Mrs. Muran's killer was set to hang."

"He is, but there are still some inquiries that need to be made," the inspector replied. "We understand that Mrs. Muran refused to sell to you; is that correct?"

"I don't know who told you that," Addison replied, "but your information is incorrect. She didn't flat out refuse to sell; she told me she'd think about it."

"That's not what we've been told, sir." Barnes pulled his notebook out of his coat pocket. "Her former factory manager claims she refused to even meet with you."

"You mean the factory manager she sacked?" Addison shrugged and smiled. He seemed to be enjoying himself. "Why would you believe anything he says? The man is a liar and probably a thief."

"So you're saying you did meet with her?" Barnes pressed.

"I met her and her husband." Addison stood up and turned toward the mirror over the washbasin. He buttoned his collar. "It was a day or so after Sutter had been sacked. I'd paid Sutter to arrange a meeting, but he'd not been able to talk Mrs. Muran into seeing me, so I went along there myself." He turned and went to the open wardrobe, reached inside, and pulled out a gray-striped waistcoat.

"If Sutter hadn't been able to arrange an appointment, why did you think Mrs. Muran would see you?" The inspector shivered slightly as a gust of wind blew in through the open window.

"She's a lady." Addison put on the waistcoat and turned back to the mirror as he buttoned it up. "I was counting on the fact that if I just presented myself at her office, she'd be too polite to toss me out. I was right." He grinned at his own cleverness. "It was my lucky day, Inspector. Her husband was there as well. When I walked in, she was polite, but I could tell she was going to show me the door fairly quickly. It was her husband that made her listen to my offer."

"So you actually made her an offer?" Barnes looked up from his notebook.

"A very good offer," Addison replied. "And as I said, she didn't flat out reject it; she told me she'd think about it."

"Our information was that she had no intention of selling under any circumstances," Witherspoon said.

"As I said earlier, your information isn't correct." He went to the wardrobe, pulled out his coat, and slipped it on.

"We've heard Mrs. Muran was more interested in protecting her workers than she was in worrying about profits," Barnes commented.

Addison turned and stared at the constable. "She might not have been interested in profits, but Mr. Muran certainly was."

"Mr. Muran didn't own the factory," Witherspoon said.

"He does now," Addison replied.

"No he doesn't," Barnes said, then he caught himself and clamped his mouth shut. Blast, maybe he ought to have let the inspector tell Addison about Russell Merriman.

Maybe Witherspoon didn't want it spread about that Merriman was now the heir to Caroline Muran's estate. He glanced at Witherspoon and was relieved to see his expression was quite calm.

Addison's demeanor changed instantly. His smile disappeared, his eyes narrowed, and his expression hardened. "What do you mean, he doesn't own it? Of course he does."

"Keith Muran doesn't own anything," Witherspoon said. "The factory belongs to his brother-in-law, Russell Merriman."

"That's impossible." Addison glared at them. "You don't know what you're talking about. Someone's having a joke at your expense, Inspector. Merriman's dead. He died last year. His obituary was in all the papers."

"No, that was a mistake." Witherspoon thought this one of the oddest interviews he'd ever had. "Mr. Merriman was the victim of mistaken identity."

"Mistaken identity?" Addison repeated. "That's absurd. That sounds like some silly nonsense from a bad West End melodrama or one of those idiotic novels people waste their time reading."

"Nevertheless, it's true," Witherspoon replied. "The American authorities incorrectly identified the victim of a shooting as Russell Merriman."

"Even Americans don't make errors like that," Addison snapped.

"Mr. Merriman is alive and back in England," Barnes added. "He's also the reason we're here."

Addison took a deep breath and got hold of his emotions. He ignored the constable's comment. "So Merriman's alive, eh. Then I'll just deal with him instead of Muran. Matter of fact, Merriman's not a businessman. I'm sure he'll be reasonable about selling the company." He pulled out his pocket watch and noted the time. "Is Mr. Merriman staying at the Muran house?"

"No," Witherspoon replied.

"Then where is he staying?" Addison snapped. "Come on, now, I've not time to waste larking about. Where is the fellow?"

Witherspoon ignored Addison's outburst. "We understand you were quite insistent about wanting to buy the business. Is that correct?"

"Ye gods, are you deaf?" Addison asked incredulously. "Answer my question. Where is Merriman?"

"We're not through asking our questions," Barnes said flatly. "I think you'll find this will go much quicker if you'll continue cooperating."

Addison sighed and folded his arms over his chest. "I wouldn't quite describe it that way. One can't be insistent when one is trying to buy something someone else has. But I did want the business, I'll admit that. Now look, I really must get going. I've answered your questions, so I'd appreciate it if you'd tell me where Russell Merriman is staying."

Witherspoon got to his feet. "I'm afraid I can't help you, sir. I've no idea where Mr. Merriman might be."

CHAPTER 9

"Do you believe him, sir?" Barnes asked as they came out of the hotel.

"I'm not sure," the inspector admitted. "What do you think?" It never hurt to obtain an additional opinion, especially from someone as astute as the constable.

Barnes thought for a moment. "He seemed to be cooperating, and he certainly answered our questions, but I'm not sure how much of it was genuine. I've got a feeling he knew the case had been reopened and was expecting us."

"I had the same feeling myself," the inspector replied. He glanced up the road and spotted a hansom heading toward the hotel. "But the case hasn't been officially reopened. I mean, it's not been in the papers, so how could he have known? Oh well, I suppose it doesn't matter whether he knew or not; what's important is whether or not he was telling us the truth."

"That's always the difficulty, isn't it, sir." Barnes waved at the hansom, but the driver didn't see him.

"Addison obviously wants to buy Merriman's, but whether or not he wanted it badly enough to murder Mrs. Muran to get it is quite another matter. It's not generally how one does business in this country."

"Murder's been done for stranger reasons, sir," Barnes muttered. He waved his arm again, and this time the driver saw him.

"I do wish someone at the hotel could verify that Addison was here that night."

"We've got lads questioning the staff, sir," Barnes said. "If he left his room that night, someone might have seen him coming or going."

"If they can remember, Constable," Witherspoon muttered morosely. "It was several months ago."

Barnes ignored that. "Where to now, sir?"

"Number Eighteen Cedar Road, Waltham Green," he replied as the hansom pulled up in front of them. He climbed inside.

Barnes gave the driver the address and swung in beside Witherspoon. He knew exactly who they were going to see, but he had to pretend he didn't. "Waltham Green, sir? Who are we going to see?"

"A woman by the name of Helen Maitland." He grabbed the handhold as the hansom lurched forward. "You've probably not heard of her, but she might have something useful to tell us. Mrs. Jeffries shared some very interesting gossip with me at breakfast. She hears things all the time. She says people actually stop her in the street to tell what they've seen or heard. It's amazing what people can find out if they keep their ears open, isn't it?"

"Uh, yes sir, it certainly is. Uh, who is—"

"Helen Maitland was the Muran housekeeper."

"Was, sir?" Barnes thought he was getting quite good at this game. "She doesn't work there now?"

"No, she quit when she found out Mrs. Muran had been murdered. I find that very peculiar."

"I didn't see her name in the case file," Barnes commented. He looked at Witherspoon out of the corner of his eye.

"Her name wasn't in the case file." The inspector didn't look pleased. "Inspector Nivens didn't interview her or anyone else from the household. I've no idea why; perhaps he didn't think it pertinent to the investigation."

As the cab made its way through the crowded London streets, they discussed the case. The constable took the opportunity to drop a few hints and plant some ideas in the inspector's willing ears. He'd had quite a long chat with Mrs. Jeffries this morning, and they'd agreed he'd pass along the information the household had managed to obtain.

By the time the cab pulled up in front of the Maitland house, Barnes was fairly sure he'd managed to convey most of the relevant facts to his superior. He got down from the cab and told the driver to wait for them. From habit, he surveyed the neighborhood as he and the inspector went up the short stone walkway to the house.

Before he had a chance to knock, the door opened and a short, plump woman stuck her head out.

"Gracious, it's Inspector Witherspoon. I didn't expect to see you here, sir."

"Er, have we met?" the inspector asked. The woman looked vaguely familiar.

"We've not actually met, sir, but you do know me. I'm Mrs. Briggs. My husband and I own the butcher shop just off the Holland Park Road. You're one of my best customers. Do come in, sir." She opened the door wider and ushered them inside.

Witherspoon moved toward the one bit of space in the tiny foyer that wasn't occupied. He squeezed past the fully loaded coat tree, banged his foot against the umbrella urn, and steadied himself by grabbing onto the newel of the staircase. Barnes slipped in next to him.

Mrs. Briggs pointed at a closed door down the hallway.

"Now go on into the parlor, sir. It's just through there and I'll go get Helen. You and the constable make yourselves comfortable." She started up the narrow staircase.

"Yes, thank you, we will." Witherspoon shook his head in amazement. "It's almost as if she were expecting us."

"Maybe she was, sir," Barnes commented. The parlor was small but very clean. There was a three-piece furniture suite upholstered in brown wool, a fireplace with a painting of a hunting lodge over the mantelpiece, and brown-and-white-striped curtains at the window. At each end of the settee there were matching tables topped with a crocheted doily. A vase of dried flowers was on one of them and a china shepherd stood on the other.

Witherspoon took one of the overstuffed chairs and Barnes sat down on the settee. Just as they'd settled themselves, the door opened and the two women appeared, causing both men to leap to their feet.

"Sit down," Mrs. Briggs said, waving them back to their places. "This is my sister, Helen Maitland. This is Inspector Witherspoon and his constable. They're going to ask you some questions about Mrs. Muran."

"How do you do." Helen Maitland nodded politely. She resembled her sister except that she was thin instead of plump and her face was pinched with worry. "I don't know what you think I can tell you," she began as she dropped into the chair opposite the inspector. "It'll not make any difference."

"You just answer their questions." Mrs. Briggs eased down on the settee next to the constable. "It'll do you good to get everything off your chest. It'll help you to sleep at night, dear. The truth always does."

"But I don't think I ought to say anything. It was really just a private matter; nothing to bother the police with," she protested.

"Why don't you let me be the judge of that," Witherspoon said gently. He'd no idea what she was talking about, but it was something that had kept her awake nights. "I understand you were so upset over Mrs. Muran's death that you've not been back to the Muran house since the funeral."

"Of course I was upset; Mrs. Muran was a saint."

Witherspoon tried to think what to ask next. He remembered the bits of gossip Mrs. Jeffries had told him, but that wasn't helping him come up with any questions.

"Why did you quit your position?" Barnes asked softly.

"Oh, I couldn't go back to that house, not after she was gone. I just couldn't." Helen's pale face had gone even whiter.

"Tell them why," Mrs. Briggs prompted. "Tell them why you didn't want to go back. Don't leave anything out, Helen. Tell them everything."

"Do you really think I ought to?" Helen looked down at her hands. "It doesn't seem right, and it makes him look such a beast and he isn't really. He's a good man, and he was very devoted to her."

"Of course you must," Mrs. Briggs said firmly. "For goodness' sakes, Helen, tell them what happened the day that Mrs. Muran was murdered. You'll not have any peace until you do, and frankly, I can't stay here forever. I've got a family to see to and a business to run."

Helen stared at her sister for a long moment and then took a deep breath. "I'm not sure where to begin."

"Why don't you start from the time you arrived at the Muran house that morning," Witherspoon suggested.

"It was terrible right from the start," Helen said softly. "As soon as I walked into the house, I knew that it was going to be a dreadful day. They were having a row, you see. Mr. Muran was shouting at her, and what was more frightening, she was yelling right back at him."

Witherspoon nodded in encouragement. "You weren't used to their quarrels?"

"They never had a cross word with one another," Helen replied. "But this time they were shouting loud enough to wake the dead."

"What were they arguing about?" Barnes asked.

"I didn't hear it from the beginning, so I've no idea what started the row." She fingered the material of her gray skirt nervously. "But I did hear him tell her she was a fool to refuse the offer. She yelled back that it was her company and she could do what she liked, that she'd thank him not to interfere. Then it would go quiet for a moment before there'd be another outburst. He yelled that he was tired of spending so much time on his own and she screamed that from what she'd been hearing, he had plenty of company." Her eyes filled with tears. "Please don't think ill of either of them. This wasn't how they usually behaved. They loved each other, and it was terrible to hear them tearing into each other like that."

"Yes, I'm sure it was very upsetting for you. Please go on," Witherspoon said.

"All of a sudden it went quiet again and Mr. Muran came tearing down the stairs. He marched right past me without so much as a word. He grabbed his coat and hat and stormed out of the house." She paused briefly. "Mrs. Muran stayed upstairs and I went on into the kitchen. Harriet, that's the scullery maid, and Charlotte, she's a housemaid, were cowering in the corner, and even cook looked worried."

Helen pulled a handkerchief out of her sleeve and dabbed at her eyes. "You've got to understand, Inspector, none of us were used to this kind of behavior. Mr. Muran was always the most considerate of men and Mrs. Muran was kindness itself. Everyone seemed frozen in shock, but I knew that wouldn't do. The Turners were coming for luncheon, so I told the girls to get the breakfast things cleared up and asked cook what she planned on serving." Helen smiled at her sister. "Believe it or not, I can take charge when I've a mind to."

"Of course you can, dear," Mrs. Briggs replied. "Go on and tell them the rest."

"Mrs. Muran stayed in her room for the rest of the morning. She didn't come down until right before Mrs. Turner and her daughter arrived for luncheon."

"Didn't she usually go to the factory?" Barnes asked.

"Yes, but she hadn't planned on going that day. That's why her cousins were invited to lunch," Helen explained. "They'd complained they never got a chance to see her. She waited for them in the drawing room, and when they arrived Mr. Muran came in with them. I was afraid there was going to be another argument. Mr. Muran barely spoke to Mrs. Muran. It was that way all through the meal—Mrs. Muran would make some remark and he'd ignore her and speak to Miss Turner."

"Were you in the dining room?" Witherspoon asked.

"I served," Helen said. "The day girl hadn't shown up and Charlotte was helping cook. It was very awkward. I've never seen Mr. Muran behave like that. I was glad when that dreadful meal ended and they retired to the drawing room. I let Charlotte bring up their coffee. I was that desperate to escape, I was."

"Did the guests appear to notice that something was wrong?" Barnes asked.

Helen thought for a moment. "I'm not sure. They kept the conversation going nicely, of course. But even if they had noticed the tension in the room, they'd have done their best to keep up appearances and pretend that nothing was amiss. That's just the way everyone behaves."

"What happened then?" Witherspoon couldn't see anything too frightening about the narrative. He'd never been married, of course, but even the most devoted of couples must occasionally have a spectacularly loud row.

"Mr. Muran excused himself and went into his study and the ladies had coffee in the drawing room." She looked at the inspector. "You're wondering why I was so frightened, aren't you?"

"Well, yes. From what I understand, all married couples sometimes have an argument."

"It wasn't the argument that upset me, sir; it was the gun."

"Gun?" Witherspoon repeated. "What gun?"

"The one that Mr. Muran took away from Mrs. Turner."

Helen shook her head in disapproval. "She was trying to get it into her muff, but it was a big thing and it wouldn't fit."

"I can understand why seeing a gun could be quite disconcerting," Witherspoon said sympathetically.

"It wasn't seeing the weapon that bothered me, sir. I've seen guns before. Mr. Muran has one that he keeps in his study. No, sir, it was what Mrs. Turner kept saying that upset me so much." Helen closed her eyes. "Ye gods, the poor woman is out of her mind half the time and doesn't even know it. I was standing on the landing—neither Mr. Muran nor Mrs. Turner knew I was there. Mrs. Muran and Miss Turner were still in the drawing room, so at least Mrs. Muran was spared hearing that woman's vile filth."

"What was she saying?" Barnes prodded.

"She kept saying that it was all Mrs. Muran's fault, that she'd stolen too much, that she'd taken it all away from them. She said it over and over and over. Mr. Muran kept watching the drawing room door while he tried to quiet her down. Finally, he grabbed her and gave her a quick shake."

"Tell them the rest," Mrs. Briggs ordered. "Tell them everything so you can get a decent night's sleep."

"Mrs. Turner's eyes rolled up in her head and I was sure she was going to collapse. But then all of a sudden she was right as rain and asking Mr. Muran what they were doing standing out in the hallway."

"What did he say?" Witherspoon asked. "Please try to remember his exact words."

"He said, 'Get a hold of yourself, Edwina. You're talking rubbish. What in the name of God has gotten into you?'"

The inspector leaned forward. "What did she say?"

"She said, 'What on earth are you talking about? I just came out to get my shawl.' Then he asked her what was the last thing she remembered, and she said it was getting out of her chair and walking toward the drawing room door."

Witherspoon said nothing for a moment. "Are you saying she'd no idea what she'd just done?"

"That's right, Inspector, she'd no idea at all." Helen

dabbed at her eyes again. "So you can understand why I don't want to go back to work for Mr. Muran. I feel sorry for him, I really do, but I refuse to be in a house with a mad-woman, and as sure as I'm sitting here, she'll be living in that house."

"Why do you think Mrs. Turner is going to be living in Mr. Muran's home?" Witherspoon asked.

"I don't think it, sir, I know it. Mr. Muran isn't the sort of man that can live on his own, and both those Turner women will take advantage of his loneliness. Take my word for it, sir, Lucy Turner has already determined that she'll be the next Mrs. Muran, and I've no doubt whatso-ever that Mrs. Turner will do everything she can to make sure that happens." She shook her head. "God forgive me, I know it's not the poor woman's fault that she's losing her mind. It happens to lots of old people, but I can't stand it."

"Our gran went that way," Mrs. Briggs interjected. "It was heartbreaking to watch, and it almost killed our poor father."

Helen turned her tear-stained face to the inspector. "I know I should have told the police all this before, and I kept waiting for someone to come. But no one did so I decided it wasn't important. Then I heard about that man being ar-rested and it should have made me feel better, but it didn't."

"Do you know if Mr. Muran told Mrs. Muran about the incident?" Barnes asked.

Helen shook her head. "I don't think so. After the Turn-ers left, Mr. Muran went into his study and spent most of the afternoon there, and Mrs. Muran went upstairs to her room. Mr. Muran didn't even come out when the Turners came back for tea that afternoon."

"They came twice that day?" Barnes asked.

"Yes, for luncheon and for tea," Helen said. "They'd been shopping in the neighborhood, you see, so Mrs. Muran had invited them back that afternoon."

"What time did you leave that day?" Witherspoon leaned back in his chair.

"At my usual time: six o'clock," she replied. "Mr. Muran had come out of his study and gone upstairs to get dressed."

"So they might have spoken about the matter after you left?"

"It's possible." Helen shrugged. "I don't know. I was just glad to be gone."

Witherspoon frowned. "Do you have any idea what Mrs. Turner meant when she was . . . uh . . ."

"Out of her mind," Helen finished the sentence for him. "I've no idea, Inspector, and neither does anyone else in the household. But I think it's something you'd do well to ask her. Even if she's out of her head, she had some reason for what she was saying, and I find it very peculiar that within a few hours of her ranting and raving, poor Mrs. Muran was murdered."

Smythe spotted Fletcher coming out of the cabshack. He hurried toward him. "Come 'ave a pint with me." he held up a coin. "I'll make it worth yer while."

Fletcher looked about, his expression uncertain. "I don't know. I ought to get back out."

"There's a pub just around the corner," Smythe coaxed.

"I know the place," Fletcher replied. "I suppose a few more minutes won't hurt."

Smythe chatted easily as they walked the short distance to the pub. He pulled the door open and they stepped inside. The place was clearing out and he spotted an empty table. "Go grab us a seat," he told Fletcher. "I'll get the pints."

A few moments later, he slipped into the chair opposite Fletcher and put their glasses on the small table. "Here's yer beer."

"Ta. I don't usually drink much." Fletcher picked up the beer and took a long, slow drink.

"Tell me more about what happened that night," Smythe said softly.

Fletcher slowly lowered his drink. "I've already told ya everything I can remember."

"Are you sure there's nothin' you've forgotten?" he pressed. He wanted the man to voluntarily tell him the truth.

Fletcher looked down at the table. "I don't know what ya mean."

"I'm just wonderin' if there was some little detail you might 'ave forgotten to mention, that's all." Smythe noticed that the man's cheeks, what you could see of them over his beard, were turning red. "It's important we know everything that 'appened that night. A man's life is at stake 'ere, and what with you bein' a decent man, a Presbyterian at that, I know you'd not want someone to hang for a crime they didn't do. That's why all these little details are important. They add up, you see."

"There is one thing I might have gotten wrong," Fletcher replied. His voice was so low that Smythe could barely hear him.

"We all forget things every now and again," Smythe said. "It's human nature. Why don't you tell me what it is you might 'ave gotten wrong when we 'ad our last little chat."

Fletcher looked up at him, his expression troubled. "He asked me to wait. The husband, he asked me to wait, but I didn't, and it's preyed on my mind something fierce."

"Why didn't you tell me this before?"

"I was afraid to tell the truth. I didn't know who you worked for, did I? You might work for the company. They send out people to watch us every now and again, and the company has strict rules about strandin' passengers. I was scared I'd lose my job." Fletcher took another quick drink. "I wanted to get back to the West End and pick up another fare. There was a music hall that was lettin' out, and I didn't want to miss a chance to make a few more coppers. When he had me drop 'em off on Barrick Street, I thought he were just larkin' about and I wasn't in the mood to put up with it. But ever since I found out what happened to that poor woman, my conscience has bothered me something fierce. I keep thinkin' it's my fault, that if I'd been sittin' there in my rig waitin' for them, maybe the killer would have left them alone." He looked at Smythe, his eyes filling with tears. "I've not had a decent night's sleep since I talked to that copper and found out that lady had been shot."

Witherspoon closed the file in front of him and shoved it to one side. "It's not very good, is it," he muttered to Barnes, who was sitting at the other desk. They were in a small, unused office at the Ladbroke Road police station. As this was the closest station to Witherspoon's home, they had let him set up an office so he wouldn't have to go all the way into the Yard.

"No, sir, it's not," Barnes agreed. "Let's face it, sir, no matter how many times you go through that file, you'll not find any evidence that's useful." He got to his feet. "Why don't I go get us a cup of tea."

"That's an excellent idea." Witherspoon reached for another stack of papers. "While you're gone, I'll start reading these statements. Maybe something useful will pop out at me."

Barnes left and the inspector began reading the top sheet. He heard the door open and without looking up said, "That was fast. Was the tea trolley in the hallway?"

"I'm not here to bring you your tea," Nigel Nivens snapped.

Witherspoon jerked his head up. "Gracious, Inspector Nivens, I didn't expect to see you here."

"No, I'm sure you didn't." He took off one of his gloves. "I'm not going to beat around the bush, Witherspoon. I don't care what kind of mandate you think you have from the chief inspector; you'd better be careful here. I'll not have you getting my conviction overturned."

"I'm not trying to get your conviction overturned. I'm trying to find out the truth," Witherspoon protested. This was a decidedly awkward situation. "I can understand that having a murder conviction on your record might seem to be advantageous, but surely you'd not want to see an innocent man hanged."

Nivens laughed harshly and took off his other glove. "I don't give a toss about the likes of Tommy Odell. He's a bloody thief."

"But that doesn't necessarily mean he's a murderer."

"You've got everyone fooled, don't you," Nivens snarled. "You act so modest and humble, as though the last thing on your mind is recognition or advancement. But I know what you're up to. You've not got me fooled."

"Inspector Nivens, I assure you I've no idea what you're talking about," Witherspoon replied. He wished the constable would return. Nivens face was going a very peculiar shade of purple. "I'm simply doing my job as best I can."

"Your job doesn't include getting my conviction overturned," Nivens cried.

"It's not your conviction. It's the Crown's," the inspector shot back.

"It's mine," Nivens shouted. "And I earned it fair and square. Tommy Odell is a murderer. He killed Caroline Muran."

"What did he do with the gun?" Witherspoon jabbed his finger on the closed file. "You searched his home but you couldn't find the weapon used in the crime. Where was it?"

"He tossed it in the river or gave it to one of his mates. The gun isn't important. He had Muran's watch."

"He lifted that watch from Keith Muran earlier that evening," Witherspoon replied. "That's what Odell does. He's a pickpocket, not a robber or a killer."

Nivens eyes narrowed dangerously. "I'm warning you, Witherspoon, I'll not have you undermining me. I have friends in high places as well, and Chief Inspector Barrows won't always be around to protect you."

Witherspoon refused to be intimidated. "It makes no difference to me how many friends you may or may not have. I'll continue to do my job to the best of my ability."

"Your ability!" Nivens laughed harshly. "Don't be ridiculous. You don't seriously believe that you've managed to pull the wool over my eyes as well. Others may be foolish enough to think you've solved all your cases on your own, but I know the truth."

"What on earth are you talking about?" Witherspoon gaped at him in amazement.

"Oh, come now, stop playing the innocent. You know as well as I do that you're not solving all these murders on your own." He smiled maliciously. "I promise you, Witherspoon, if you blot my record with a bad conviction, I'll expose your secret to the whole world."

"What secret? I've no secret."

"Don't play me for a fool," Nivens shouted. "I'm on to you. If you harm my service record, I'll find out who is helping you if it takes me the rest of my life."

"Is everything all right, sir?" Barnes followed by two uniformed lads had quietly entered the room. The constable was holding two cups of tea, but his attention was focused on Nivens. "We heard shouting out in the hall."

"Everything is fine, Constable," Nivens snapped out the words, turned on his heel, and stalked toward the door. The two constables standing behind Barnes moved aside to let him pass.

"Are you all right, sir?" one of the younger lads asked as soon as the door had slammed shut behind Nivens. "We heard the voices and we weren't sure what to do so we went and fetched Constable Barnes.

"I'm fine." Witherspoon forced a smile. In truth, the confrontation had upset him dreadfully. "Inspector Nivens and I were simply having a difference of opinion."

"Yes, sir." They nodded and turned to leave.

"Thanks, lads," Barnes called over his shoulder. He handed a cup to Witherspoon. "You look like you could use this."

The inspector took a quick sip, closed his eyes for a brief moment, and then sat down. "Honestly, Barnes, I don't know what Inspector Nivens is thinking. We can't ignore facts. We can't just pretend he's done a decent job when his investigation was so bad it should embarrass a first-year man on the force. What does he expect me to do, let an innocent man hang in order to bolster his service record?" He shook his head. "I don't care what he threatens; I can't do it."

Alarmed, Barnes said, "He threatened you, sir?"

Witherspoon sighed heavily. Sometimes he wished he were still back in the records room. It was so very nice and peaceful there. "He didn't actually threaten my person, but he did say that Chief Inspector Barrows wouldn't always be around to protect me."

Barnes almost laughed. "The chief isn't protecting you. Your record is, sir, and that won't change no matter who is our chief inspector. You've solved more homicides than anyone on the force, sir, and you've done it fair and square. You've never roughed a suspect or threatened a source for information. Don't worry, sir. As long as you keep on catching killers, Nivens can't touch you."

Witherspoon smiled faintly. He was tempted to tell the constable that Nivens had accused him of having help with his cases, but the idea was so outlandish he wouldn't dignify it by repeating it. There were times, though, when he did think that providence had smiled upon him with inordinate favor. Often he was at the right place at just the right time to make an arrest or stop a suspect from fleeing. He'd also noticed that clues and concepts and different ways of approaching a problem often seemed to come to him quite readily; but surely that was the result of good police work, his instincts, and his inner voice. He wished his inner voice would do a bit of talking about this case. "I do hope you're right, Constable, because right now I don't have a clue as to who murdered Caroline Muran."

The elderly woman came out of the side door of the Turner house and started toward the Kings Road. Betsy followed after her. The woman wore clothes that had seen better days—her brown bombazine dress was faded in spots and the burgundy feathers on her black bonnet drooped sadly.

The edges of the brown-and-burgundy-plaid shawl draped over her shoulders were badly frayed and some of the fringe was completely gone.

When she reached the corner, instead of turning right toward the shops, she turned left. Betsy, who'd been walking a good distance behind, hurried after her. She reached the corner just in time to see the woman stepping into a building halfway down the block.

Betsy ran toward the spot where her quarry had disappeared and then stopped. Blast, she thought, it's a ruddy pub. She didn't like pubs. They reminded her too much of her impoverished childhood in the East End of London. She'd seen too many poor women ruined by places like this; places were they could go and trade their misery and hopelessness for the numbness of alcohol. Her grandmother had called them gin palaces. Her family had been poor, but unlike most of their neighbors, none of them had been drinkers. She guessed she'd been lucky. Pubs might be a bit more respectable than some of the places of her childhood, but she hated them nonetheless. Yet she'd gone into such places before and she'd do it again. She reached for the handle, pulled the door open, and stepped inside.

The pub was the old-fashioned kind with a raw-hewn bench along each wall and a bar at the end. A barmaid stood behind the counter, pulling pints and chatting with two rough-looking workmen. On a bench along the far wall two bread peddlers, both of them women, sat talking quietly as they drank their beer. The long, flat baskets they used for their stock lay on the floor at their feet.

Betsy gathered her courage, walked boldly up to the counter, and eased in beside her quarry. "Can I speak to you a moment?" she asked the rather startled woman. "I promise I'm not selling anything."

"Do I know you?" the woman asked. She'd recovered and was staring at Betsy with a rather calculating expression.

"No, but I need some information you might have,"

Betsy replied. "And I'm willing to pay for it. Let me buy you a drink and then let's take a seat over there." She pointed to the empty bench on this side of the pub.

"I'll have a gin." She picked up her shopping basket and moved over to the bench.

"Two gins," Betsy called to the barmaid. She had plenty of coins in her pocket, and rather than try to worm anything useful out of the woman, it had suddenly seemed that it might be easier to just offer her money. Older ladies weren't susceptible to flirtatious smiles and stupid flattery.

"Here you go, dear," the barmaid said, putting the two drinks on the counter.

Betsy paid her, grabbed the glasses, and made her way to the bench. "Here you are." She handed the woman her gin and sank down next to her. "Thank you for talking to me."

The woman shrugged. "I'll talk as long as you keep buyin'. My name is Selma Macclesfield. What's yours?"

"I'm Laura Bobbins," Betsy lied. "I work for a private inquiry agent and I need some information."

Selma Macclesfield stared at her skeptically. "A private inquiry agent. But you're a woman."

"I didn't say I *was* one." Betsy smiled. "I said I *worked for* one. I know it's odd, but the pay is better than doing domestic work, and my employer has found that often a woman such as yourself will talk more freely with another woman." She leaned closer. "Especially about the more delicate matters that crop up every now and again. If you know what I mean."

"What do you want to know?" Selma took a quick drink.

"Do you work for Mrs. Edwina Turner and her daughter, Lucy?" Betsy asked.

Selma nodded and drank the rest of her gin. "That's right."

Betsy stared in dismay at the now empty glass in the woman's gnarled hand. "Uh, would you like mine?" She handed Selma her glass. "I'm not really thirsty."

"Neither am I, but I like gin." She took Betsy's glass. "I work for the Turners because it's the only job I can get. I can't stand either of them. Mrs. Turner is going crazy as she gets older, and Miss Turner is a nasty sly boots that I wouldn't trust further than I could throw her. They don't like me much, either, but they keep me on because they're too cheap to pay a decent wage and I'm all they can get. It works well for all of us."

Betsy was taken aback. "Uh, well, can you tell me if either of the Turner ladies were home on the night of January thirtieth? You might remember, it was the night—"

"I know what night it was," Selma interrupted. "That's when their cousin was murdered. Miss Lucy was out that night, but I don't know about the old lady. I wasn't there myself."

"Then how do you know about Miss Lucy being out?" Betsy asked.

"Because she flounced out before I left that night. They'd been gone most of the day, you see. They'd been shopping and had tea with Mrs. Muran. That always put Miss Lucy in a foul mood. When they come in, there was a note from Mr. Samuels sayin' he'd not be callin' around for Miss Lucy that night. That put the cat amongst the pigeons, I can tell you. Mrs. Turner was furious."

"Who is Mr. Samuels?" Betsy suspected she already knew the answer.

Selma smiled slyly. "Alexander Samuels was Miss Turner's uh—what's the best way to say it—gentleman caller. Exceptin' that he weren't much of a gentleman, if you get my meanin'."

"I'm afraid I don't."

"He's got plenty of money but no breedin' to speak of," Selma said bluntly.

"Did Mrs. Turner disapprove of him?

Selma laughed. "Course not, the old witch wouldn't have disapproved of the devil himself if he had enough money, and Samuels is rich as sin."

"I don't understand. Why was Mrs. Turner so furious?"

"Because he wasn't goin' to be comin' around anymore," Selma explained. "Miss Lucy had been seein' him quite regularly like, but he'd been showin' signs he was losin' interest. That's what got Mrs. Turner all het up. That's what caused the row that evening. Mrs. Turner told Miss Lucy she was a fool, that she wasn't getting any younger, and that she'd ruined her chance to grab a rich one. Mind you, I'm not sure she ever had much of a chance. Men like Samuels aren't fools. But the old woman didn't see it that way. She kept screamin' at Miss Lucy that she'd ruined it and now they were goin' to be stuck for the rest of their lives playin' the poor relations. I almost felt sorry for Miss Lucy."

"Is that when Miss Turner left the house?"

Selma looked pointedly at her empty glass.

Betsy leapt to her feet. "Let me get you another one."

"Get me another two," Selma ordered. "I've got lots to say."

CHAPTER 10

It had started to rain by the time the household gathered for their afternoon meeting. Ruth arrived just as the others were sitting down. She shook the water off her jacket, hung it on the coat tree, and slipped into her chair. "I won't make a habit of being late, I promise."

"We've only just sat down." Mrs. Goodge put a plate of apple tarts next to the teapot.

"I'm sure you had a good reason." Mrs. Jeffries began to pour.

Ruth smiled uncertainly. "I think perhaps I might. I'm not certain that what I heard has anything to do with our case. But as you've all told me, everything could be important."

"What did you find out?" Mrs. Jeffries handed her a cup of tea.

"Most of our suspects know how to use a pistol." She looked around the table at their faces. They all stared at her politely. "Oh dear, you already knew that, didn't you."

"We didn't," Wiggins declared, "and that's right important. Dr. Bosworth says most people are such bad shots it's a wonder anyone actually hits their mark, and whoever shot poor Mrs. Muran knew what they was doin'."

"Or they got lucky," Smythe muttered. "Bosworth said that was possible as well."

"Why don't you start from the beginning." Mrs. Jeffries put a tart on a dessert plate and gently pushed it toward Ruth.

"Today I had lunch with my friend Marianna Bibbs," Ruth continued. "Right after Caroline's murder, she happened to be at a dinner party and several of the other guests knew both the Murans and the Turners. Naturally, the talk turned to crime in the streets and how dreadful it was. You know, the sort of polite but rather stupid things people say in those circumstances." She took a quick sip of her tea. "One of the men happened to mention that it was too bad that Keith Muran hadn't been armed. That if he'd had a weapon with him, he might have saved his wife's life. Someone else at the table made the comment that having a gun wouldn't save you unless you knew how to use it. Then the other fellow, I believe Marianne said his name was Jackson Miller, said that Muran did know how to use a weapon. That he'd gone shooting with him, and Muran was a good shot with both a rifle and a pistol."

"He wouldn't have missed then," Smythe commented.

"But it couldn't be him," Betsy protested. "Dr. Bosworth said that Muran's head wound was so bad that he spent several days in hospital. He couldn't have shot his wife, got rid of the weapon, and then banged himself on the head hard enough to give himself a concussion."

"Why not?" Mrs. Goodge demanded. In her book, husbands were naturally suspect. "There was no one about. The street was empty. He'd have had plenty of time to do as he pleased, and what's more, those buildings were all empty. I'll bet they were never searched. He could have hidden the gun somewhere in one of them then come out, coshed himself on the head, and toppled over next to his poor wife's body. It would have been as easy as baking a treacle tart."

"More likely, if Muran did it, he had an accomplice," Smythe said. "But Mrs. Goodge's theory is possible. Maybe we ought to put a flea in the inspector's ear about searching the empty buildings."

"I'll have a quick word with Constable Barnes," Mrs. Jeffries said. "I wonder if Lucy Turner could have been the accomplice. She was his mistress."

"We don't know that for sure," Betsy said. "I heard something today that suggests she might not have been. She was seeing another man. His name is Alexander Samuels, and he's rich as sin."

"Cor blimey, guess she wasn't so crazy about Mr. Muran as we thought," Wiggins said.

"Gracious, that does cast a different light on the matter." Mrs. Jeffries caught herself. Speculating like this wasn't going to help them. "We're getting ahead of ourselves. Let's let Ruth finish."

"There isn't much else to tell," she said. "Once I found out that Keith Muran knew how to handle a gun I decided to find out if the Turner women were decent shots. That's why I was so late—I went see my friend Harriet Turnbull and had a word with her. Harriet's the widow of General Roland Turnbull. Edwina Turner's husband served under him in India. But Harriet's been out of town so today was the first time I was able to speak to her. Harriet claims that both the Turner women can shoot."

"She was certain of this?" Mrs. Jeffries pressed.

"Oh, yes," Ruth replied. "During one of the uprisings in India, Edwina helped out in the field hospital. Harriet told me that Edwina was known for keeping a loaded pistol on her lap as she nursed the wounded. She bragged she knew how to use it."

"What about Lucy?"

"Lucy knows how to use a gun," Ruth replied. "Harriet was certain of that, but she didn't know how skilled she was with the weapon. I know it isn't much, but I hope it helps us."

"Everything helps," Mrs. Goodge said. "And you've learned a sight more than me. All I heard was that Edwina Turner has been going wrong in the head for months now. She's taken to burying things in the back garden."

"Maybe she buried the gun," Wiggins suggested excitedly.

The cook shook her head. "No, she'd need a shovel or a spade to do that properly, and my source told me that the woman digs in the dirt with her bare hands. She's not right in the head."

"But that doesn't mean she didn't commit the murder," Mrs. Jeffries mused. "Apparently, she's able to function normally most of the time." She glanced around the table. "Who'd like to go next?"

"I will." Betsy told them about her meeting with Selma Macclesfield. She didn't mention that she'd followed the woman into a pub and plied her with gin to loosen her tongue. "She says that Mrs. Turner was furious at Lucy that afternoon. The old woman was convinced that Alexander Samuels wasn't going to see Lucy anymore. They had a terrible row about it." She gave them all the ugly details and then she sat back in her chair, shaking her head in amazement. "It must be awful when your own mother speaks to you like that. It must have made Lucy Turner feel utterly worthless. I feel sorry for her."

"I don't think either woman has had a very happy life," Mrs. Jeffries murmured. Something niggled in the back of her mind, but it was gone so fast she couldn't grasp what it meant. "Wiggins, did you learn anything today?"

"No," he admitted morosely. "I didn't hear a bloomin' thing exceptin' Charlotte complainin' that she was bein' loaned out to the Turners tomorrow to help serve at a luncheon for Mr. Muran."

"I take it you've had no further luck on finding out where all our suspects were that night?" Mrs. Jeffries asked.

"It's right 'ard tryin' to find out where people where," he said defensively. "I spent bloomin' 'ours walkin' about and talkin' to anyone who'd stand still for thirty seconds. But I didn't 'ave much luck today."

"I'm sure you'll do better tomorrow." Betsy patted him on the arm.

"Of course you will," the housekeeper reassured him. Mrs. Jeffries had actually been hoping that Wiggins would find out a few more details about who had been where on the night of the murder. It would have helped sort things out a bit. But he'd done his best and she didn't want him feeling bad about his abilities. "You always come through in the end."

The footman beamed proudly. "I do my best."

"I found out something useful," Smythe said. "I 'ad a word with the driver, and he admitted to me that Muran had asked him to wait that night."

"Then Muran was telling the truth," Mrs. Jeffries mused.

"Not only was he tellin' the truth, but I don't see 'ow he could be the killer unless he was workin' with an accomplice." Smythe declared. "If the driver had waited like he was supposed to, he'd have been a witness."

"None of this makes sense," Mrs. Jeffries muttered. "You're right, if the cab had waited, there would have been a witness to the whole thing."

"Not necessarily," Wiggins said. "I mean, if the hansom was turned the wrong way, he'd have not been lookin'. The killer could 'ave come up, banged Muran on the head, shot Mrs. Muran, and disappeared before the cabbie even turned his head to look. It's a dark road and the only gas lamp is on the corner. Seems to me whoever did this killin' is right bold and brazen. They'd not make much noise coshin' someone on the skull, and they could be gone in the blink of an eye after the shots were fired."

The inspector was late getting home, but despite being exhausted he was quite happy to tell Mrs. Jeffries about his day. She handed him a sherry and took her usual spot opposite him. "Are you making progress, sir?"

"It's difficult to tell." Witherspoon frowned. "But we're doing the very best that we can."

He looked away for a moment. "And I'm now virtually certain he didn't do it. It's not that I've uncovered evidence or anything like that; it's more a feeling. Mrs. Jeffries, what am I going to do if I fail? I don't think I could live with myself if that man hangs for a murder I'm sure he didn't commit."

"You simply have to find the real killer," she said stoutly. Deep inside, she shared the same fears as the inspector, but right now wasn't the time to wallow in her own doubts. Witherspoon worked best when he was sure of himself and confident in his own abilities. "You're very good at what you do, sir. I'm sure you're making progress."

"Do you really think so?" He stared at her hopefully. "Today it didn't seem like I was making any sort of progress at all. There was nothing in the second set of reports from the constables that we sent out to speak to potential witnesses. They only found two people who were in the area that night. One of them was drunk and the other was a watchman who was doing his rounds and didn't see or hear anything."

"But at least you sent lads out to make certain there were no witnesses," she pointed out. "That's very important, sir. As you always say, details can make or break a case." He'd never said any such thing, or if he had it was because he'd heard it from her first, but it was the truth. "What else did you do today, sir?"

Witherspoon hesitated. "I had a rather unsettling meeting with Inspector Nivens."

"What did he want?" she asked in alarm.

"He was very upset, actually," he said, draining his glass. "He seems to think that I'm deliberately trying to reverse his conviction."

"It's not his conviction," Mrs. Jeffries forced herself to keep calm. "It's the Crown's. He was merely the officer on the case." She now understood what had upset her inspector so badly. Nivens had obviously been his usual obnoxious and threatening self. "But you've dealt with Nivens before and I'm sure you handled him properly today."

"Well, I did my best to make him understand I wasn't out to harm his career." He was glad he'd told her about the altercation. He was beginning to feel ever so much better. "But I couldn't tell Chief Inspector Barrows I'd not look into the matter, could I. Furthermore, my conscience wouldn't let me ignore the issue. Right after Nivens left, Russell Merriman came to see me."

"At the Yard?"

"Oh, no, I was at Ladbroke Station, but he'd been to the Yard and they'd told him where we were. Naturally, he wanted to know if we were making progress."

"I hope you told him you were, sir." Mrs. Jeffries believed in taking every opportunity to boost the inspector's confidence.

"I told him the investigation was moving along as well as could be expected, but that we still had a great deal more work to do. He seemed satisfied with the reply. He was on his way to the solicitor's office. He said he was going to do what was right and take over running the estate. He said that was the way his sister would have wanted it." Witherspoon shook his head. "It should have been an awkward conversation, but it wasn't. Merriman's eyes filled with tears when he mentioned his sister, but somehow it wasn't a sad moment. It's odd, isn't it, what you can sense about people."

"Not everyone can do that, sir. But then, that's why you're such an excellent detective. You're very good at getting people to talk freely, and, of course, you're very perceptive." She got up and reached for his empty glass. "Would you like another, sir?"

Witherspoon flushed with pleasure. "Oh, I shouldn't, but as it's been such a distressful day, I will have another. We interviewed Helen Maitland. She was the Murans' housekeeper."

"She no longer works there?" Mrs. Jeffries baited the hook.

"Oh, no, she hasn't worked there since Mrs. Muran was murdered. She had quite a tale to tell, though I'm not certain what it might mean." He told her about his meeting with the housekeeper.

Mrs. Jeffries took her time pouring his sherry, but even moving at a snail's pace, she finally had to hand him his glass. "That's very interesting, sir. Did you see anyone else today?"

"We interviewed John Addison. His firm was, well, actually still is, trying to buy Merriman's." He leaned back in his chair and sipped his drink. "He's a rather peculiar fellow."

"In what way, sir?"

"Our coming to see him didn't seem to bother him in the least. His whole manner was odd. It was almost as if he considered the whole enterprise nothing more than a challenge." He told her about their encounter with Addison.

The hall clock struck the hour as Betsy stuck her head into the drawing room. "Good evening, sir," she said to Witherspoon. "Are you ready for your dinner?"

"Oh, yes." He got up. "I'm actually quite hungry."

"Go ahead and bring it up," Mrs. Jeffries told her. "I'll serve tonight."

Mrs. Jeffries stayed in the dining room while the inspector ate his meal. She chatted as she served him his leg of mutton and stewed apples with clotted cream. By the time she poured his after-dinner cup of tea, he was relaxed and she'd learned every detail of his day. During the meal, she'd also managed to convey practically all the information the household had gathered. She'd save the few bits she hadn't been able to mention to the inspector for Constable Barnes.

"I'll take my tea up with me." Witherspoon got to his feet. "Ask Wiggins to take Fred for his walk. Poor old fellow. I've not spent much time with him lately." He put his hand over his mouth to cover a yawn.

"I'm sure you'll make it up to him." Mrs. Jeffries handed him his cup. "Sleep well, sir."

As soon as he'd gone upstairs, she piled the dirty dishes on a tray and took them down to the kitchen. As they cleared up, she told the others everything she'd learned.

"It's all useful, I suppose," Mrs. Goodge muttered as she headed for her room. "But let's face it, we're still no closer on figurin' out who actually murdered Caroline Muran."

"I wouldn't say that," Wiggins said. "We've learned lots and lots. It'll all come together and make sense when it's supposed to. Come on, Fred, time for bed."

"Is the back door locked?" Mrs. Jeffries asked of no one in particular as she went toward the back stairs.

"It's locked and bolted." Smythe took Betsy's hand and fell in step behind the housekeeper.

The household went up to their beds.

Mrs. Jeffries went into her quarters and closed the door. She leaned against the cold wood for a moment as Mrs. Goodge's last words rang in her ears. Despite everything, the cook was right. They weren't any closer to finding the killer. Her worst fears were going to be realized and they were all going to be racked with guilt for the rest of their lives. They'd let an innocent man hang. Oh, don't be daft, she told herself as she pushed away from the door. We've still time.

From the landing outside, she heard Betsy say, "Thank goodness I've not missed my chance."

"What do you mean, lass?" Smythe's voice was a harsh whisper through the heavy door.

"Lucy Turner is a beautiful woman, but if she was Muran's mistress, she missed her chance to have a husband and children by wasting her whole life pining after a man she couldn't have."

"We've neither of us missed our chance." Smythe's voice faded.

Mrs. Jeffries got undressed, doused the lights, and then went to sit in her chair by the window. She stared at the gas lamp across the road and tried to make her mind go blank, but nothing happened. She simply couldn't stop herself from thinking.

She decided it was no use, and she might as well go to bed. She got up and slipped beneath her covers. Closing her eyes, she tried her best to sleep, but she lay there wide awake. She was annoyed with herself for being unable to put herself in that state that usually helped her see the true nature of the crime. Instead, she was laying here in the dark staring at the ceiling while unrelated bits and pieces popped willy-nilly in and out of her head. John Addison hadn't been bothered at all by the police turning up and questioning him. Perhaps that meant he was one of those people who considered themselves so much cleverer than the rest of the human race. People like that never thought they'd be caught. Then again, now that Russell Merriman was back, perhaps that had put a damper on Addison's plans. Perhaps Merriman's return changed a lot of plans.

She rolled over onto her side and stared at the window. And Addison had been in town on the night of the murder. It was really too bad they didn't know for certain if he'd left the hotel that night. She closed her eyes and sighed. She might as well let her mind do what it wanted. Obviously, she wasn't going to be able to control her thoughts in any sort of coherent, logical fashion.

Muran might have had an accomplice. That certainly could have worked if he'd really wanted to rid himself of his wife, but then again, there also seemed to be ample evidence that he genuinely loved Caroline. Yet appearances could be deceiving, and the fact was, the man had been widowed twice before the age of fifty. She rolled onto her back and stared up at the ceiling again. Perhaps he didn't have an accomplice. She thought of Mrs. Goodge's explanation. It was a tad far-fetched, but it was certainly possible. And what's more, by coshing himself over the head,

Muran instantly took himself off the suspect list. Even the inspector hadn't seen any reason to doubt the man's story. She made a mental note to be sure to mention to Constable Barnes that they ought to search the empty buildings near the murder scene.

She felt her eyelids grow heavy and she began to drift toward sleep. Wiggins was right, she thought. What we've got to do is find out who wanted Mrs. Muran dead and Mr. Muran alive. But that's the trouble, she told herself sleepily. All of our suspects benefit with Mrs. Muran dead and Mr. Muran alive. John Addison will be able to buy the business, Mr. Muran will have lots of money, Roderick Sutter would have revenge for being fired, and the Turner women might get to be ladies of the manor and not poor relations.

She drifted off to sleep. In her dreams, she walked in a heavy fog and she was frightened. She knew she was near the river. The fog would drift about, sometimes heavy, sometimes so wispy she could see the embankment. She knew she had to find the way home, that she had something important to do, something that was a matter of life and death.

From all around her, came the sound of voices. "I lost my position over twenty quid," a man's hard tone rang out. She whirled about, but all she could see was heavy mist. "I stepped out to get my shawl," a woman replied. Even in her sleep she knew dreams didn't need to make sense.

"She threw the salt cellar at the day girl." That voice sounded a bit like Wiggins. "We're no closer to finding who murdered Caroline Muran," Mrs. Goodge declared. "He must 'ave had an accomplice," Smythe added.

Mrs. Jeffries sighed in her sleep. She wanted to tell them she was sorry, that she'd tried her best to solve the case, but it was simply too difficult. But naturally, as she was asleep, she couldn't get her voice to work properly.

Betsy suddenly appeared at her side. "Do you think I'll miss my chance?"

Mrs. Jeffries awoke with a start and sat up. Her pulse pounded and her mind raced as Betsy's words repeated themselves in her head. Facts, theories, and ideas all came together in that lightning bolt fashion that made things make perfect sense. "Good gracious, that's it. He changed everything."

She looked toward the window and saw that it was still dark outside, but she knew she couldn't go back to sleep. She got up, lighted the lamp on her desk, and then sat down. She had to think. She had to be sure. Yet even if she was sure, how on earth was she going to prove it?

Betsy was sitting at the kitchen table when Smythe came downstairs. A teapot, two cups, and a plate of buns were in front of her. "I was beginning to think you'd forgotten," she said softly.

"Course I didn't forget. I just had to be extra careful coming downstairs so I don't wake that silly dog. Even with a door between us, Fred's got sharp ears." He leaned over and dropped a quick kiss on her lips. "I thought I saw a crack of light comin' from Mrs. Jeffries' rooms as well." He slipped into the chair next to her. "I think she might be up and about."

"Do you think she knows?" Betsy looked toward the back staircase.

Smythe shrugged. "Even if she did, she wouldn't care. We deserve a bit of time to ourselves, and the only way we can be alone together is early of a mornin' when everyone else is asleep. She'd understand."

Since their engagement, they had gotten in the habit of occasionally getting up early so they could have some time together. The others in the household tried their best not to constantly intrude upon the couple, but between their work and the inspector's cases, it was almost impossible to have any privacy. So they'd hit upon this idea, and so far, it had worked well.

"We do have a wedding to plan." Betsy poured the tea and handed him his mug. "That takes time. There are a lot of decisions that have to be made. Speaking of which, we do need to pick the day."

"Pick the one you like. Any day will do me." He took a quick sip of the hot liquid.

"You can't just pick any old day." Betsy stared at him irritably. Sometimes men were such dolts. "We've got to see what else people have planned for the month."

"What's that got to do with it?" Smythe had noticed that when it came to wedding plans, he frequently said the wrong thing.

"It's got everything to do with it," she sighed. "I want people to come, not send their regrets because we picked the wrong day and they had other plans. That's why we've got to think it through carefully. We don't want to pick a day there's an important social event. Isn't Ascot in June? I'll want Lady Cannonberry there and Luty and Hatchet. But they've got social obligations, too, and we've got to take that into account."

"Rubbish," he said, putting his mug down. Sometimes Betsy didn't realize her own worth. Sometimes the insecure, frightened girl who'd collapsed on the inspector's doorstep took over and made her say silly things. "You're more important than a flower show or a race meeting. It's our wedding! Other people can make their plans around us. Do you think Luty or Hatchet or Ruth would go to a bloomin' race meeting rather than come to our wedding?"

"Well, no, but there's no need to make things awkward for anyone." She looked down at her lap, embarrassed that she'd made a fuss. Of course their friends would put them first. "I just want everything to be perfect."

"It will be." He lifted her chin, forcing her eyes to meet his. "It's going to be the best day of your life, Betsy. I promise you. You can have anything you want. You know that. We can have a reception at the Palace Hotel or we can take a grand tour of the Continent, go to America, or do anything you like. You just tell me what you want and I'll give it to you."

Smythe had made a fortune in Australia and invested it wisely and well. He'd been good friends with the inspector's late aunt, Euphemia Witherspoon. When he'd come back from Australia, he stopped in to see his old friend. He'd found her in very poor health and surrounded by a pack of servants that were taking terrible liberties. They'd been robbing her blind and practically imprisoning her in her own home. Smythe had run all of them off except for the youngest, Wiggins. When Euphemia had realized she was dying, she'd made him promise to stay on for a bit and watch out for her nephew, Gerald Witherspoon. He'd agreed and he'd stayed. Inspector Witherspoon had moved in and hired Mrs. Jeffries and Mrs. Goodge. Betsy had come, and before you could say bobs-your-uncle, they were investigating murders and looking out for one another. They'd become family.

Unfortunately, Smythe hadn't told them he was rich. He'd then been stuck with the problem that as he'd not said anything about having so much money, the others in the household might not take kindly to thinking he'd deceived them all these years. When he and Betsy had fallen in love, he'd finally told her. Mrs. Jeffries had guessed the truth, but the others still thought he was just a coachman.

"All I want is you," she said softly. "But a nice wedding wouldn't hurt, either. You know we can't make too big a fuss, don't you?"

He sighed. "I know, but we don't have to skimp, either. We'll have us a proper wedding and do it right."

"You said you might have a way for us to keep on with our investigations," she said hopefully.

They'd known that once they were married, things at Upper Edmonton Gardens would change. Smythe would want to give her a home of their own and he'd not want her working as a maid, not even for someone as good as Inspector Witherspoon.

"There might be." He hesitated. He'd still not thought the whole thing through, and it might not work out. Like Betsy, he knew that once they wed, things would change. He liked investigating murders as well, and he was determined that he'd find a way for them to continue their work, even if they no longer lived in the inspector's household. "I've got an idea."

"What is it?" she asked.

"Gracious, you two are up early." Mrs. Jeffries swept into the kitchen. "Oh dear, am I intruding?" She'd given them as much privacy as she possibly could, but if her theory about the murder was correct, they had much to do and she had to get started.

"That's all right, Mrs. J." Smythe grinned broadly. He'd not been ready to share his thoughts on how they could continue their investigations with his beloved quite yet. "You're up early yourself."

"I couldn't sleep." She looked hopefully at the teapot. "Is there enough in there for me?"

"There's plenty." Betsy was already up and moving to the sideboard for another cup. "Why couldn't you sleep? Is your stomach bothering you again?"

"It wasn't indigestion." Mrs. Jeffries sat down. "It was this case. Something is going to happen today, and we've got to prepare as best we can."

"Bloomin' ada, you know who did it!" Smythe exclaimed.

"Thank goodness. I was terrified we weren't going to solve this one." Betsy smiled happily and handed Mrs. Jeffries her mug.

"Well, I don't precisely know who did it," Mrs. Jeffries explained. "But I've narrowed the field a bit."

"What does that mean?" Mrs. Goodge asked. She was standing in the doorway, holding a smug-looking Samson in her arms. Her tone had been just a tad irritated.

"Excellent, you're up," Mrs. Jeffries said. "We must get Wiggins up as well. I'm going to need all of you."

"What's going on?" The cook put the cat down and came on into the kitchen. She stared suspiciously at the teapot. "Have you been meetin' without me?"

"No, Betsy and I just snuck down early to make some weddin' plans." Smythe got to his feet. "Mrs. Jeffries come down because she's figured it out, and I've got to go get Wiggins."

"I'll put more water on to boil," Betsy said.

Mrs. Goodge looked at the housekeeper. "Thank goodness you've figured it out. This case has been keeping me awake at nights."

"I'm not precisely sure," Mrs. Jeffries explained. "But I've a feeling we're on the right track, so to speak." Blast, what if she were wrong.

Samson, who'd walked over to his empty food bowl, meowed loudly.

"Just a minute, precious," the cook called over her shoulder.

"I'll explain everything as soon as we're all assembled," Mrs. Jeffries said firmly.

By the time the cat was fed and the fresh tea brewed, Wiggins and Smythe had come downstairs.

"Should I go get Lady Cannonberry?" the footman asked.

"Not yet, but we will need her later," Mrs. Jeffries replied. "Now, I'm going to have to ask all of you to do some very specific tasks today. Wiggins, I want you to get over to the Muran household and find your friend Charlotte."

"I don't think she'll be up this early," he said.

"Don't be daft, lad. By the time you have your tea and get over there, she'll be in the kitchen helping to get breakfast," Mrs. Goodge said. "Not all households are like this one. Most places make the servants get up at the crack of dawn."

"Once you speak to Charlotte," Mrs. Jeffries interjected, "you must tell her the truth about us, about what we do, but then you must swear her to secrecy. What we need her to do might be very important."

"You want me to tell her about our snoopin'?" Wiggins asked incredulously. "About our workin' on the inspector's case?"

"Tell her you work for a private inquiry agent, and then promise to help her find a new position," Betsy suggested quickly. "That's what I always do and it generally works fairly well."

"That's an excellent idea," Mrs. Jeffries said to Betsy. She turned back to Wiggins. "Tell Charlotte that once she's inside the Turner house, she's to keep watch. If she sees either of the Turner women adding anything to the food that's to be served at luncheon, she's to come and get you. You'll need to be standing watch close by. Can you do that?"

Wiggins nodded. "What'll I do if she tells me she's seen something?"

Mrs. Jeffries thought for a moment. "You'll find the inspector and tell him what you know."

They all began to protest at once, but she held up her hand for silence. "Don't worry, I've come up with a story to mask our actions on this case. We're in a position where we may have to let him know we've been helping. But if that happens, we'll deal with the consequences as best we can."

"You think one of them is going to use poison?" Mrs. Goodge asked.

"I think it's very possible," Mrs. Jeffries replied. She looked at Smythe. "Can you find Russell Merriman?"

"I've no idea what he looks like," he replied. "But if you give me a description, I can suss 'im out. Do we even know where he's staying?"

"He's staying at the Muran house," Mrs. Goodge interjected. "Sorry, I forgot to mention that yesterday. He moved in a day or so ago."

"Then findin' 'im will be pretty easy. What do you want me to do?"

"Keep an eye on him," she replied. "If my theory is correct, someone is going to try to kill him today. The trouble is, I'm not exactly sure who it's going to be, so we've got our work cut out for us."

"You don't know who it is?" Mrs. Goodge pulled her shawl tighter against the early morning chill.

"I'm fairly sure it's one of three people," Mrs. Jeffries said. "Betsy, can you get to the Turner house and find Selma Macclesfield?"

"I can," Betsy said uncertainly. "Mrs. Jeffries, it's not like you to be so unsure of the identity of the killer. Are you sure we're not moving too quickly. We don't want to make a mistake." She was voicing the doubts she could see on the faces of the others.

Mrs. Jeffries looked around the table. "I know it sounds as if I don't know what I'm doing, but you've got to trust me."

"We do trust you," Mrs. Goodge said. "But you've just admitted the killer could be one of three people. We don't want to expose ourselves without need. If we go tearing about and interferin' in the inspector's case and the killer isn't caught, it'll not go down very well."

"I do understand that," Mrs. Jeffries said quickly. "I wouldn't ask any of you to expose yourselves if I wasn't sure it was absolutely necessary."

"But you don't know exactly who the killer is?" Smythe pressed.

"It's one of three people," she repeated, picking the pot up and starting to pour. She could understand their concerns, but really, you'd think by now they'd have learned to trust her. She wasn't sure if she was offended or not.

Mrs. Goodge cocked her head to one side and stared at the housekeeper speculatively. "In the past you've always been sure."

"I'm certain the killer is going to strike today," she said. She handed Wiggins his tea. "But that's all I'm sure of, and that's why I'm going to need everyone's help."

"You've not steered us wrong yet," Wiggins declared as he took his tea. "You know what's what. I trust you, Mrs. Jeffries."

"As do I." Betsy got to her feet. "What do you want me to tell Selma Macclesfield?"

"I'll go and start shadowin' Russell Merriman," Smythe said.

Mrs. Goodge looked at the housekeeper. "What do you need me to do?"

Mrs. Jeffries smiled gratefully at her staff and then gazed at the cook. "I'm afraid I'm going to have to ask you to spend your day being at the ready, so to speak."

CHAPTER 11

———

"We've got to get to the Turner household today, sir," Constable Barnes said to Witherspoon. He'd spent the last hour in the kitchen with Mrs. Jeffries, and he wasn't certain he understood what was going on, but he'd decided to trust her. The worst that could happen was that they'd end up asking all the principals in the case a few more questions. Mrs. Jeffries had given him a list. Just in case.

"We've a meeting with the chief inspector this morning and I'd like to go to Barrick Street and search those empty building near the scene of the crime," Witherspoon replied. "But if you think your source was sure of his information, we can interview the Turner women, too. Perhaps we'll have another word with Roderick Sutter as well."

Barnes had told the inspector that a "source" had come forward with some new information about the whereabouts of some of the suspects on the night of the murder. "He was sure, sir, and he's generally been reliable in the past."

"What took him so long to come forward?" Witherspoon asked. They were standing in the foyer. The inspector reached for his heavy overcoat and slipped it on.

"He doesn't like Inspector Nivens," Barnes lied. "Nivens arrested him once and was excessively rough, so he kept what he knew to himself until the word got that we were having another look at the case. But he definitely saw both the Turner women leave their house that night. He was working that neighborhood, sir. I expect he was casing the whole area looking for a nice empty house to rob."

"And he's sure it was them he saw?" Witherspoon reached for his bowler and popped it onto his head.

"Oh yes, he noticed the address when Miss Turner came out. As I said, sir, he was watching the area. Then a few minutes later, Mrs. Turner left. He told me he crept around the back of the house and had a look through the window. He was hoping the place would be empty, but he spotted the housekeeper so he left." Barnes opened the front door and they stepped outside. "He was going to rob the place, sir. But as he didn't actually do the deed, we'd no reason to hold him. Why do you want to interview Sutter again, sir?"

"I want to get a better sense of the man." Witherspoon went down the stairs. He'd thought about how Mrs. Jeffries had told him he was very perceptive and quite good at getting people to talk freely. He wanted to have another chat with Sutter and see if his "inner voice" could sense anything. "We might as well ask him to tell us again where he was that night. After all, he was very angry with Mrs. Muran."

Barnes waved at a hansom that had turned the corner. He hoped he'd be able to get the inspector to the Turner house by the time Merriman got there. He'd do his best.

Betsy shed her jacket and hat as she hurried down the hall. Mrs. Goodge was sitting at the table when she came into the kitchen. "No one else is here," the cook said. "But Wiggins has reported in that he's done his bit. I sent him back to keep watch on the house."

"What about Smythe?" Betsy asked.

"I've not heard from him. But I'm expectin' Mrs. Jeffries back any moment now." She glanced anxiously at the clock and noted that it was past noon. "Leastways, I hope she's back soon."

"Where did she go?"

"To the Muran house," she replied. "She sent Ruth along to the Fortune Hotel. But I think she only did that so Ruth would feel useful."

Betsy flopped down in her chair, a worried look on her face. "I hope she knows what she's doing."

"So do I," Mrs. Jeffries said from the doorway. "Were you able to have a word with Selma Maccelesfield?" She took off her cloak and gloves.

Betsy's cheeks flushed with embarrassment. "I only meant that I hope this goes right . . ."

Mrs. Jeffries held up her hand. "I know what you meant and I took no offense. What did you learn?"

"She told me that the gun is still in the house. Apparently, when Mrs. Turner had her little spell at the Muran house, Mr. Muran neglected to take the weapon from her."

"That was foolish of him," Mrs. Goodge muttered.

"It wouldn't have mattered if he had taken it away from her. Miss Turner keeps a derringer," Betsy continued.

Mrs. Jeffries sighed. "Well, my news isn't much better. Keith Muran knows that Merriman is taking over the estate."

"How did you find that out?" The cook stared at Mrs. Jeffries in admiration.

"I bribed the day girl for information when she put the laundry basket out the back," she replied. "Muran told Merriman over dinner last night that he was going to honor his sister's wishes with the company. He made it clear he was going to sign the contracts to complete the purchase of the row houses. He's an appointment with the solicitors later this afternoon. I expect he'll sign the contracts then."

. "You learned a lot of details," Betsy exclaimed. "That's amazing."

"Not really," Mrs. Jeffries sighed. "As the girl was serving dinner, she heard the whole conversation."

"How did Mr. Muran react?" Mrs. Goodge asked.

"He was polite, but the girl said it was obvious he wasn't pleased. But he could hardly make a fuss as both the Turners were there as well. Has Wiggins reported back?" Mrs. Jeffries took her seat.

"He popped in to say that he managed to get the message to Charlotte and she's agreed to come get him if she sees anyone playing about with the food."

Barnes got down from the hansom and tried to figure out what in the name of thunder he was going to do next. It was almost one o'clock, and it had taken every bit of ingenuity he possessed to get the inspector here. Now what? He stared at the outside of the Turner house and wondered if he'd made a big mistake.

"I do hope the ladies are at home," Witherspoon said. "I hope to speak to Sutter again today."

"This shouldn't take long, sir," Barnes replied. He looked around, wondering where Smythe and Wiggins were hiding. Mrs. Jeffries had told him they'd be close by. She'd seemed convinced that something was going to happen today. Mind you, she hadn't told him what that something might be, merely that it was important to get the inspector to the Turner house. He straightened his shoulders and started up the walkway.

They were three feet from the front door when there was a loud bang from inside the house.

"That was a shot, sir!" Barnes flung open the front door and charged inside. Witherspoon was right behind him.

A woman's screams pierced the air as they raced down the hall. The door at the end of the hall suddenly burst open and Keith Muran, his face white with fear, came running out.

"This way," he called to the two policemen. He threw himself at a set of double doors and shoved them open. The three men rushed inside.

"Oh my God, oh my God, it was an accident. I told him to leave the wretched gun alone, but he insisted on picking it up." Lucy Turner was standing next to the dining table staring down at Russell Merriman. There was blood pouring out of a wound in his chest.

Witherspoon pushed her aside and knelt down beside Merriman. "Get everyone out of here," he ordered Barnes.

"Oh my God, he's dead," Lucy weeped.

"Get ahold of yourself!" Mrs. Turner ordered her daughter. "And tell us what happened."

"Barnes, send one of the servants out for a constable," Witherspoon yelled. "Have them send along a doctor right away."

"A doctor!" Lucy cried harder. "What good will a doctor do? He's dead and it's my fault. I told him to leave the gun alone, but he said he wanted to have a look at it, he wanted to examine the handle."

"It was an accident, Lucy." Keith put his arm around her and gently tugged her toward the door. "Come along now. Let's do what the policeman says."

"We need to clear this room," Barnes instructed. Two maids, both the Turner women, and Keith Muran hovered just inside the dining room. He herded all of them out into the hallway.

Barnes looked at the maid closest to him. She had plastered herself against the wall and was staring at him out of wide, frightened eyes. "Go to the corner and find a constable," he ordered. "Tell him there's been an accident and that Inspector Witherspoon is on the scene. Ask them to send for a doctor and to come along here straightaway. Tell him to bring plenty of help."

She nodded and charged for the front door.

Barnes ushered them into the drawing room. Keith Muran led Lucy to a chair and knelt down next to her. She was weeping quietly.

Mrs. Turner took a seat on the settee. She looked at Lucy and then turned her attention to the other maid. "Get her some brandy."

"That's probably a very good idea." Barnes nodded at the girl and she rushed out of the room.

"Do be quiet, Lucy," Mrs. Turner snapped. "You're making a spectacle of yourself."

"Oh my God, he's dead," Lucy cried. "Poor Russell, he was covered in blood. It's dreadful, simply dreadful. But I told him to leave it alone. I told him it wasn't safe."

The door opened and the maid slipped back in carrying a glass of amber liquid. She gave the glass to Keith Muran and he put it up to Lucy's lips. "Drink this. It'll make you feel better."

Barnes watched her closely. Her fingers trembled as they closed around the glass, but she managed to swallow. She coughed delicately and lay back against the chair. "He shot himself in the chest. He'd turned the gun to look at the handle and it went off. I'd told him to leave it alone. I'd told him, but he didn't listen."

"Could you please tell us what happened?" Barnes said. He didn't care how distraught she was; he wanted her statement.

Lucy looked at him with tear-filled eyes. "I'm not sure what to say. It all happened so quickly."

"Why don't you start from when Mr. Merriman arrived," Barnes suggested.

"For goodness' sake, Constable." Muran stood up, but he kept his hand on her shoulder. "She's had a terrible shock. Must you question her this very minute?"

"My poor cousin is dead." She dabbed at her eyes with a handkerchief she pulled from the sleeve of her sapphire blue dress. "I'm not sure I can speak of it. It's too horrible."

"I'm afraid you'll have to," Barnes said flatly. He looked at Muran. "I suggest you either leave the room or be quiet, sir. This is a very grave matter. A man is dead."

"How dare you," Muran snapped.

"It's all right." Lucy reached up and patted his hand. "I want to tell them what happened. I want to get it over with." She took a deep breath. "Russell was the first to arrive, so we chatted while we waited for Keith to get here. I happened to mention that I was using our grandmother's silver, and Russell asked if he could see it."

"Where was Mrs. Turner?" Barnes asked.

"She was still upstairs," Lucy replied.

"I had to go up and change my shoes," Mrs. Turner volunteered. "The others were bothering my feet."

"Go on," Barnes instructed. He wished more help would arrive. They needed the doctor here. Poor Witherspoon was dreadfully squeamish about corpses, so it didn't seem fair that he should get stuck with Merriman's body.

"I took him into the dining room. The table was already set and he had a look at our grandmother's silver. Just then Keith arrived and I heard the girl put him in the drawing room. I didn't want to keep him waiting, so I tried to hurry Russell up a bit. I told him he'd have plenty of time to look at the silver while we ate our lunch. He laughed"—she stopped as her eyes filled with tears yet again—"but as we were walking out, he spotted my derringer."

"You had a gun just laying about in your dining room?" Barnes pressed.

"It was in a gun box, Constable. It was lying on the desk. Russell saw it, and before I could stop him he'd lifted the lid and taken the thing out. It's quite a fancy weapon. My father had it made in India. It's got a carved ivory handle. Russell picked it up. I told him to put it back, that I'd brought it down to take it to a gunsmith for repairing—the wretched gun has a loose trigger. But before I could explain, he'd turned the gun toward himself and it went off."

"Why did he turn the gun?" Barnes asked softly.

"He wanted to have a closer look at the handle. He was muttering something about the carving . . . then it went off and I started screaming. Oh God, poor Russell . . ." she broke off and buried her face in her hands.

"That's quite a story, Lucy. Too bad it's all a lie." Russell Merriman, propped up by Witherspoon, stood in the open doorway and stared sadly at Lucy Turner.

She raised her head, an expression of horror on her face.

"Thank God you're alive." Keith Muran started toward Russell. "We thought you were dead."

Suddenly, Lucy Turner leapt to her feet and charged at her cousin. Holding her hands out as claws, she flew across the room. "Why won't you stay dead?" she screamed. "Ye gods, you bloody Merrimans have caused me no end of trouble. I finally got rid of that damned sister of yours and then you had to come back from the grave and ruin everything."

Witherspoon pulled Merriman out to the hall at the same time that Barnes hurled himself after the screaming woman. He tried grabbing her shoulder, missed, and stumbled to his knees. It was Mrs. Turner who stopped her daughter.

She grabbed her arm, whirled her about, and slapped her across the face. "Stop it. Just stop it. It's over. It's all over."

"No!" Lucy screamed. "He's mine, it's all mine! I worked for it, I put up with that sanctimonious chit for years. I'm sick of being the poor relation. She stole him from me and now her bloody brother is stealing everything else. I'll not have it, I tell you. I'll not have it!" She shook her mother's arm off and started for the hallway.

Witherspoon was dragging Merriman toward the front door as quickly as he could. He wasn't sure what was happening, but the look in that woman's eyes convinced him he needed to get the man out of there as fast as possible.

Barnes grabbed Lucy from behind just as the front door opened and two police constables burst inside. Lucy, her gaze locked on Russell, punched and kicked at Barnes as she tried to get to her prey.

"Help the constable!" Witherspoon yelled.

The two constables rushed toward Barnes as he grappled with Lucy, but just then, Mrs. Turner jumped into the fray. "Leave my daughter alone, you monsters," she cried. "She can't help herself. She's out of her mind."

"I'm no more out of my mind than you are," Lucy screamed at her mother. She yanked one arm out of Barnes' grasp, balled her hand into a fist, and punched one of the constables in the eye.

"Lucy, please stop," Keith Muran pleaded. He was ineffectually waving his hands at the struggling mass of bodies.

"Shut up," she snarled at Muran as one of the constables forced her to her knees. "This is your fault, you bloody twit. If you'd married me instead of her, we'd not be in this fix. I should have hit you hard enough to kill you when I had the chance."

Witherspoon leaned Merriman up against the wall. "Will you be all right here?" he asked anxiously. "I must help. I'm afraid she's going to make a run for it."

"It's the mother you've got to worry about," Russell commented. He could see everything. "She just kicked one of the constables in the knee. Uh-oh, he's going down. Go on. I'll be fine here."

"I do wish the doctor would hurry," the inspector complained. He didn't like leaving a bleeding man propped against a wall, but from the drawing room he could hear bumps, screams, grunts, and the sound of furniture breaking.

Russell looked at his shoulder. "Don't worry. It's only a flesh wound. I'll be all right. Go and lend them a hand. I do believe she's going to whip all three of them."

And she almost did. But in the end, they managed to get Mrs. Turner out of the way and a pair of cuffs on Lucy.

"Lucy Turner," Witherspoon said. "You're under arrest for the murder of Caroline Merriman Muran and the attempted murder of Russell Merriman."

"Go to hell," she said, sneering.

Wiggins and Smythe arrived home a little past four in the afternoon. "Where have you been?" Betsy demanded. "I've paced so much I've almost worn a hole in the floor."

"We got away as soon as we knew what 'appened." Wiggins grinned broadly. "Mrs. Jeffries, you ought to be one of them fortune tellers they 'ave at the music hall. Somethin' did 'appen today, and that's why we're so late gettin' back."

"Lucy Turner tried to kill Russell Merriman," Smythe announced. He grabbed Betsy's hand and pulled her toward the table, which had been set for tea. "She confessed to killing Caroline Muran as well. It was quite a dustup, it was. Both them Turner women have pretty powerful punches."

"What happened?" Mrs. Goodge demanded. She and Ruth Cannonberry were already seated.

"Is Inspector Witherspoon all right?" Ruth asked anxiously.

"He's fine, but one of the other constables is goin' to 'ave a black eye," Wiggins said cheerfully. He slipped into his chair. "Miss Turner popped him one right in the face, she did."

"And Mrs. Turner got another one in the knee, but I expect he'll be fine in a day or two," Smythe added.

Mrs. Jeffries, who'd been pacing the floor along with Betsy, took her seat at the head of the table. "Smythe, tell us what happened. Start from the time you and Wiggins arrived at the Turner house to keep watch."

Smythe nodded. "Well, as you know, I was followin' Russell Merriman this morning, but that didn't take much doin' as both he and Keith Muran were home until half past twelve. Then they went to the Turner house in Chelsea. I followed along and met up with Wiggins."

"I 'ad us a good hidin' place all sussed out," Wiggins interrupted. "The house across the road had one of them tangled overgrown gardens, so we just nipped in behind the bushes. There was no one about, so it was right easy. Mind you, it did get a bit cold."

"We watched the men go in and then we settled down to wait. Just before one o'clock a hansom pulls up. The inspector and Constable Barnes gets out. Nothin' had 'appened up until then, and I've got to tell ya, Constable Barnes looked worried. But just as they was walking to the door, a shot rang out."

"How dreadful," Ruth muttered.

"Inspector Witherspoon and the constable rushed the door and barged straight in." Smythe shook his head. "I've got to tell ya, we weren't sure what to do, so we just stayed put. A few minutes later, Charlotte came rushing out and ran down the street like the hounds from hell was at her heels."

"I went after her," Wiggins interjected. "But I couldn't catch her, she went that fast."

"She went to fetch more help," Smythe continued. "We heard the constable's whistle blast and knew he was summoning more men. But then all of a sudden we heard a great ruckus comin' from the house. The girl had left the door partially open and we could hear all this shoutin' and thrashin' about." He nodded his thanks as Mrs. Jeffries handed him a cup of tea. "It went on for a few moments, and once again we didn't know whether or not to barge in and help. But as there weren't any guns goin' off, we thought we'd best stay hid."

"Then what happened?" Mrs. Jeffries asked.

"Then Charlotte and two more constables came running back and into the house. A few minutes later, a doctor arrived. But by then they'd led Lucy Turner off in handcuffs."

"When the ruckus died down a bit, I managed to sneak around the back of the house and talk to Charlotte. Accordin' to what the other maid said, Miss Turner went mad and shot Mr. Merriman and then claimed it was an accident. She thought she'd killed him."

"But that didn't work, as Merriman wasn't dead," Smythe added. "Apparently, he didn't take kindly to being shot. I've got to say, Mrs. Jeffries, I had my doubts today. I didn't think anything was goin' to 'appen."

"I knew we'd catch the killer," Wiggins said smugly. He helped himself to a treacle tart.

"I wasn't sure," Mrs. Jeffries admitted. "As a matter of fact, I didn't know which of the three had actually done the murder, but I was fairly confident it had to be either Keith Muran or one of the Turner women."

"You really didn't know?" Betsy asked.

"I'm afraid not," Mrs. Jeffries replied. She helped herself to a tart. "I was fairly certain it was one of those three, and I was also sure it would happen today."

"Why today?" Smythe took a sip of his tea.

"Because Russell Merriman was going to sign the contracts to complete the purchase of the row houses. He was going to honor his sister's wishes. Once those contracts were signed, all the company's money would be tied up. I knew that the killer would strike today because I was sure that the main reason Caroline had been murdered was to keep the company's capital from being spent on worker housing. I just wasn't sure who the killer actually was."

"But how could you know?" Betsy asked. "You only found out this morning that Merriman had told Muran and the Turners of his plan."

"No, I had it *confirmed* this morning," Mrs. Jeffries replied. "Yesterday the inspector said that Merriman had told him he was going to honor Caroline's wishes. Once I realized that Merriman was sharing that sort of information with a policeman, I decided there was a good chance he hadn't been keeping it a secret. He'd probably told any number of people, so it seemed logical that the killer might have already heard of Merriman's plans."

"But he only told Muran last night," Mrs. Goodge

insisted. "So how could you know this morning that Merriman was going to be murdered by one of those three?"

"Because Merriman was the key," she explained. "I kept asking myself who wanted Caroline Muran dead. Well, there were a number of people who wanted her dead, but as Wiggins once said, the killer had to be someone who wanted her dead and Keith Muran alive. At first glance, you could make the case that that circumstance was applicable to all our suspects. But upon closer inspection, it became obvious to me that Sutter didn't particularly want Keith Muran alive. Muran wouldn't have given him his job back."

"What about Addison?" Smythe asked. "He made it clear that the husband was easier to deal with than the wife."

"Yes, but at the time of Caroline's murder, everyone thought Russell Merriman was dead, so that means if Addison was prepared to do murder to acquire the company, why not kill both of the Murans and deal with the estate? That would have been the easiest of all. No, there were only three people who wanted her dead and him alive."

"I'm glad it wasn't him," Betsy said. They all knew who she meant.

"I think Keith Muran loved his wife," Mrs. Jeffries said. "And I know that the Turners were angry and bitter over being poor relations. I think Lucy murdered Caroline knowing full well that she'd be the next Mrs. Muran. She wanted it all. She wanted the man, the house, and the money. Then Russell Merriman came back, and all of a sudden the house and the money might not come with marriage to Muran. The only way to be sure to get it all was to make sure Merriman didn't sign those contracts. She'd gotten away with murder once; she was sure she could do it again."

"I still don't see how she did it that night," Mrs. Goodge complained. "I mean, she couldn't have known that Caroline was going to insist on going to Barrick Street to look at those buildings."

"But I think she did know," Mrs. Jeffries countered. "Remember, Caroline'd had a terrible row with her husband that day and neither of them was in a forgiving mood. The Turners came back to the house that afternoon for tea. Caroline might have mentioned she was thinking of looking over the buildings."

"But what if she didn't?" Betsy frowned in confusion. "How could Lucy have known to be there?"

"She could have walked. Several witnesses mentioned that the traffic was so bad that night that you could probably have walked somewhere faster than a hansom would carry you," Mrs. Jeffries replied. "We know she left the house that night after she'd argued with her mother, and we know she knew where the Murans were going to be. She could easily have seen them come out of the concert hall and get into a hansom. She could have followed the cab, seen them get out, slipped up behind them, and done her worst."

"That would explain why she knocked him out before she murdered the wife," Betsy murmured. "She didn't want him to recognize her."

"She hit him pretty 'ard," Smythe commented.

"Only hard enough to knock him out," Mrs. Jeffries pointed out. "Not hard enough to do any permanent damage. Another reason I thought of the Turner women—whoever murdered Caroline Muran probably knew something about fast death. Mrs. Turner had worked in a field hospital in India, and I'm sure she passed some of her knowledge on to her daughter."

"Why'd you send me along to talk to Charlotte about the food?" Wiggins asked.

"Because I wasn't sure if she'd use a gun or poison," Mrs. Jeffries said. "Actually, I was fairly sure it would be the gun—both women are good shots."

"Not quite good enough," Smythe muttered.

"I'm afraid we'll have to wait until the inspector gets home to find out the rest," Mrs. Jeffries said. "And I imagine he'll be quite late today."

But oddly enough, he was home before dark and surprised them all by coming directly down to the kitchen.

Fred, who'd reclaimed his favorite spot on the rug near the stove, leapt up and bounced eagerly around the kitchen. Samson, who'd been sitting on the footstool, jumped down and ran off to the safety of the cook's room.

Witherspoon stared at the departing cat. "Why is Samson running away?"

"It's not you, sir." Wiggins rose to his feet. "It's Fred. Samson gets a bit nervous whenever Fred starts his bouncing about the kitchen."

"Sit down, lad." Witherspoon waved him back to his chair and slipped into the empty spot next to Mrs. Jeffries. "I could do with a cup of tea. It's been a rather extraordinary day."

"Would you share your news with us, sir?" Mrs. Jeffries motioned for Betsy to fetch another cup. "You know how we love hearing about your cases."

"That's why I've come down," he exclaimed. "Lucy Turner has confessed to the murder of Caroline Muran. Mind you, I don't think the woman's sane. She seemed to think it quite all right to murder someone if they were in the way of her getting what she wanted. While we were taking her statement she kept saying over and over that the Merrimans were the cause of all her troubles. She tried to murder Russell Merriman, but she only wounded him in the chest."

"Gracious, sir." Mrs. Jeffries handed him his cup. "Does that mean that Tommy Odell will be released?"

"Indeed it does," he said. "We've sent word to the Home Office. As soon as the formalities have been attended to, he'll be released." He took a quick sip of tea. "I must say, we had a bit of luck with this one. It's amazing how often I happen to be at the right place at the right time."

"Whatever do you mean, sir?" Betsy asked.

Witherspoon told them what had happened that afternoon. They listened closely, taking care not to ask too many questions or do anything that would give the game away. "I must say, it was very fortunate that Constable Barnes' informant saw Miss Turner leave the house that night."

"Otherwise, you'd not have been anywhere near the Turner house at just the right moment and you wouldn't have heard the gunshot," Wiggins said. "And you'd not have solved this one so quickly. Good thing you were there, sir."

"Yes, quite right." Witherspoon finished his tea and got to his feet. "I believe I'll take Fred for a walk."

"Why don't you take him over to Lady Cannonberry's," Mrs. Jeffries suggested. "I'm sure she'd love to hear your good news, sir."

"That's a splendid idea," Witherspoon agreed. "Come along, Fred. Let's go walkies."

As soon as they were gone, Smythe got up. "I've got to see Blimpey. Now that I know for certain they're lettin' Tommy out, I can tell him the good news."

"We'll leave the back door unlocked for you," Mrs. Jeffries said.

"I'll walk you to the door." Betsy grabbed his hand and they disappeared down the hall.

"I'd best get that roast out of the oven," Mrs. Goodge said as she got up. "The inspector will want his dinner when he gets back."

"I expect he'll eat with Lady Cannonberry," Mrs. Jeffries muttered. "I think I'll go up to my room for a rest."

"I'll send Betsy up when we're ready for supper," Mrs. Goodge said.

Mrs. Jeffries went upstairs and into her room. She sat down in her chair by the window and stared out into the twilight. She was glad an innocent man wasn't going to hang, but something was bothering her.

She hadn't known until the men had returned which of the three suspects was the killer. Perhaps that was what was making her so uneasy. She closed her eyes and told herself that no one was perfect, that people did the best they could. And what did it matter? The killer had been caught. So what was bothering her?

Inspector Nivens.

Her eyes flew open. That was it. He'd always been a thorn in their sides, but now that he was going to have his conviction rescinded, it would be much, much worse. He would be out to get Witherspoon.

He'd watch their inspector's every move, and she suspected he'd have his minions watch the household. But what could be done about it?

Mrs. Jeffries sighed heavily. She'd worry about Nivens on their next case. For right now, she simply needed a nap.

Smythe was grinning from ear to ear when he walked into the Dirty Duck. Blimpey waved him over. "I take it you've got good news for me."

"Don't be daft, man. Who do you think you're foolin'." He sat down. "You already know. I've just come along to confirm it and make it official like. Your boy ought to be gettin' out in a few days."

Blimpey laughed. "It's good news, Smythe. Good news indeed. I knew I could count on you lot." He waved at the barmaid.

"I can't stay long," Smythe protested.

"You can stay long enough to celebrate with me," Blimpey replied. "And to tell me what you lot want."

"We're not wantin' anythin'." Smythe smiled at the woman who brought them their pints. "We don't do this for money," he continued when she'd gone out of earshot.

"I know that, but there's got to be somethin' I can do fer you," Blimpey protested.

"You can tell me why you wanted Odell out so badly," Smythe said bluntly. "You're a decent sort, Blimpey, but you're not a bleedin' heart."

Blimpey's smile faded and he looked down at his beer. "If I tell ya, will ya promise it'll go no further? I'd not like to embarrass my Nell or Tommy's mum."

"You've my word."

"He's mine," Blimpey replied softly. "But I didn't know it until he was arrested. His mum got out of her sickbed and come to me, told me the truth of it and said I had to keep our son from hangin'."

"You're sure she was tellin' the truth?"

Blimpey nodded. "Oh yes, I've always suspected he was mine, but she never said anything and I was too stupid to ask. I've decide that when he gets out, I'll set him up with a little shop or somethin' like that."

"Make him a shopkeeper, eh," Smythe laughed. "Don't worry, your secret's safe with me. I'd not embarrass either lady by ever mentioning the subject again."

"You're a good man, Smythe." Blimpey chugged his beer. "I'll tell ya what, to show my appreciation for what you've done for me and the lad, in the future, I'll give you as much information as you need."

"For free?"

"Nothing is free in this old world, mate," Blimpey replied. "But I'll only charge you half as much as before."

A week later Inspector Witherspoon walked out of the front door of Scotland Yard. A strong wind from the river tugged at his bowler and he shoved it harder down onto his head. He headed for the river. He was feeling very pleased. Tommy Odell had been released, they had a confession out of Lucy Turner for both crimes, and he was having dinner that night with Ruth. He rounded the corner and started onto the bridge.

"Hello, Witherspoon." Nivens stepped directly in front of him.

"Inspector Nivens," he said, stumbling to a halt. "Gracious, I didn't expect to see you here. Did you wish to speak to me? Why don't we go back to the Yard and—"

"This won't take long," Nivens interrupted. "You've made me look a fool, you know."

"I assure you, sir," Witherspoon replied, "I intended no such thing, but I couldn't let an innocent man hang. I had to do my duty."

"You made a big mistake, Witherspoon." Nivens smiled faintly. "From now on, I'm going to be watching every single thing you do. I know you've had help on every case you've solved, and I'm going to find out who has been helping you. When I expose the truth, I'm going to tell everyone. I'm going to make you the laughingstock of this town. You'll be sorry you crossed me."

"No, sir, I don't think I will." Witherspoon straightened his spine. "I use ordinary police procedures in my investigations, and I don't get any more help than any other police officer. Your investigation into the Muran murder was shoddy and criminally incompetent."

"How dare you."

But Witherspoon was tired of worrying about stepping on Nivens' toes. "I'd hoped to avoid further conflict with you, sir. But I will not neglect my duty in order to advance your career. Now, if you're through making idle threats, I really must be going."

Nivens gaped at him in surprise and quickly stepped back. Witherspoon pushed past him and kept on walking across the bridge. He knew that Nivens would make good on his threat, but for once, he didn't care. Let him do his worst. Witherspoon didn't mind making enemies in the pursuit of justice.

MYSTERY'S #1 BESTSELLER

MISS MARPLE
solving crimes for more than 70 years

___0-451-19992-8 A CARIBBEAN MYSTERY

___0-451-19986-3 A POCKET FULL OF RYE

___0-451-19993-6 AT BERTRAM'S HOTEL

___0-451-19987-1 THE BODY IN THE LIBRARY

___0-451-19990-1 THEY DO IT WITH MIRRORS

___0-451-19989-8 THE MIRROR CRACK'D

___0-451-20018-7 NEMESIS

___0-451-20019-5 SLEEPING MURDER

___0-451-20020-9 THE THIRTEEN PROBLEMS

___0-451-20051-9 4:50 FROM PADDINGTON

**AVAILABLE WHEREVER BOOKS ARE SOLD OR AT
PENGUIN.COM**

(B0098)